SONIC THE HEDGEHOG™

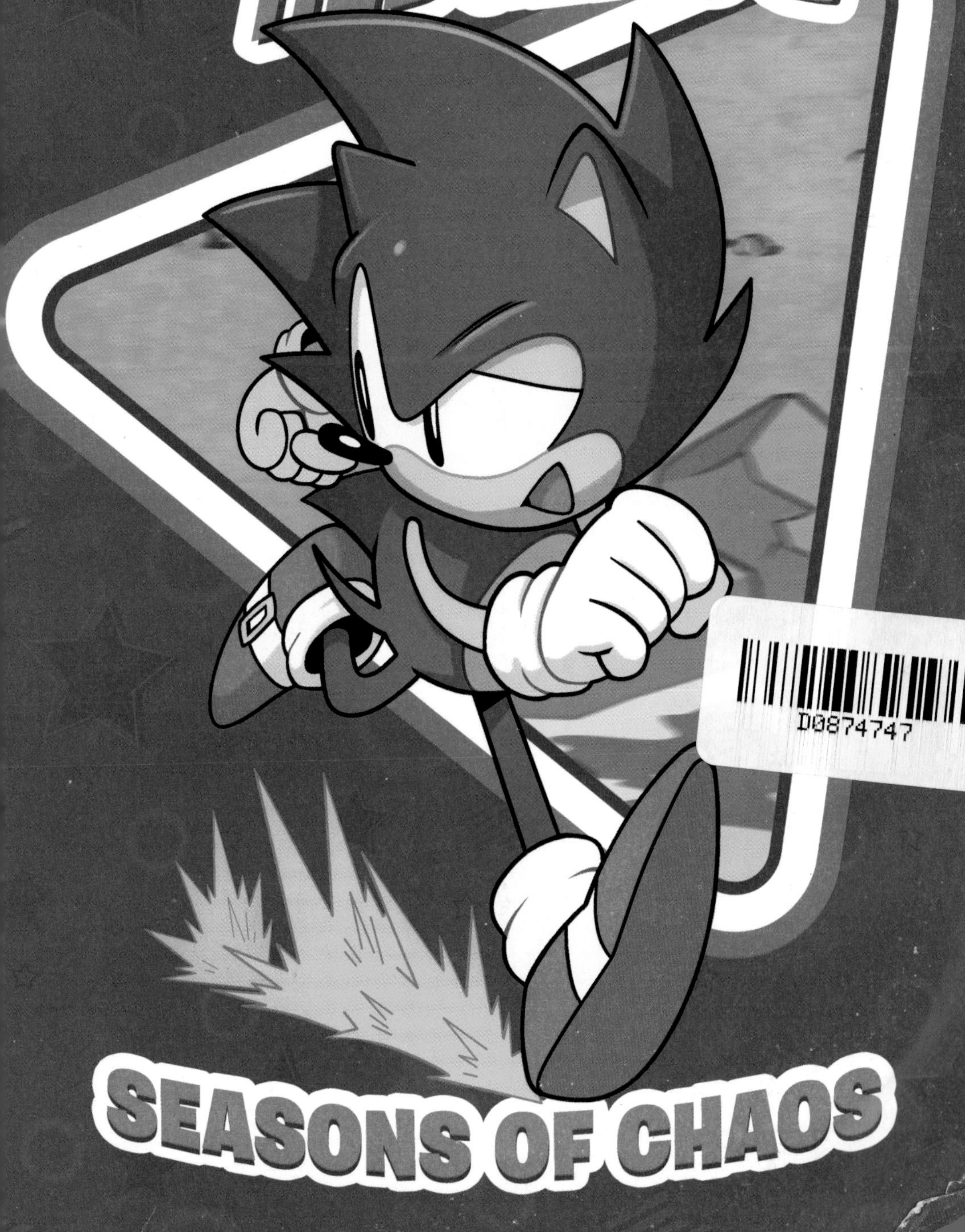

SEASONS OF CHAOS

IDW @IDWpublishing
IDWpublishing.com

Cover Art by
Patrick Spaziante

Series Assistant Edits by
Riley Farmer

Series Edits by
David Mariotte

Collection Edits by
Alonzo Simon

Collection Group Editor
Kris Simon

Collection Design
& Lettering by
Shawn Lee

Davidi Jonas, CEO
Amber Huerta, COO
Mark Doyle, Co-Publisher
Tara McCrillis, Co-Publisher
Jamie S. Rich, Editor-In-Chief
Scott Dunbier VP Special Projects
Sean Brice, Sr. Director Sales & Marketing
Lauren LePera, Sr. Managing Editor
Shauna Monteforte, Sr. Director of Manufacturing Operations
Jamie Miller, Director Publishing Operations
Greg Foreman, Director DTC Sales & Operations
Nathan Widick, Director of Design
Neil Uyetake, Sr. Art Director, Design & Production

Ted Adams and Robbie Robbins, IDW Founders

For international rights, contact licensing@idwpublishing.com.

ISBN: 979-88-87240-30-5
26 25 24 23   1 2 3 4

Special thanks to Mai Kiyotaki,
Michael Cisneros, Sandra Jo,
Sonic Team, and everyone at Sega
for their invaluable assistance.

SEASONS OF CHAOS 7

Story
IAN FLYNN

Pencils
AARON HAMMERSTROM
7-39, 43-45, 50-59, 63-66

Lineart
THOMAS ROTHLISBERGER
40-41, 46-49, 60-62
TRACY YARDLEY
42, 66

Inks
REGGIE GRAHAM
7-39, 43-44, 50
MATT FROESE
45, 51-59, 63-65

Colors
REGGIE GRAHAM

SONIC LEARNS TO DRIVE 67

Story
CLINT, JUSTIN, TRAVIS & GRIFFIN McELROY

Art
MAURO FONSECA

Colors
VALENTINA PINTO

DR. EGGMAN'S BIRTHDAY 77

Story
GALE GALLIGAN

Art
THOMAS ROTHLISBERGER

Colors
NATHALIE FOURDRAINE

AMY'S NEW HOBBY 87

Story
GALE GALLIGAN

Art
THOMAS ROTHLISBERGER

Colors
NATHALIE FOURDRAINE

INTRODUCTION

My first encounter with Sonic occurred very young within a '90s video rental store, not on the screen but eyeing a simple poster. Wagging his finger at me with his trademark 'tude and casually crossed shoes, his electric-blue presence instantly connected with me; "Who is that blue cat?!" (Sonic is a Hedgehog). At this point in time I had no idea what videogames were, but his silhouette and expression were strong enough that *Sonic 2* was the immediate pick when my school friend invited me over to play on his Sega console.

The first moments were intoxicating. Here was a character who rocketed through vibrant geometric worlds like a living embodiment of a skateboard, rolling and ricocheting off robotic enemies and other Rube Goldberg contraptions in a way that felt gravity defying. Sonic doesn't need wheels to go fast, because he himself is the wheel, reinvented! Opposing him is Dr. Eggman (aka Dr. Robotnik), who while being a malicious mad scientist bent on world domination, clearly is also a child at heart, with modular vehicles that would be the envy of any meccano enthusiast. And perhaps crucially for me, beating the game was only the beginning; the real way to play *Sonic* was to turn on the debug mode cheat and spend hours causing untold havoc within the game! This is rather fitting given Sonic's own rebellious devil-may-care attitude, and served as my first glimpse behind the smoke and mirrors (or sprites and tiles) of game development…

So, unless you've been living in Hidden Palace Zone, you're probably keenly aware that 2021 is the 30th anniversary of our favorite blue fella. Sonic's world has evolved significantly since the heyday of the '90s and means different things to people depending on who you ask. As someone who both grew up with and has been able to contribute to the series as lead developer on *Sonic Mania*, the signature style and sensibilities of the classic 16-Bit era of Sonic is a world woven from a tapestry of many pop-culture influences from the 20th Century. From pinball and parlor games, to Art Deco and Memphis Milano, to New Jack Swing and the Manchester music scene, it is a world that I feel is still rich for exploration in the here and now.

Okay, okay! You want to know what's so special about this collection, right? This is IDW's first foray into the world of Classic Sonic and…

It's got lots of colorful Classic Zones old and new!

It's got lots of characters! (even some deep cuts for you super fans)

It's the first Hard Boiled Heavies comic debut! (I'm so proud of those eggheads)

If you are learning to draw your favorite characters in the classic

style, this collection has got so many legit poses! (shout-out to SATAM Robotnik confusing me very much as a kid)

Sonic is 30 now, so let's not keep him waiting any longer. His next adventure begins with but a turn of the page!

Christian Whitehead
Creative Director @ Evening Star

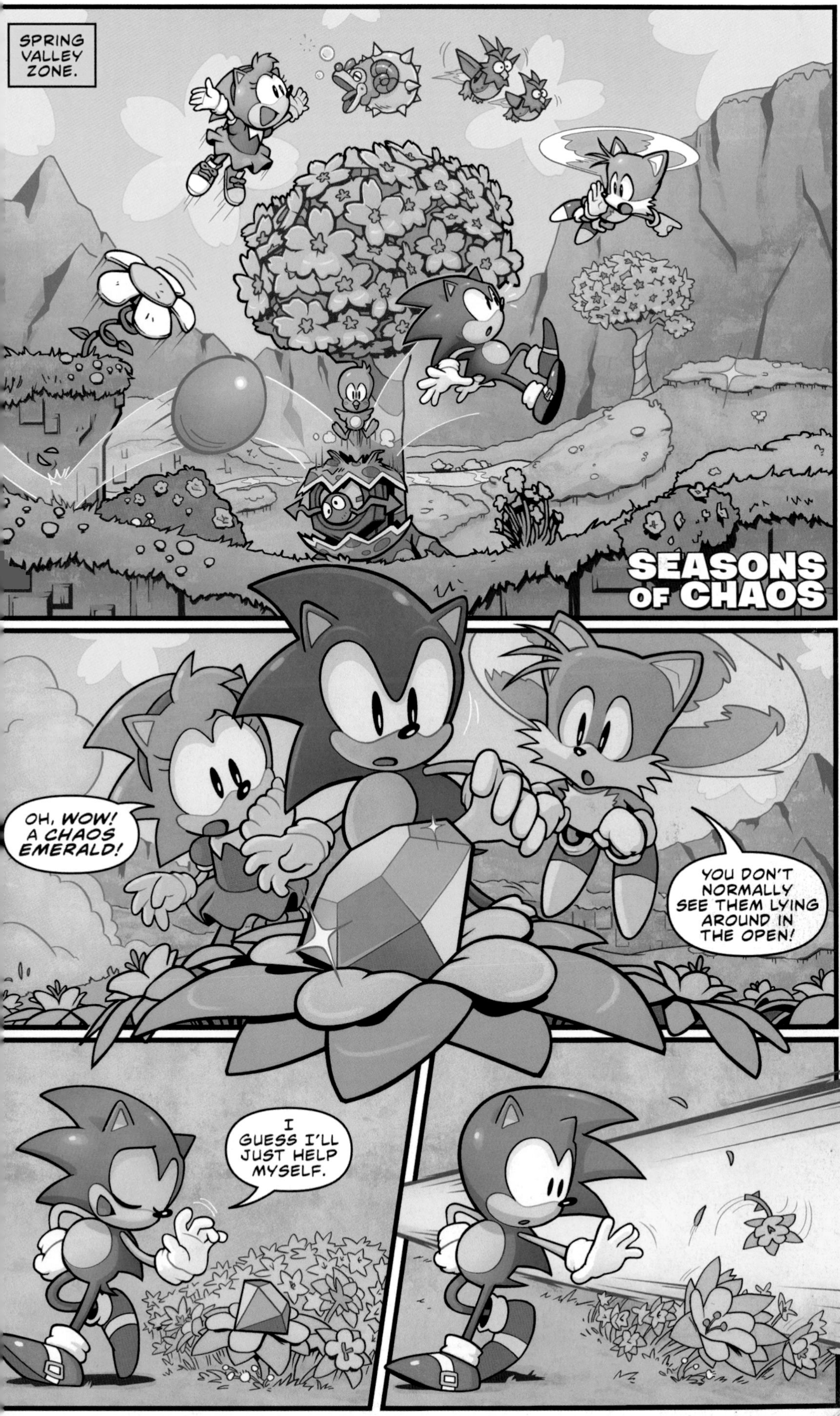
SPRING VALLEY ZONE.
SEASONS OF CHAOS
OH, WOW! A CHAOS EMERALD!
YOU DON'T NORMALLY SEE THEM LYING AROUND IN THE OPEN!
I GUESS I'LL JUST HELP MYSELF.

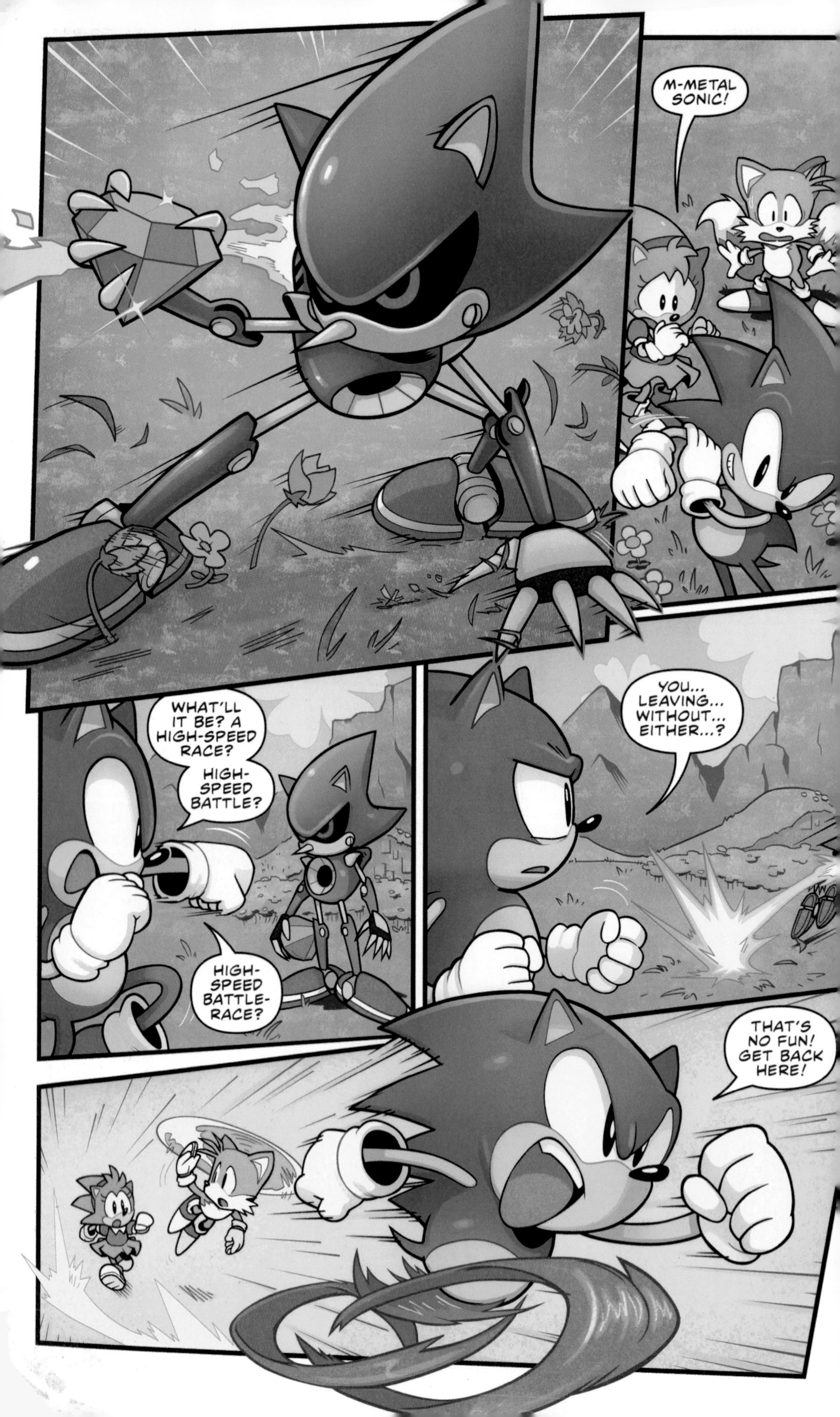
M-METAL SONIC!
WHAT'LL IT BE? A HIGH-SPEED RACE?
HIGH-SPEED BATTLE?
HIGH-SPEED BATTLE-RACE?
YOU... LEAVING... WITHOUT... EITHER...?
THAT'S NO FUN! GET BACK HERE!

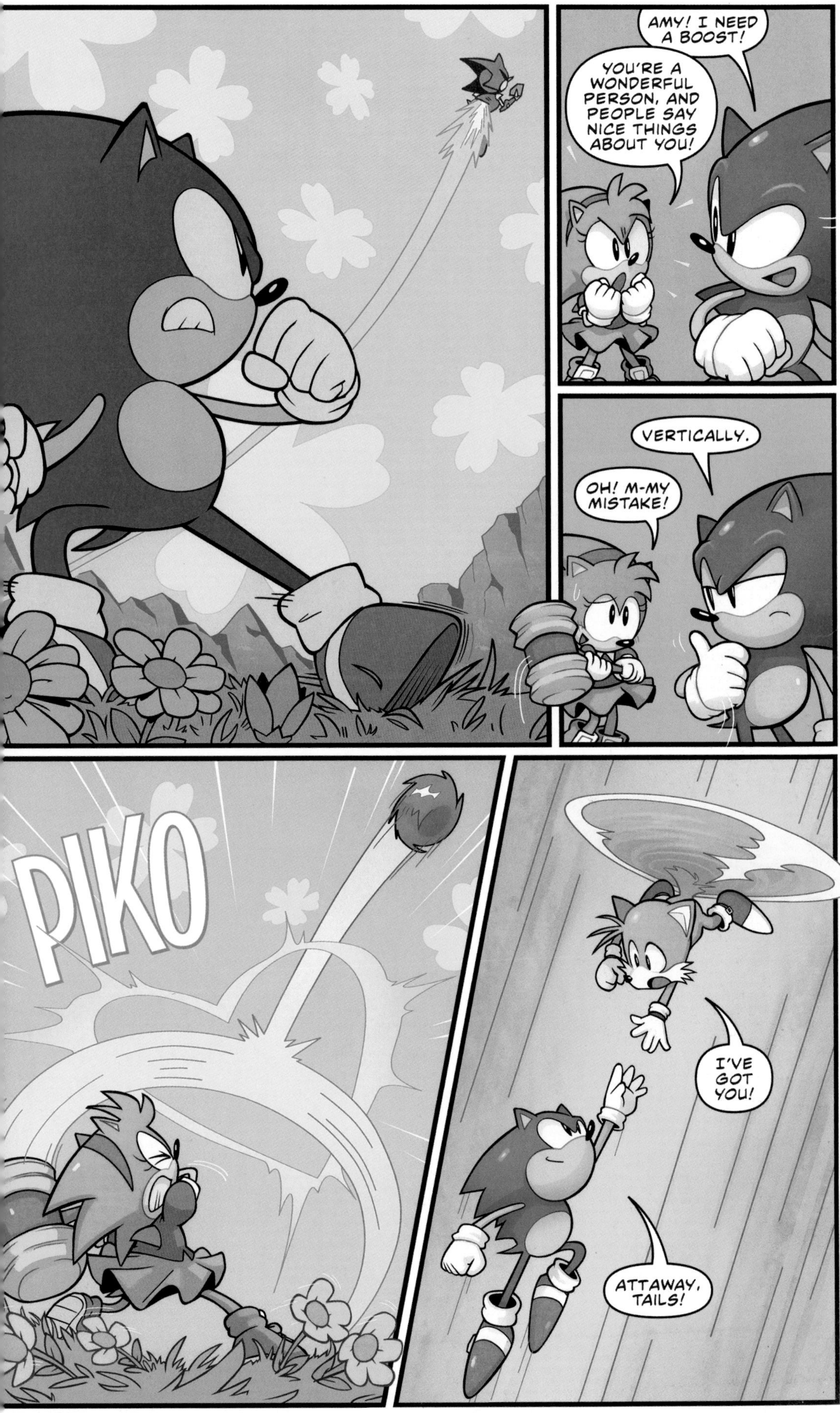
AMY! I NEED A BOOST!
YOU'RE A WONDERFUL PERSON, AND PEOPLE SAY NICE THINGS ABOUT YOU!
VERTICALLY.
OH! M-MY MISTAKE!
PIKO
I'VE GOT YOU!
ATTAWAY, TAILS!

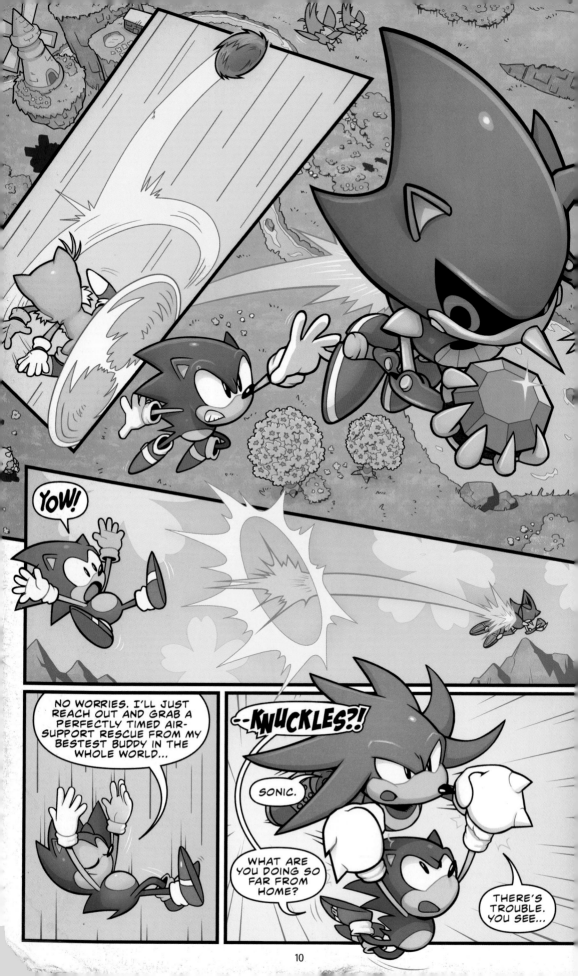

YOW!

NO WORRIES. I'LL JUST REACH OUT AND GRAB A PERFECTLY TIMED AIR-SUPPORT RESCUE FROM MY BESTEST BUDDY IN THE WHOLE WORLD...

--KNUCKLES?!

SONIC.

WHAT ARE YOU DOING SO FAR FROM HOME?

THERE'S TROUBLE. YOU SEE...

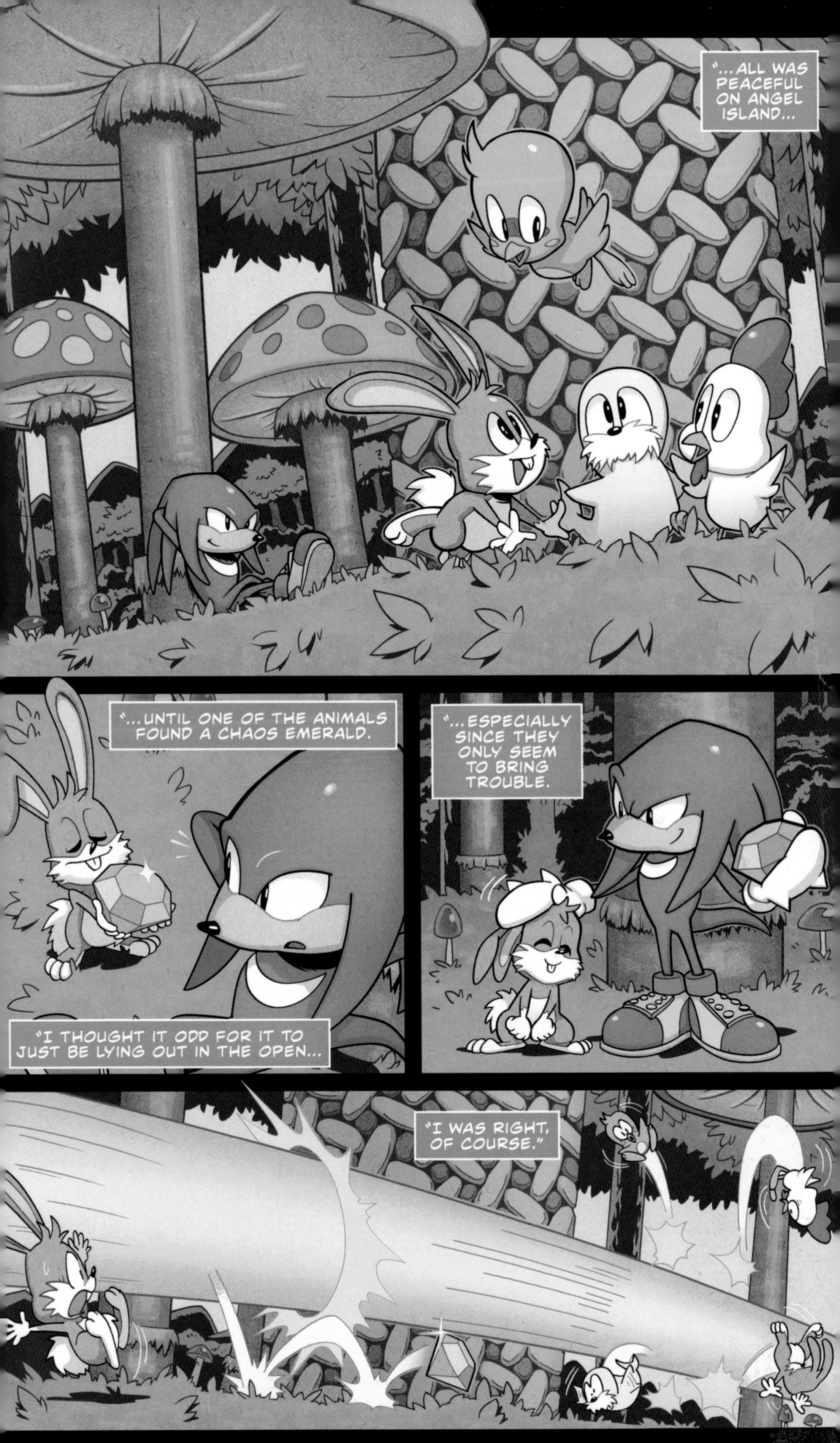
"...ALL WAS PEACEFUL ON ANGEL ISLAND...
"...UNTIL ONE OF THE ANIMALS FOUND A CHAOS EMERALD.
"I THOUGHT IT ODD FOR IT TO JUST BE LYING OUT IN THE OPEN...
"...ESPECIALLY SINCE THEY ONLY SEEM TO BRING TROUBLE.
"I WAS RIGHT, OF COURSE."

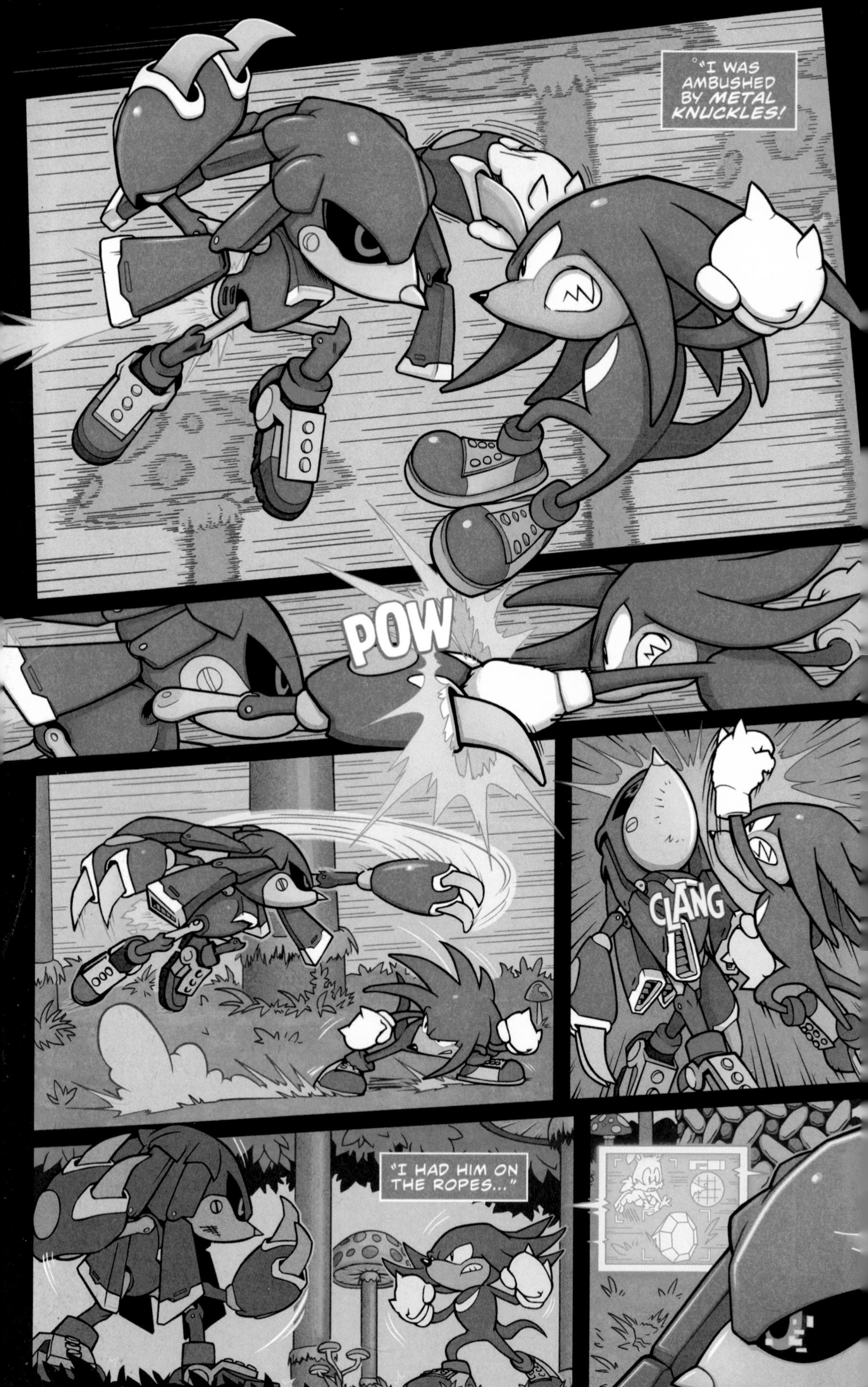
"I WAS AMBUSHED BY METAL KNUCKLES!
POW
CLANG
"I HAD HIM ON THE ROPES..."

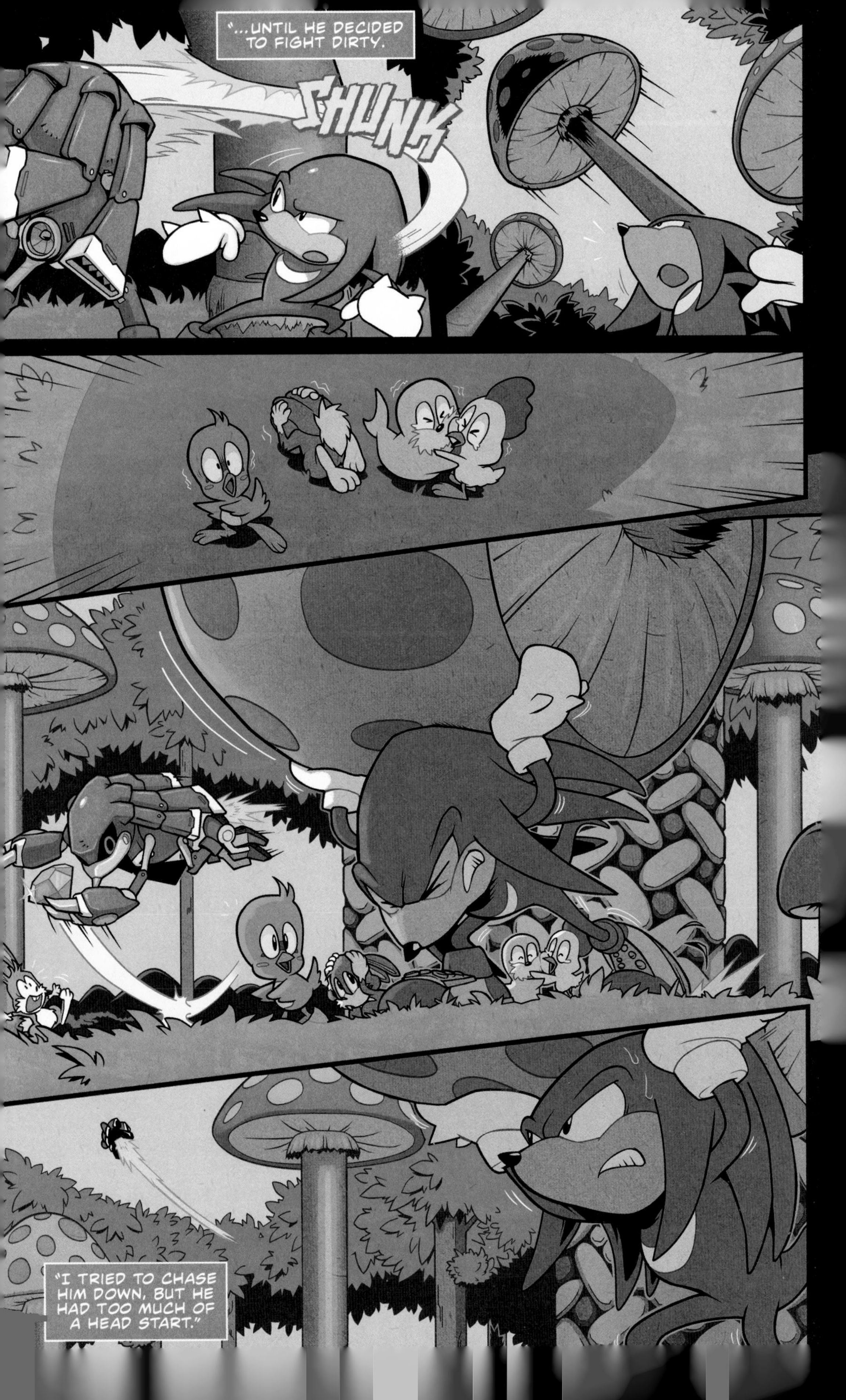
"...UNTIL HE DECIDED TO FIGHT DIRTY.
CHUNK
"I TRIED TO CHASE HIM DOWN, BUT HE HAD TOO MUCH OF A HEAD START."

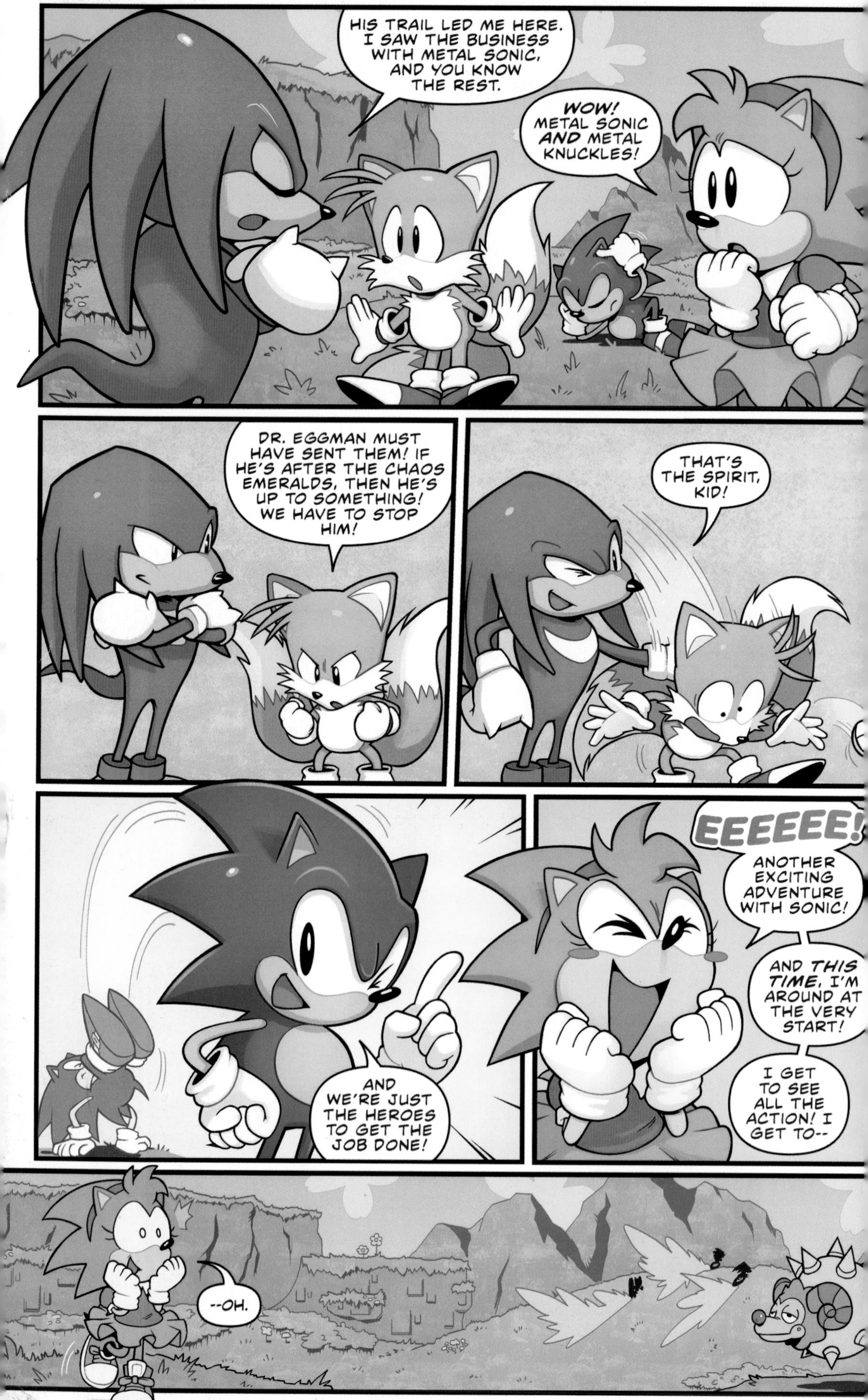
HIS TRAIL LED ME HERE. I SAW THE BUSINESS WITH METAL SONIC, AND YOU KNOW THE REST.
WOW! METAL SONIC AND METAL KNUCKLES!
DR. EGGMAN MUST HAVE SENT THEM! IF HE'S AFTER THE CHAOS EMERALDS, THEN HE'S UP TO SOMETHING! WE HAVE TO STOP HIM!
THAT'S THE SPIRIT, KID!
AND WE'RE JUST THE HEROES TO GET THE JOB DONE!
EEEEEE!
ANOTHER EXCITING ADVENTURE WITH SONIC!
AND THIS TIME, I'M AROUND AT THE VERY START!
I GET TO SEE ALL THE ACTION! I GET TO--
--OH.

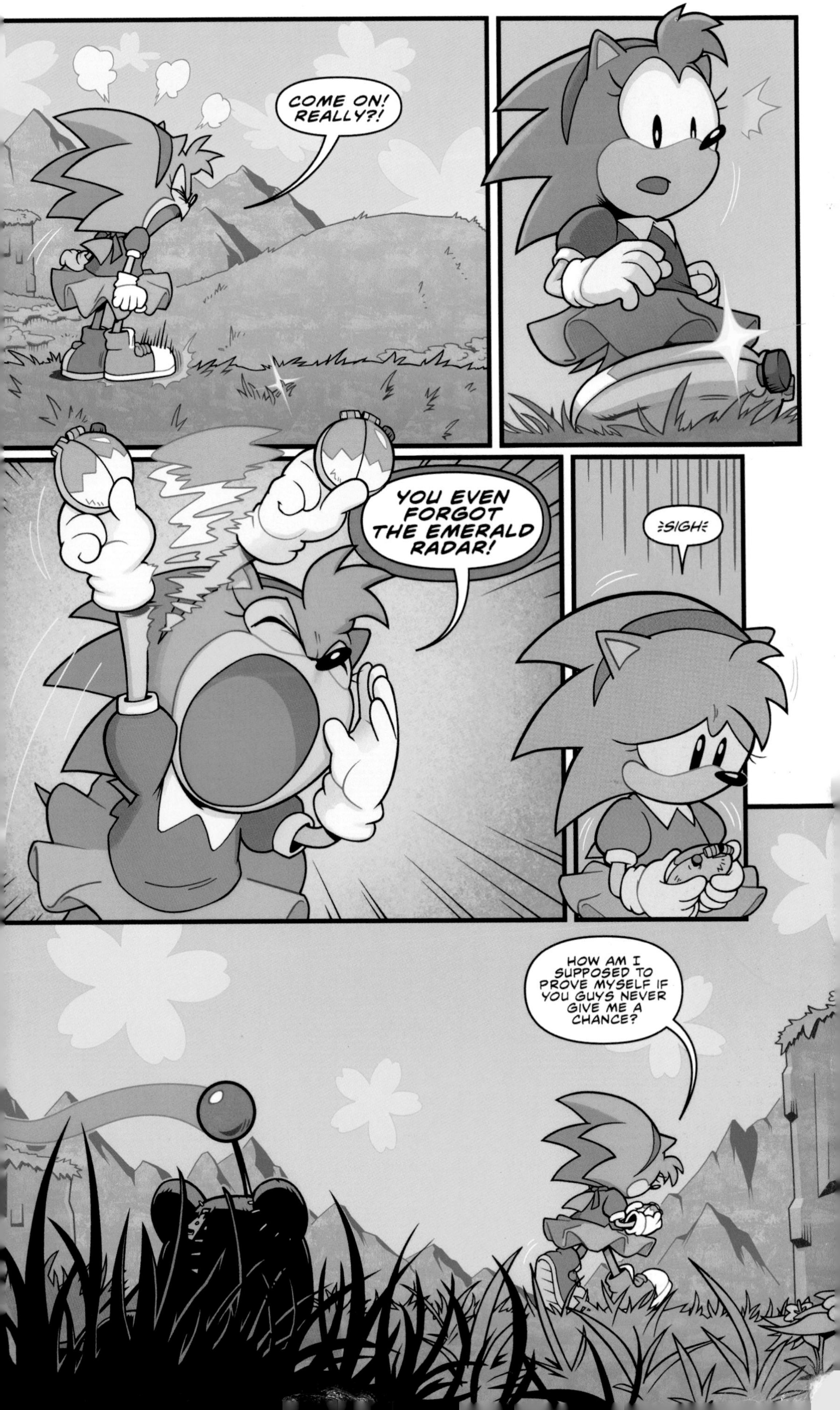
COME ON! REALLY?!
YOU EVEN FORGOT THE EMERALD RADAR!
SIGH
HOW AM I SUPPOSED TO PROVE MYSELF IF YOU GUYS NEVER GIVE ME A CHANCE?

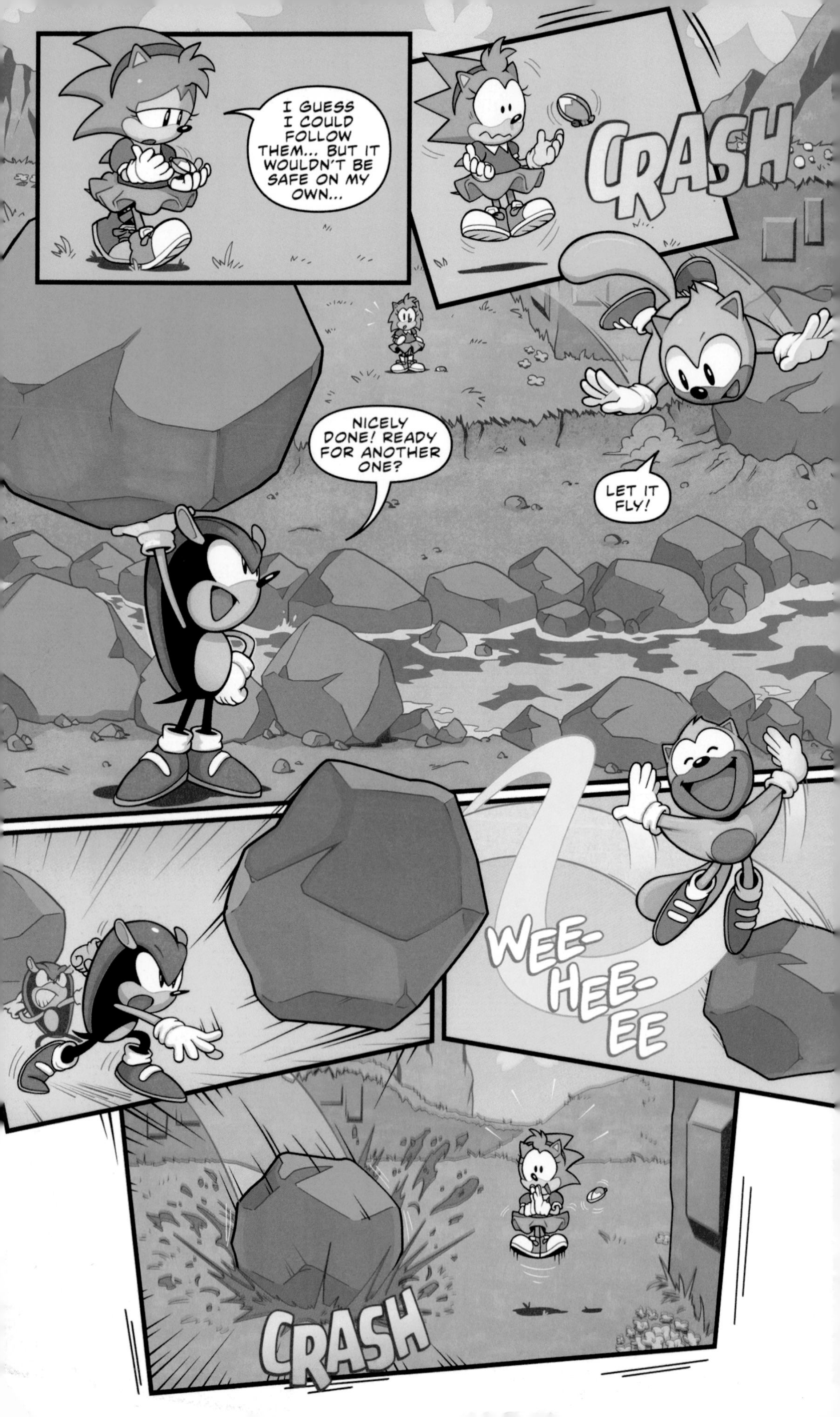
I GUESS I COULD FOLLOW THEM... BUT IT WOULDN'T BE SAFE ON MY OWN...
CRASH
NICELY DONE! READY FOR ANOTHER ONE?
LET IT FLY!
WEE-HEE-EE
CRASH

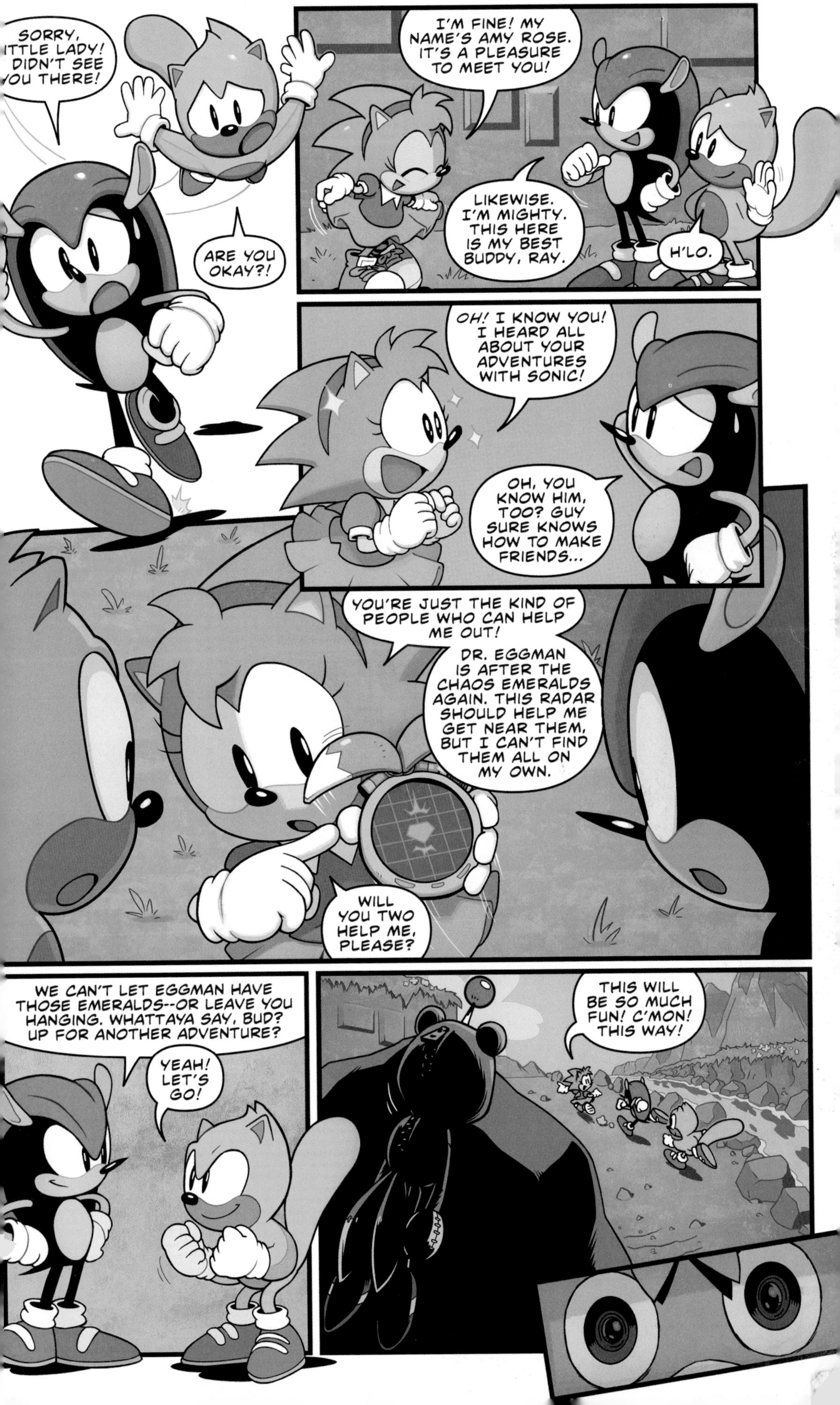
SORRY, LITTLE LADY! DIDN'T SEE YOU THERE!
ARE YOU OKAY?!
I'M FINE! MY NAME'S AMY ROSE. IT'S A PLEASURE TO MEET YOU!
LIKEWISE. I'M MIGHTY. THIS HERE IS MY BEST BUDDY, RAY.
H'LO.
OH! I KNOW YOU! I HEARD ALL ABOUT YOUR ADVENTURES WITH SONIC!
OH, YOU KNOW HIM, TOO? GUY SURE KNOWS HOW TO MAKE FRIENDS...
YOU'RE JUST THE KIND OF PEOPLE WHO CAN HELP ME OUT!
DR. EGGMAN IS AFTER THE CHAOS EMERALDS AGAIN. THIS RADAR SHOULD HELP ME GET NEAR THEM, BUT I CAN'T FIND THEM ALL ON MY OWN.
WILL YOU TWO HELP ME, PLEASE?
WE CAN'T LET EGGMAN HAVE THOSE EMERALDS--OR LEAVE YOU HANGING. WHATTAYA SAY, BUD? UP FOR ANOTHER ADVENTURE?
YEAH! LET'S GO!
THIS WILL BE SO MUCH FUN! C'MON! THIS WAY!

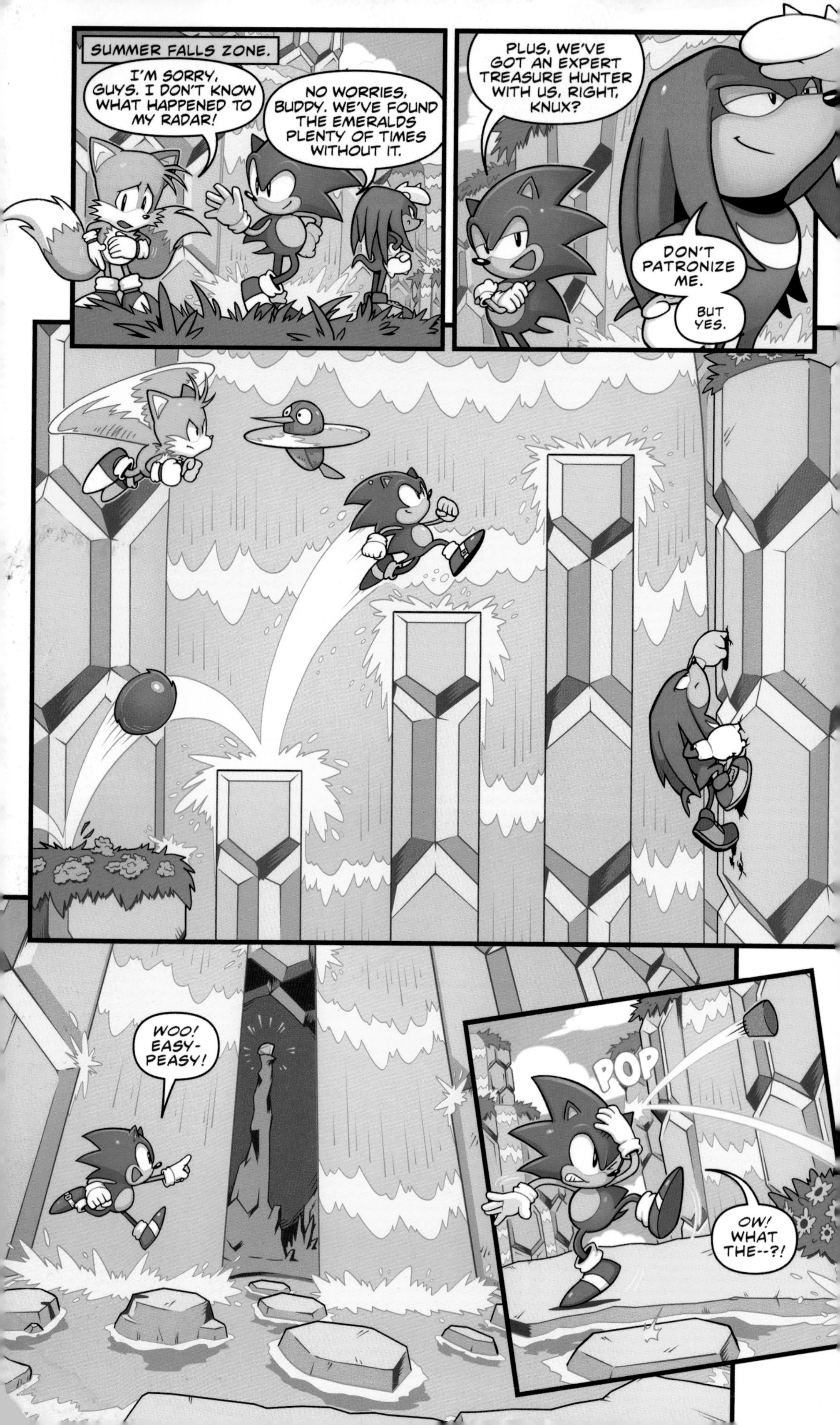
SUMMER FALLS ZONE.
I'M SORRY, GUYS. I DON'T KNOW WHAT HAPPENED TO MY RADAR!
NO WORRIES, BUDDY. WE'VE FOUND THE EMERALDS PLENTY OF TIMES WITHOUT IT.
PLUS, WE'VE GOT AN EXPERT TREASURE HUNTER WITH US, RIGHT, KNUX?
DON'T PATRONIZE ME.
BUT YES.
WOO! EASY-PEASY!
POP
OW! WHAT THE--?!

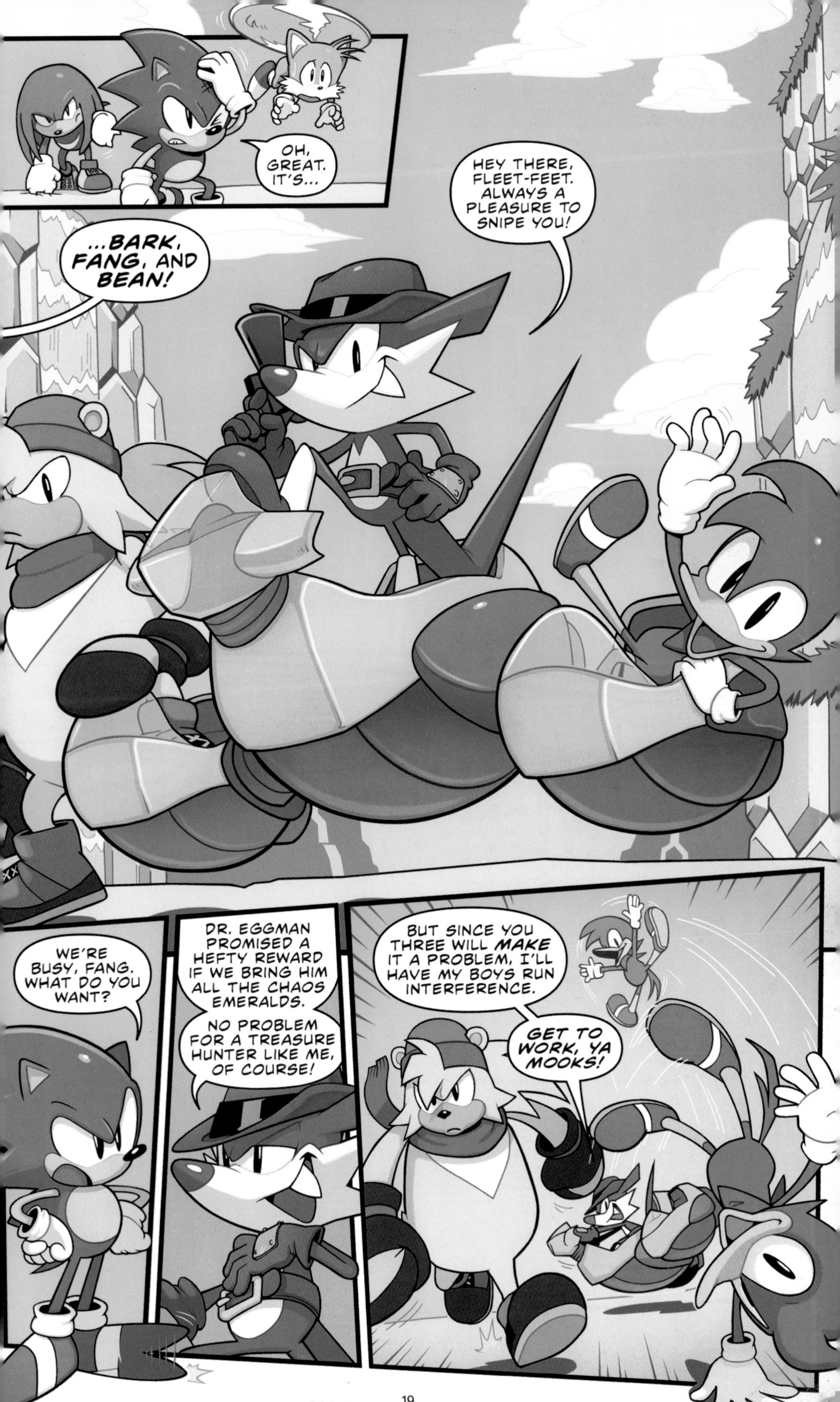
OH, GREAT. IT'S...
...BARK, FANG, AND BEAN!
HEY THERE, FLEET-FEET. ALWAYS A PLEASURE TO SNIPE YOU!
WE'RE BUSY, FANG. WHAT DO YOU WANT?
DR. EGGMAN PROMISED A HEFTY REWARD IF WE BRING HIM ALL THE CHAOS EMERALDS.
NO PROBLEM FOR A TREASURE HUNTER LIKE ME, OF COURSE!
BUT SINCE YOU THREE WILL MAKE IT A PROBLEM, I'LL HAVE MY BOYS RUN INTERFERENCE.
GET TO WORK, YA MOOKS!

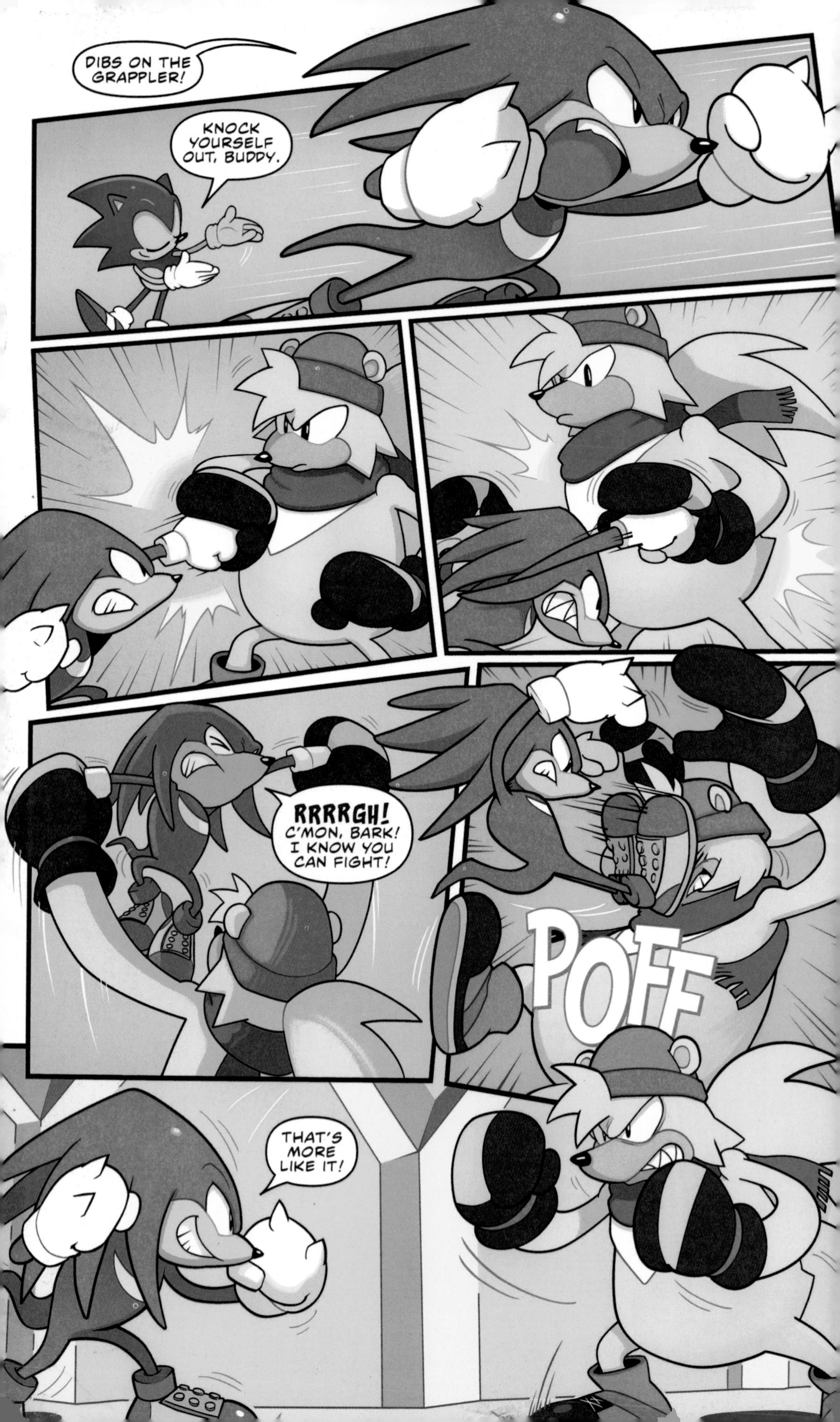
DIBS ON THE GRAPPLER!
KNOCK YOURSELF OUT, BUDDY.
RRRRGH! C'MON, BARK! I KNOW YOU CAN FIGHT!
POFF
THAT'S MORE LIKE IT!

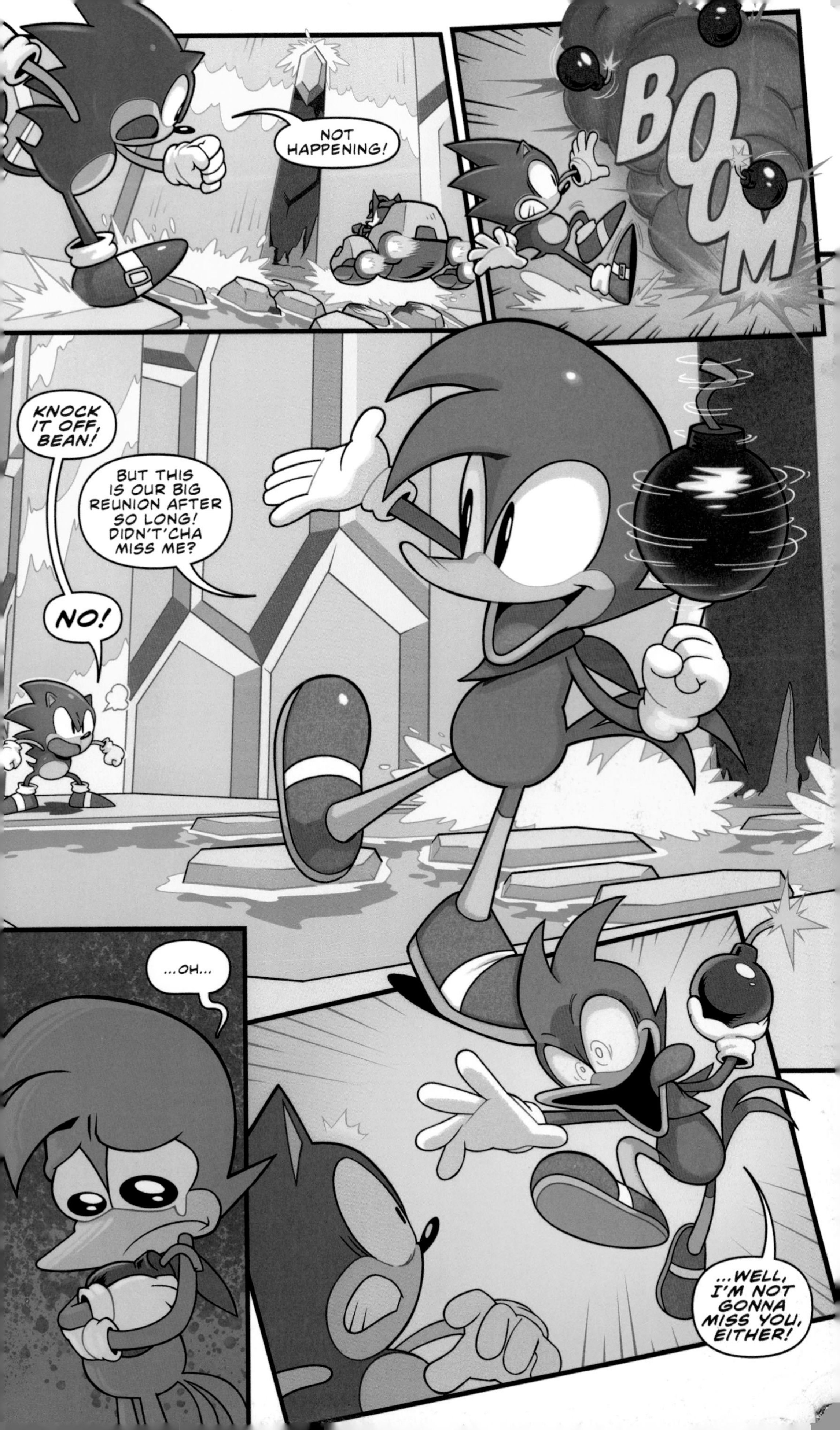
NOT HAPPENING!
BOOM!
KNOCK IT OFF, BEAN!
BUT THIS IS OUR BIG REUNION AFTER SO LONG! DIDN'T'CHA MISS ME?
NO!
...OH...
...WELL, I'M NOT GONNA MISS YOU, EITHER!

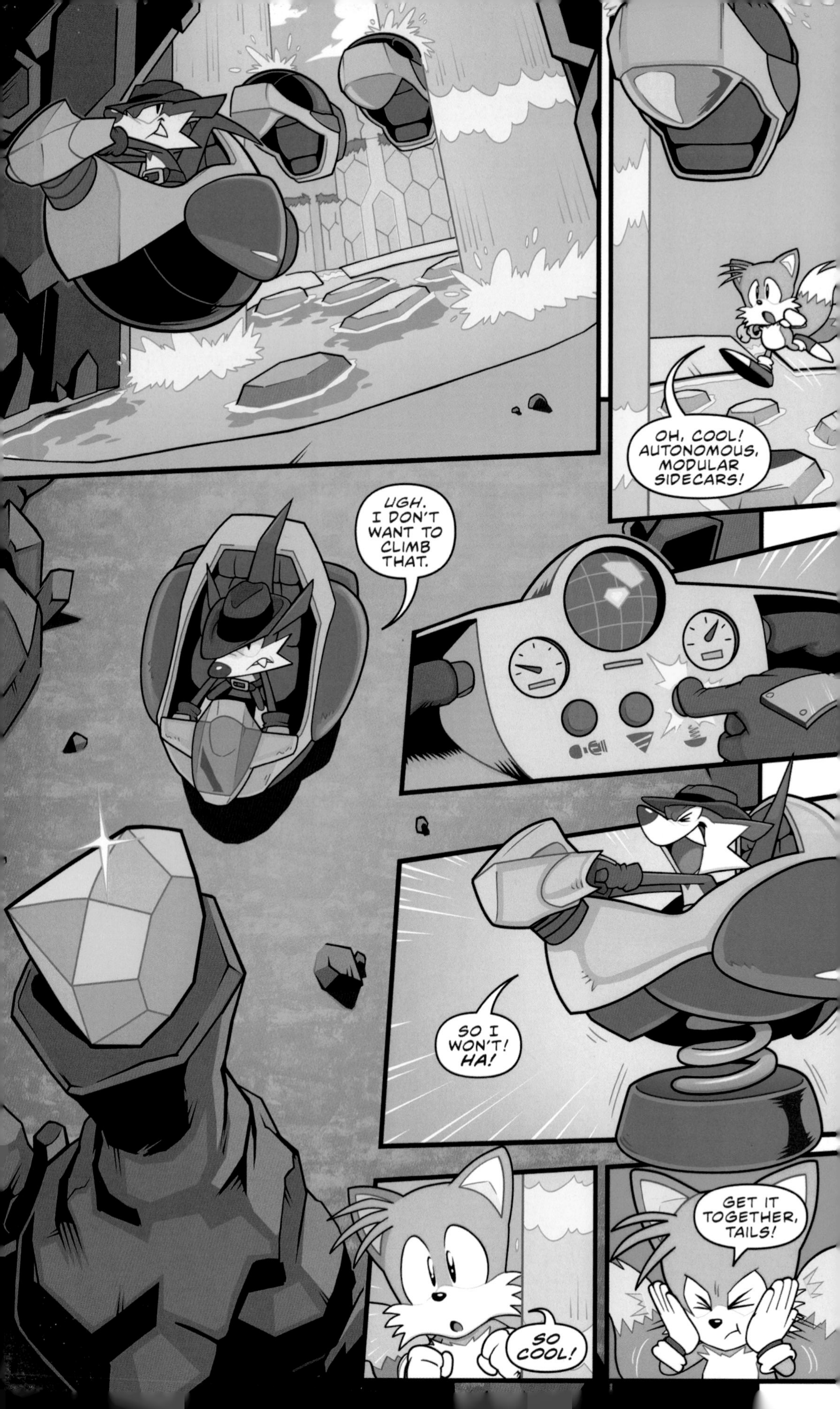
OH, COOL! AUTONOMOUS, MODULAR SIDECARS!
UGH. I DON'T WANT TO CLIMB THAT.
SO I WON'T! HA!
SO COOL!
GET IT TOGETHER, TAILS!

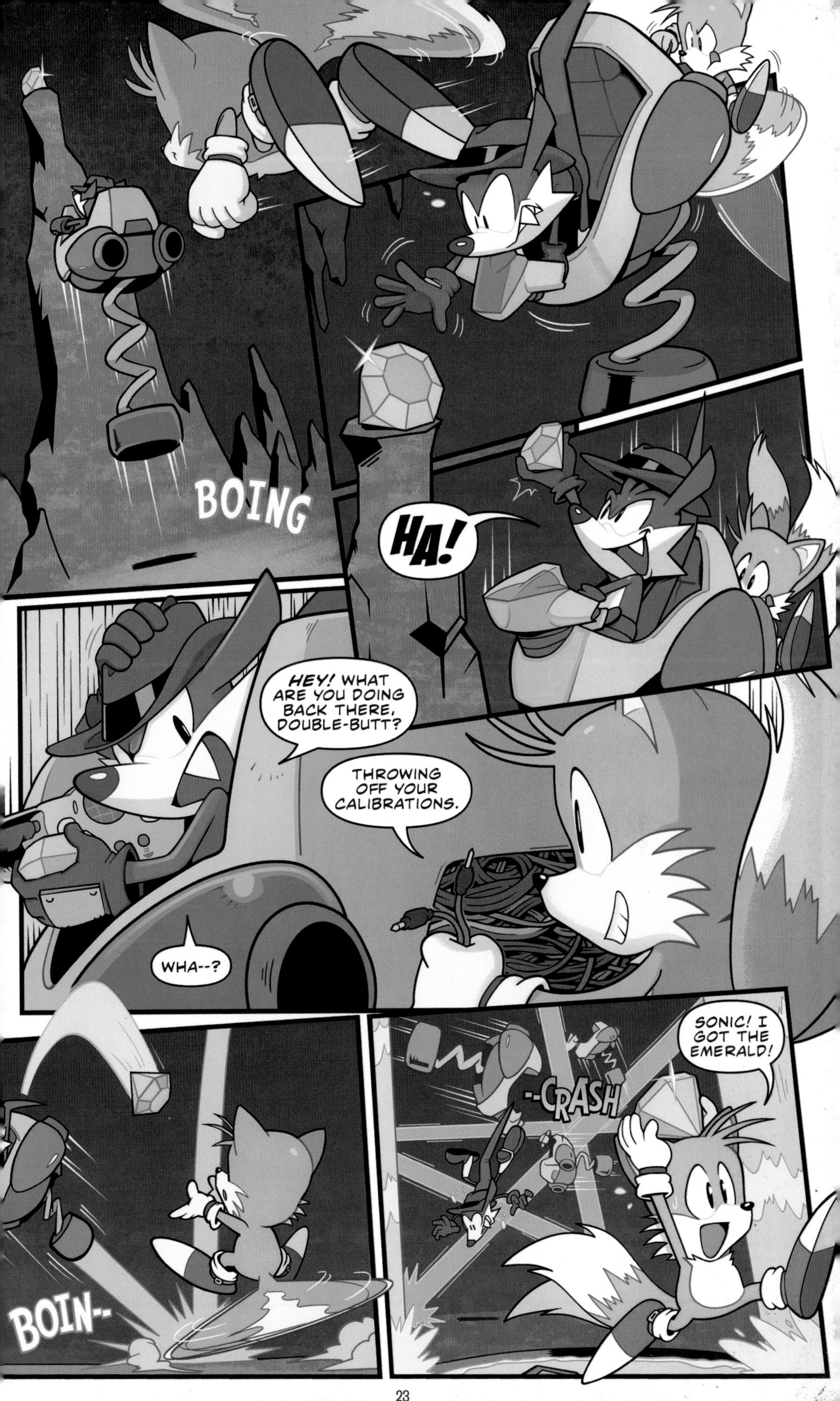
BOING
HA!
HEY! WHAT ARE YOU DOING BACK THERE, DOUBLE-BUTT?
THROWING OFF YOUR CALIBRATIONS.
WHA--?
BOIN--
--CRASH
SONIC! I GOT THE EMERALD!

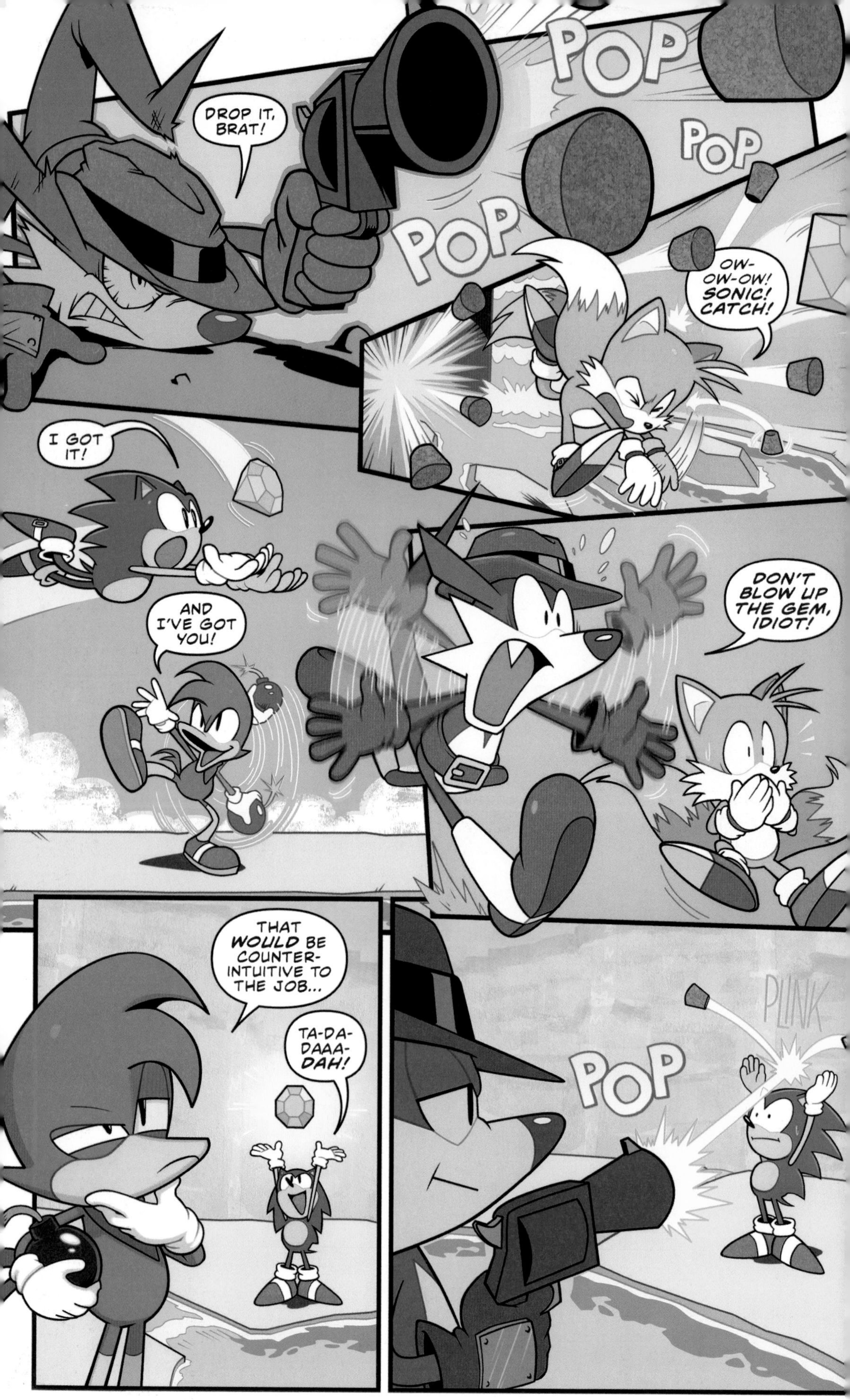
DROP IT, BRAT!
POP
POP
POP
OW-OW-OW! SONIC! CATCH!
I GOT IT!
AND I'VE GOT YOU!
DON'T BLOW UP THE GEM, IDIOT!
THAT WOULD BE COUNTER-INTUITIVE TO THE JOB...
TA-DA-DAAA-DAH!
PLINK
POP

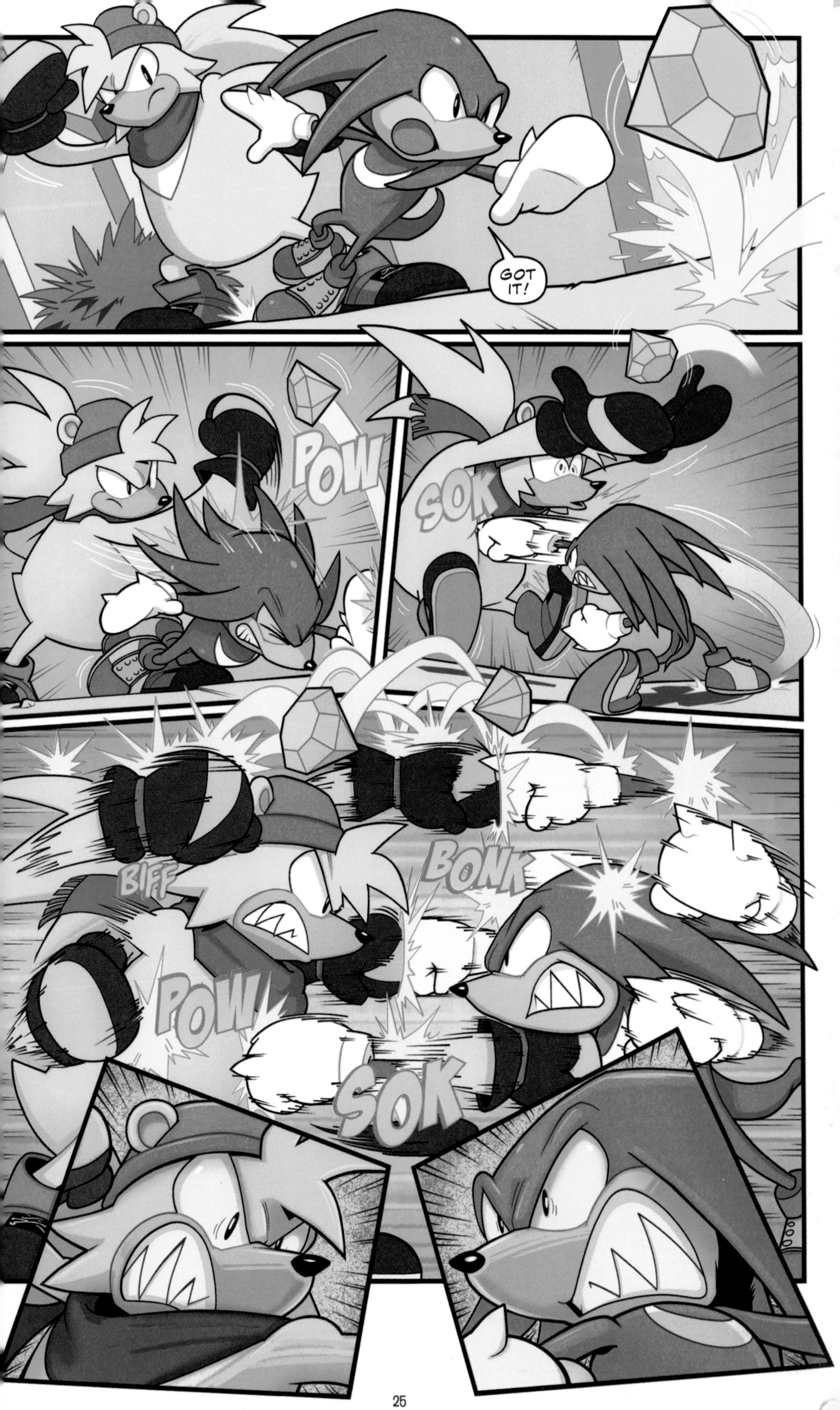
GOT IT!
POW
SOK
BIFF
BONK
POW
SOK

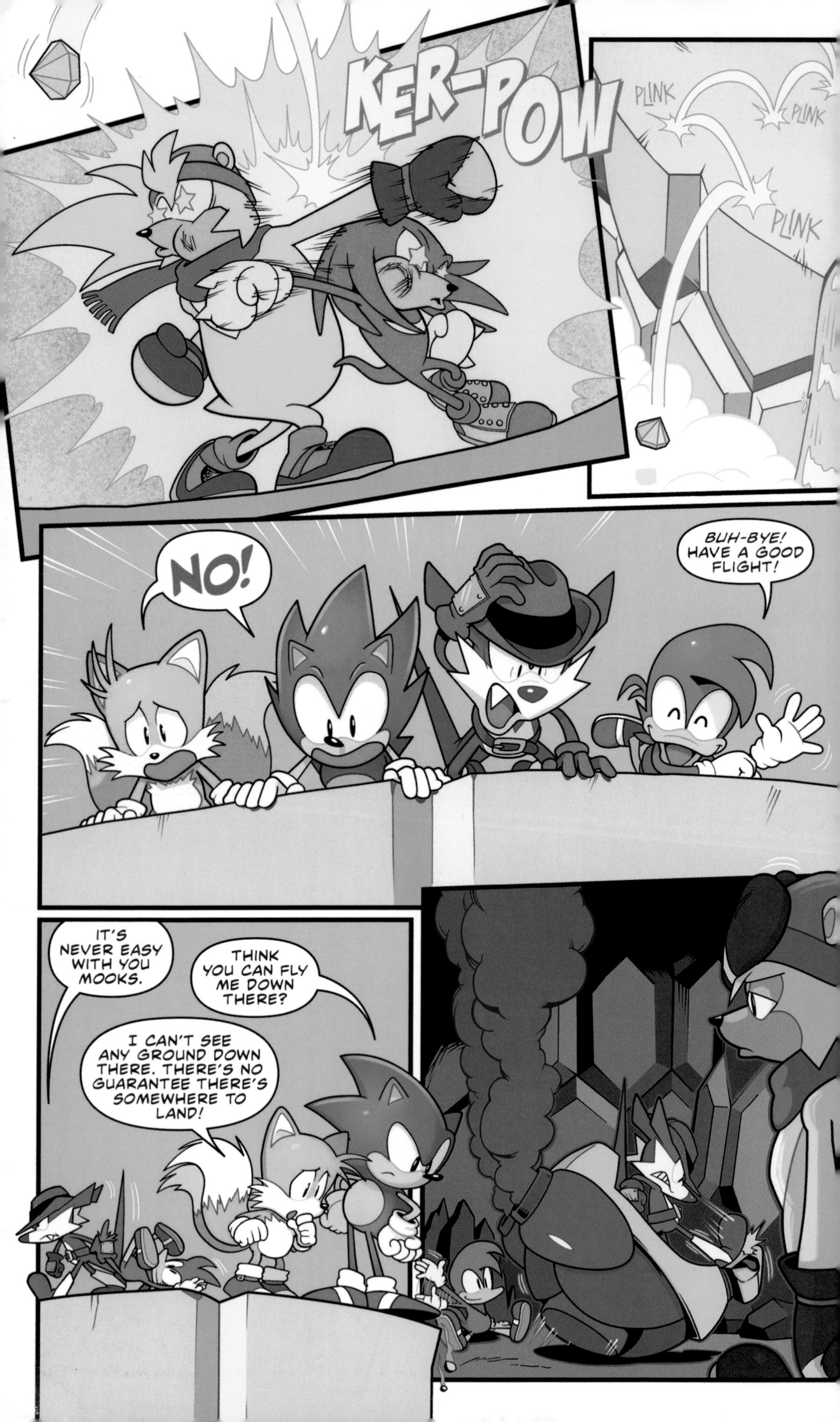
KER-POW
PLINK
PLINK
PLINK
NO!
BUH-BYE! HAVE A GOOD FLIGHT!
IT'S NEVER EASY WITH YOU MOOKS.
THINK YOU CAN FLY ME DOWN THERE?
I CAN'T SEE ANY GROUND DOWN THERE. THERE'S NO GUARANTEE THERE'S SOMEWHERE TO LAND!

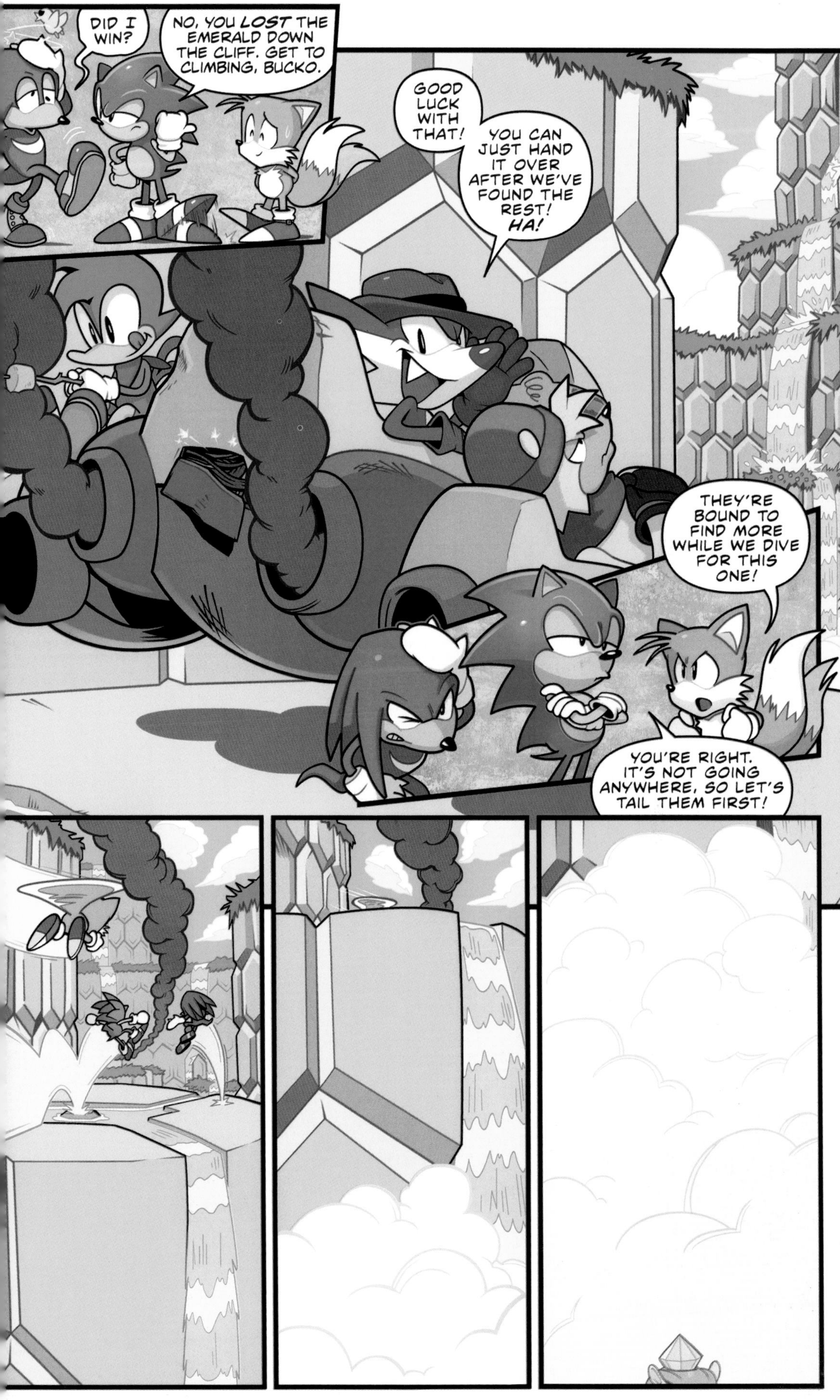
DID I WIN?
NO, YOU LOST THE EMERALD DOWN THE CLIFF. GET TO CLIMBING, BUCKO.
GOOD LUCK WITH THAT!
YOU CAN JUST HAND IT OVER AFTER WE'VE FOUND THE REST! HA!
THEY'RE BOUND TO FIND MORE WHILE WE DIVE FOR THIS ONE!
YOU'RE RIGHT. IT'S NOT GOING ANYWHERE, SO LET'S TAIL THEM FIRST!

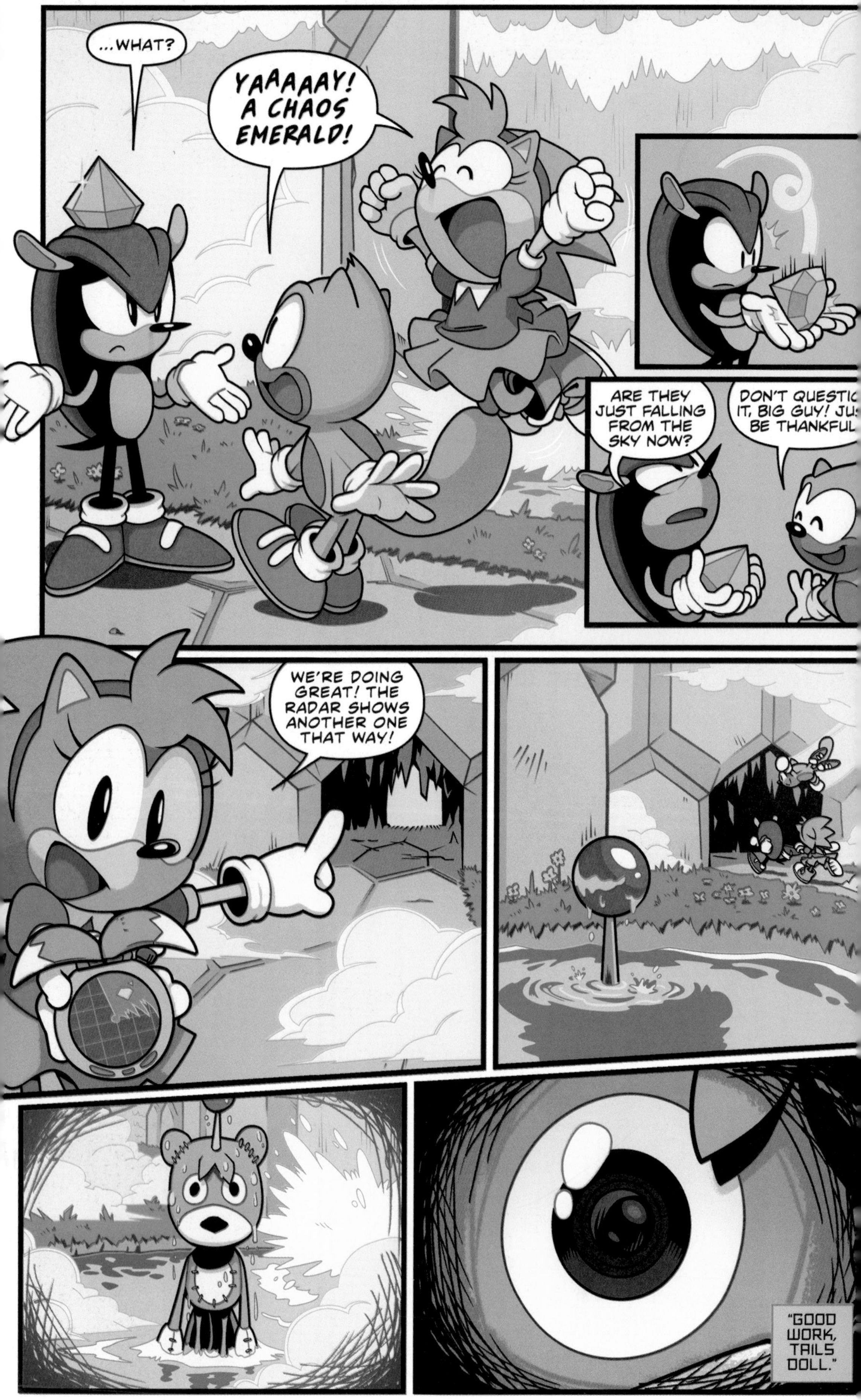
...WHAT?
YAAAAAY! A CHAOS EMERALD!
ARE THEY JUST FALLING FROM THE SKY NOW?
DON'T QUESTIC IT, BIG GUY! JUS BE THANKFUL
WE'RE DOING GREAT! THE RADAR SHOWS ANOTHER ONE THAT WAY!
"GOOD WORK, TAILS DOLL."

WITH THAT, ALL THE CHAOS EMERALDS ARE ACCOUNTED FOR.

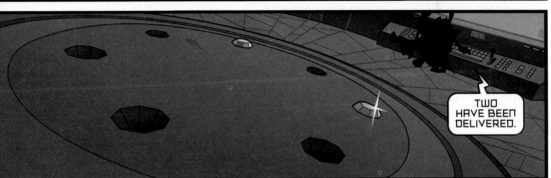

TWO HAVE BEEN DELIVERED.

THE THIRD IS HELD BY THE AMATEURS.

METAL KNUCKLES IS BRINGING THE FOURTH.

THE BUFFOONS ARE CLOSING IN ON THE FIFTH.

METAL SONIC HAS ACQUIRED THE SIXTH AND MOVES TO ACQUIRE THE SEVENTH AND FINAL GEM...

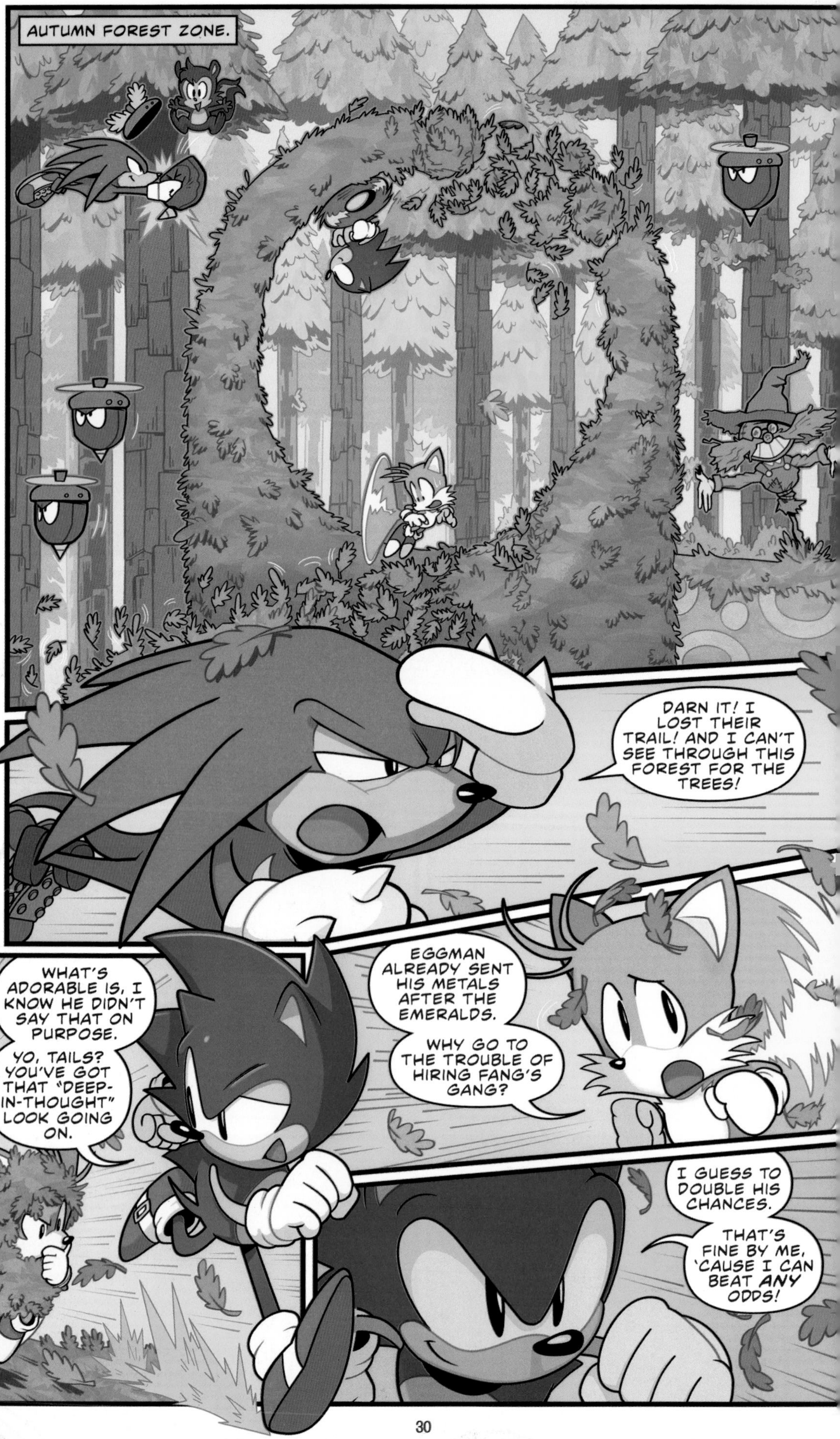
AUTUMN FOREST ZONE.
DARN IT! I LOST THEIR TRAIL! AND I CAN'T SEE THROUGH THIS FOREST FOR THE TREES!
WHAT'S ADORABLE IS, I KNOW HE DIDN'T SAY THAT ON PURPOSE.
YO, TAILS? YOU'VE GOT THAT "DEEP-IN-THOUGHT" LOOK GOING ON.
EGGMAN ALREADY SENT HIS METALS AFTER THE EMERALDS.
WHY GO TO THE TROUBLE OF HIRING FANG'S GANG?
I GUESS TO DOUBLE HIS CHANCES.
THAT'S FINE BY ME, 'CAUSE I CAN BEAT ANY ODDS!

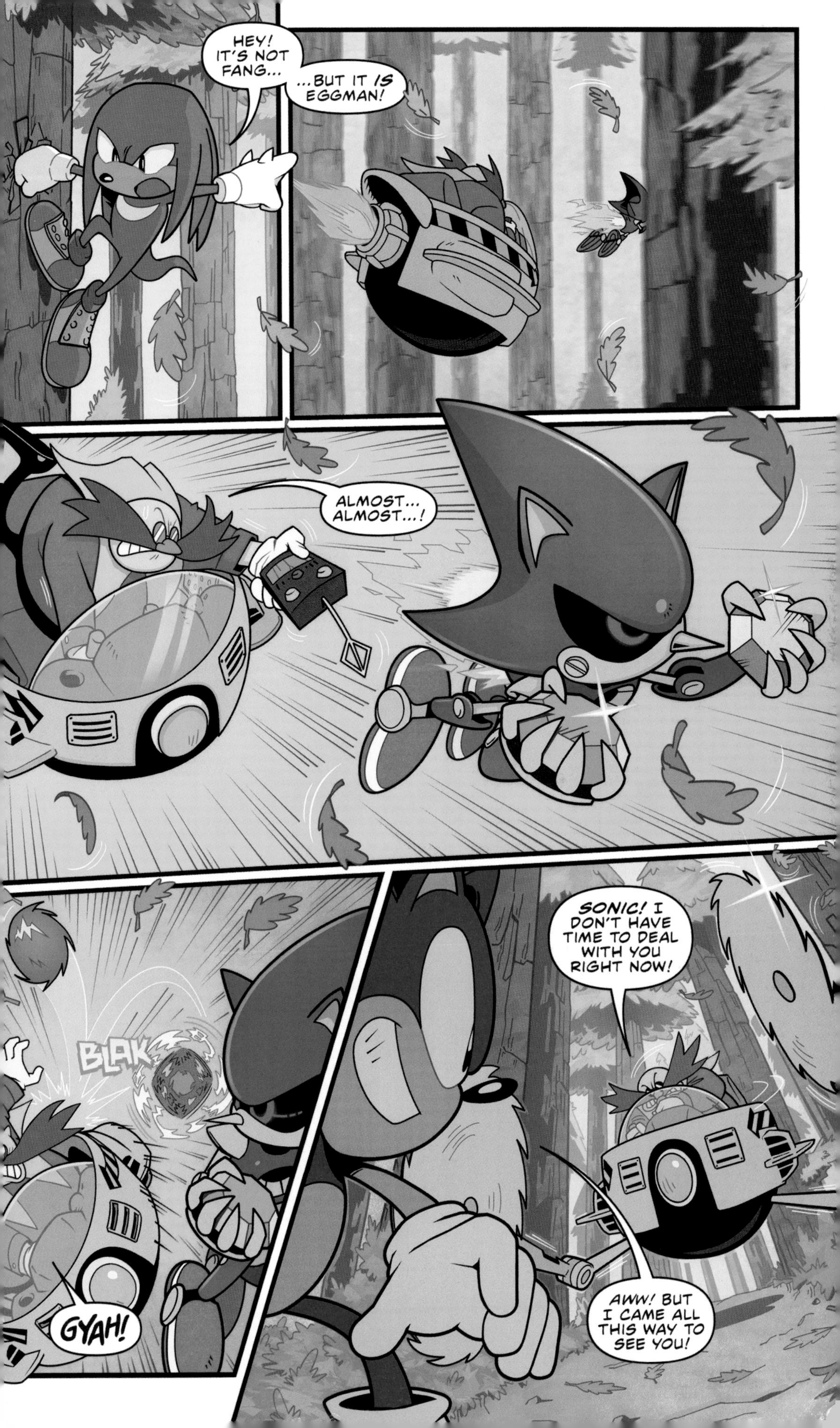
HEY! IT'S NOT FANG...
...BUT IT IS EGGMAN!
ALMOST... ALMOST...!
BLAK
GYAH!
SONIC! I DON'T HAVE TIME TO DEAL WITH YOU RIGHT NOW!
AWW! BUT I CAME ALL THIS WAY TO SEE YOU!

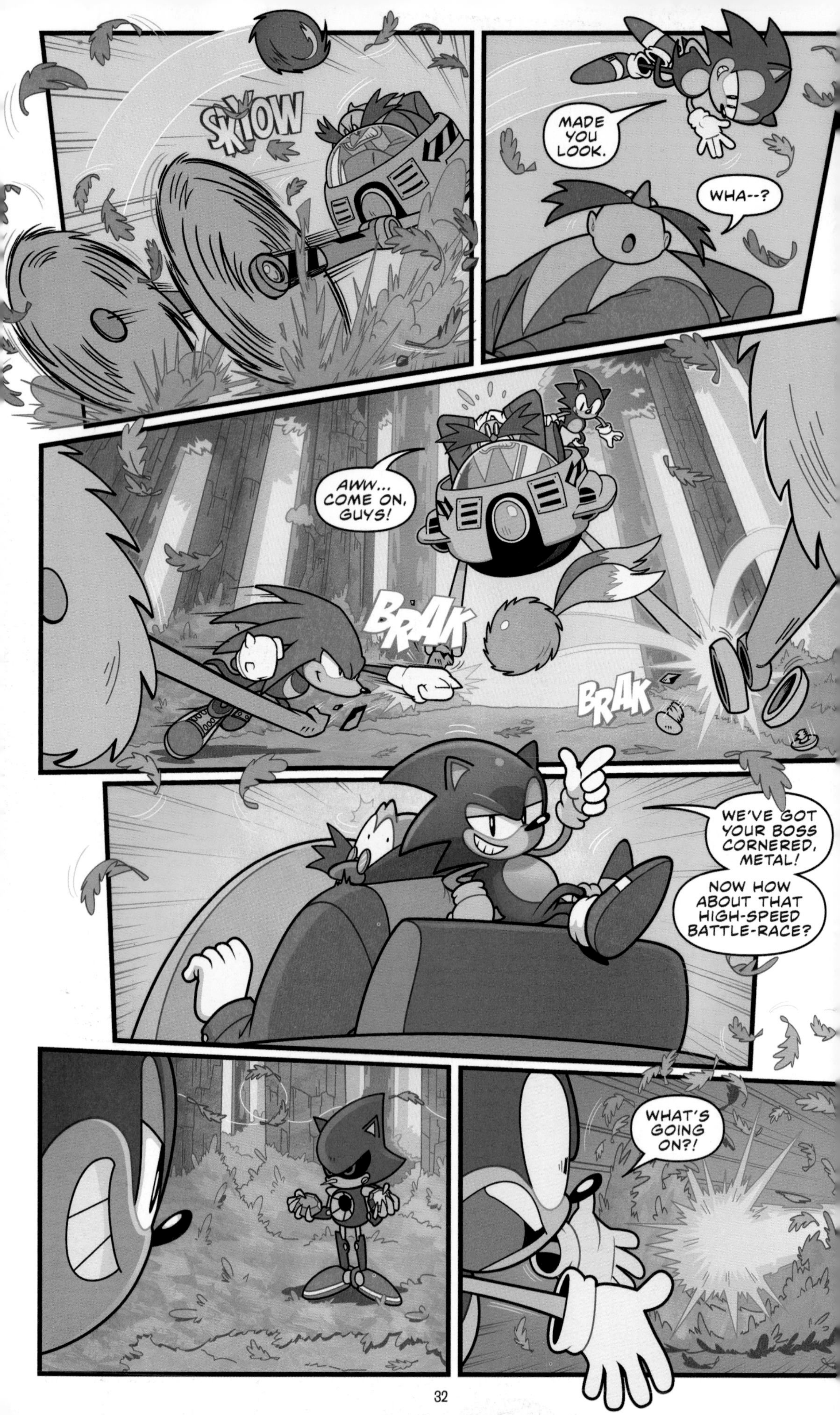
SKIOW
MADE YOU LOOK.
WHA--?
AWW... COME ON, GUYS!
BRAK
BRAK
WE'VE GOT YOUR BOSS CORNERED, METAL!
NOW HOW ABOUT THAT HIGH-SPEED BATTLE-RACE?
WHAT'S GOING ON?!

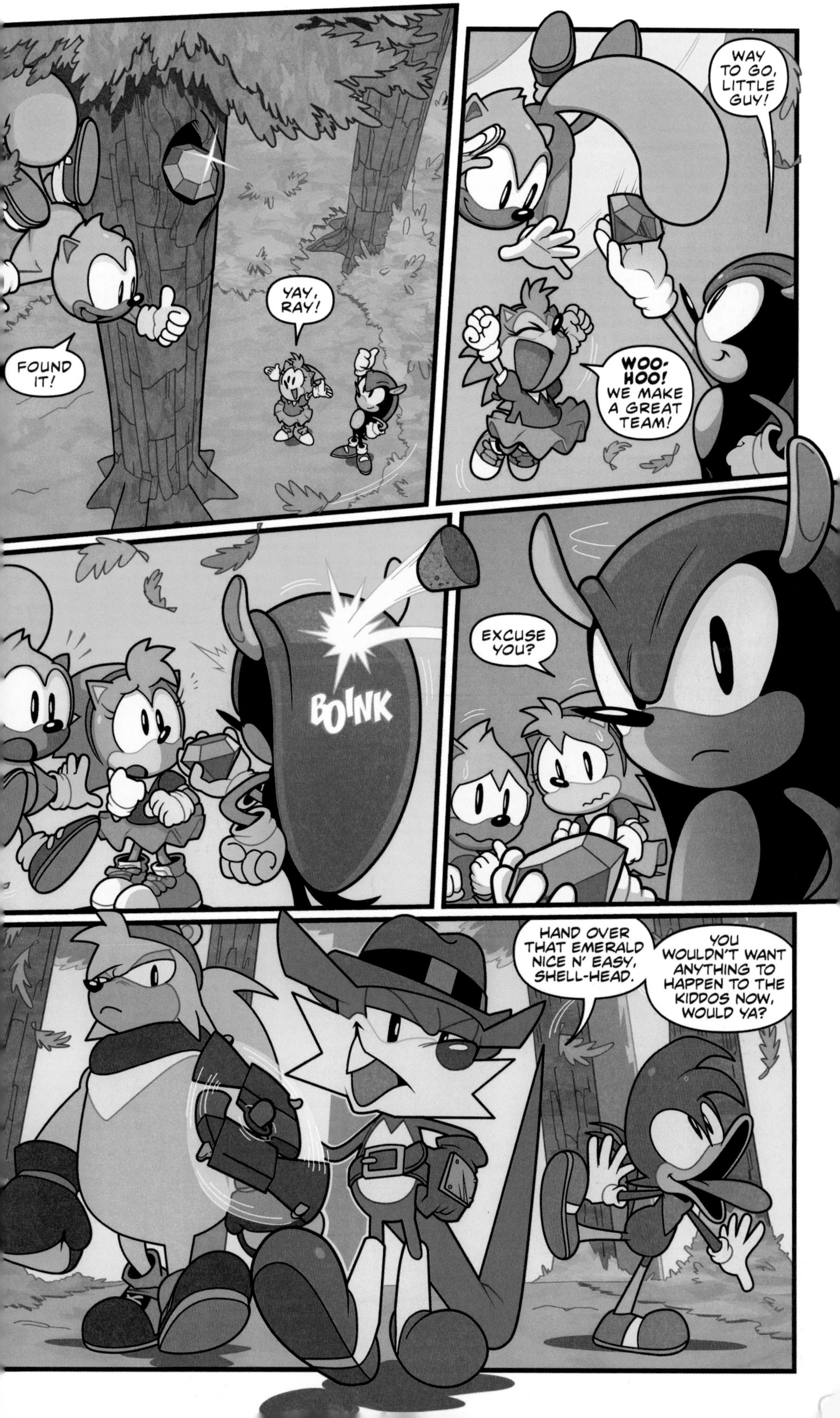
FOUND IT!
YAY, RAY!
WAY TO GO, LITTLE GUY!
WOO-HOO! WE MAKE A GREAT TEAM!
BOINK
EXCUSE YOU?
HAND OVER THAT EMERALD NICE N' EASY, SHELL-HEAD.
YOU WOULDN'T WANT ANYTHING TO HAPPEN TO THE KIDDOS NOW, WOULD YA?

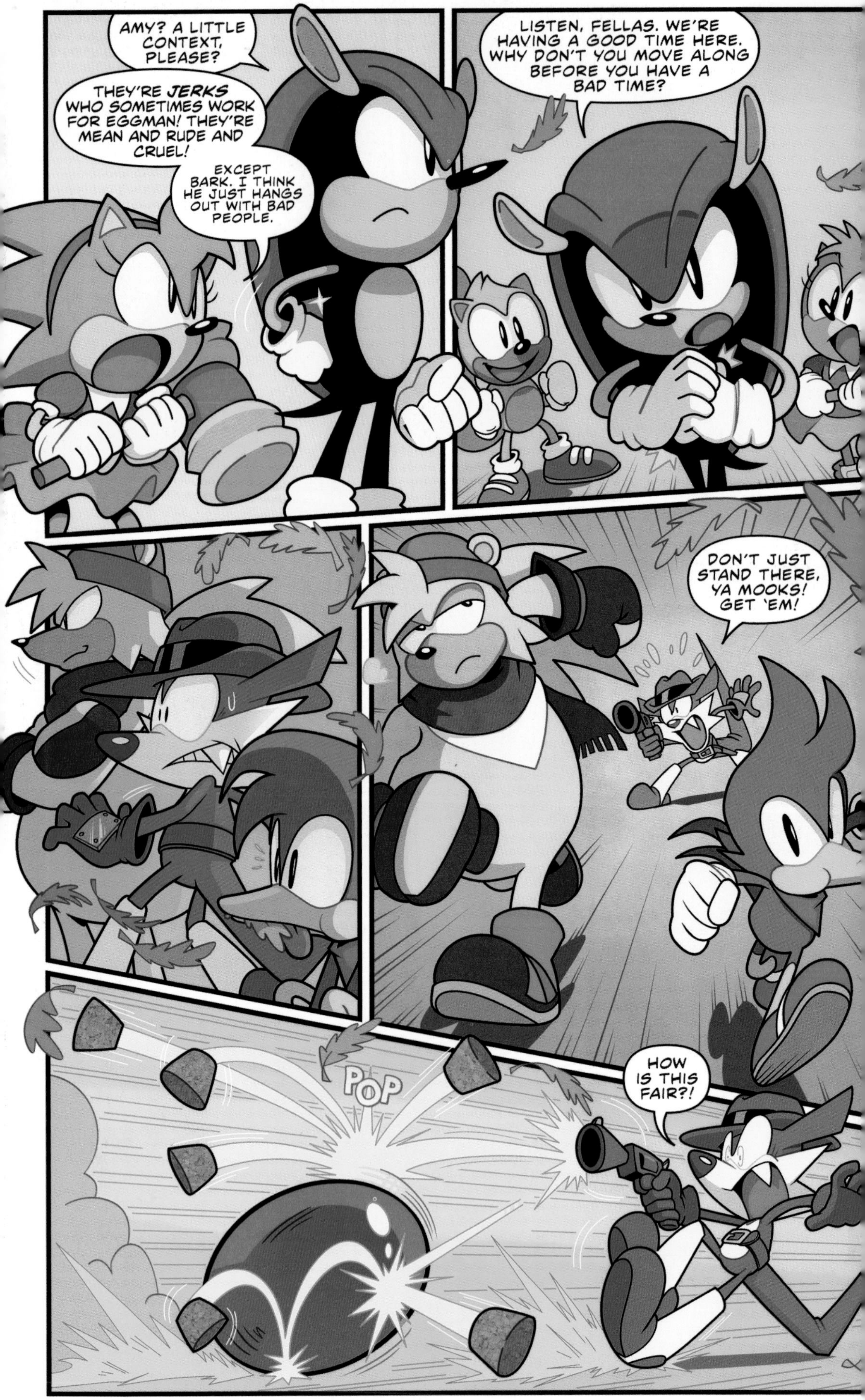

AMY? A LITTLE CONTEXT, PLEASE?
THEY'RE JERKS WHO SOMETIMES WORK FOR EGGMAN! THEY'RE MEAN AND RUDE AND CRUEL!
EXCEPT BARK. I THINK HE JUST HANGS OUT WITH BAD PEOPLE.
LISTEN, FELLAS. WE'RE HAVING A GOOD TIME HERE. WHY DON'T YOU MOVE ALONG BEFORE YOU HAVE A BAD TIME?
DON'T JUST STAND THERE, YA MOOKS! GET 'EM!
POP
HOW IS THIS FAIR?!

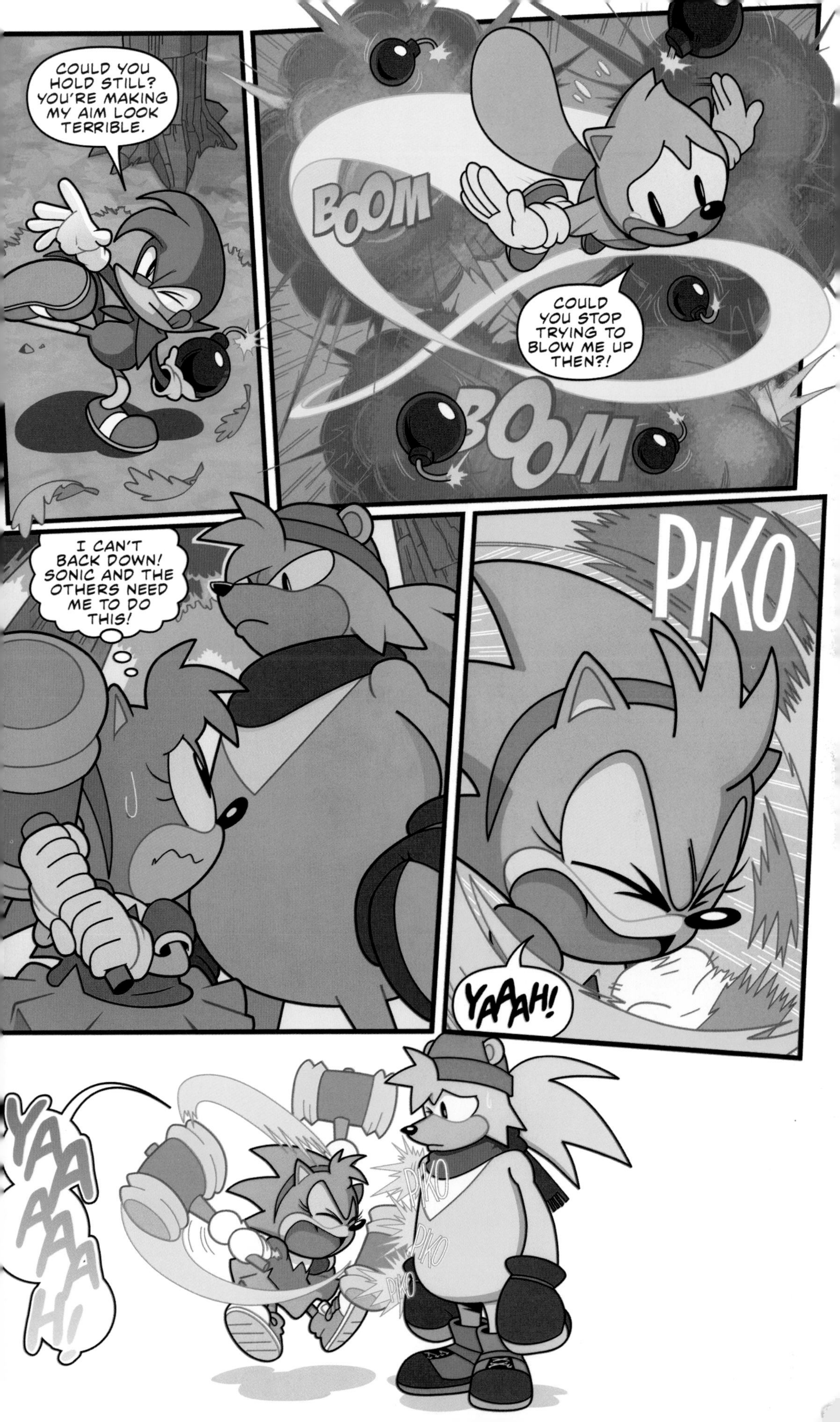
COULD YOU HOLD STILL? YOU'RE MAKING MY AIM LOOK TERRIBLE.
BOOM
COULD YOU STOP TRYING TO BLOW ME UP THEN?!
BOOM
I CAN'T BACK DOWN! SONIC AND THE OTHERS NEED ME TO DO THIS!
PIKO
YAAAH!
YAAAAAAH!
PIKO
PIKO
PIKO

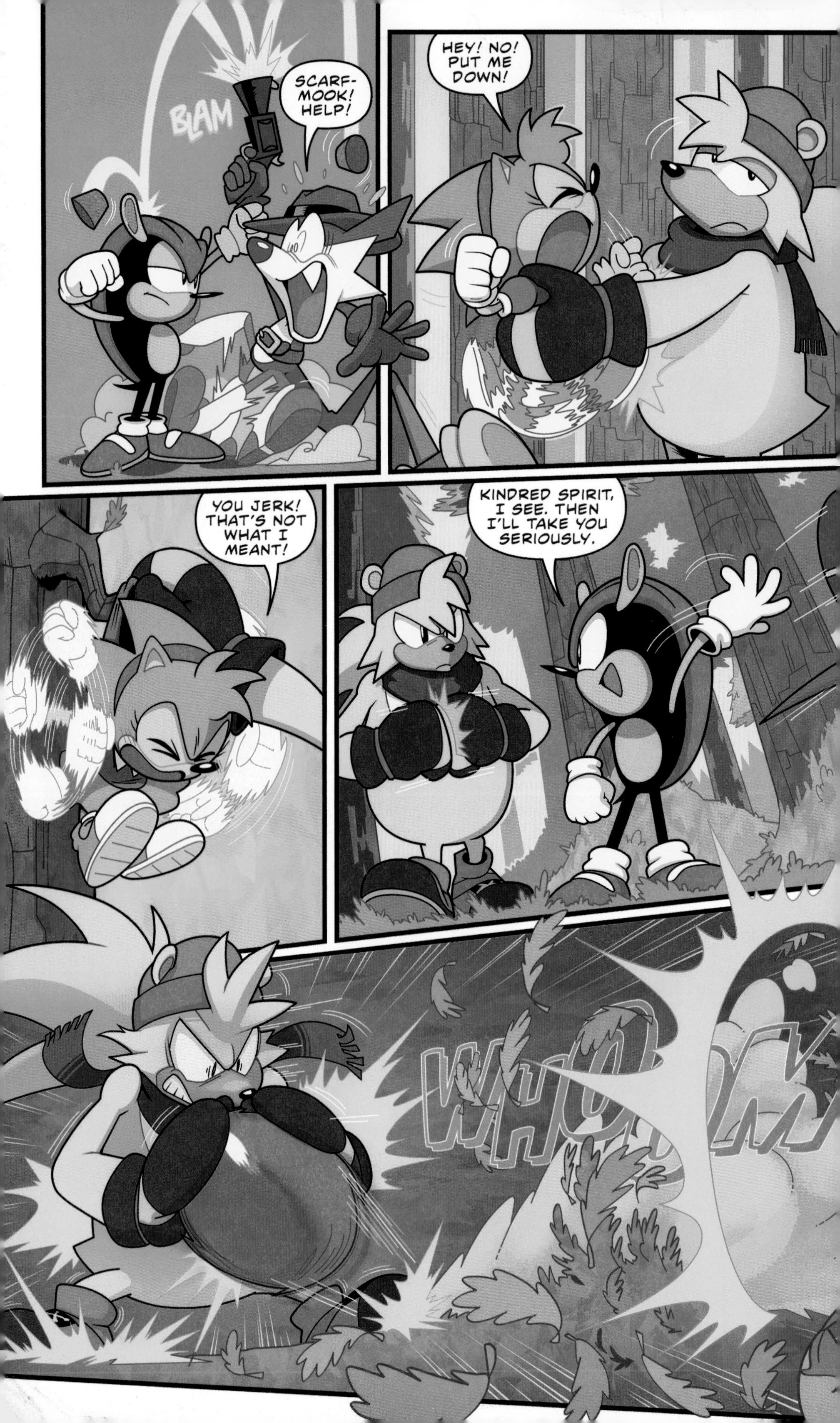
BLAM
SCARF-MOOK! HELP!
HEY! NO! PUT ME DOWN!
YOU JERK! THAT'S NOT WHAT I MEANT!
KINDRED SPIRIT, I SEE. THEN I'LL TAKE YOU SERIOUSLY.

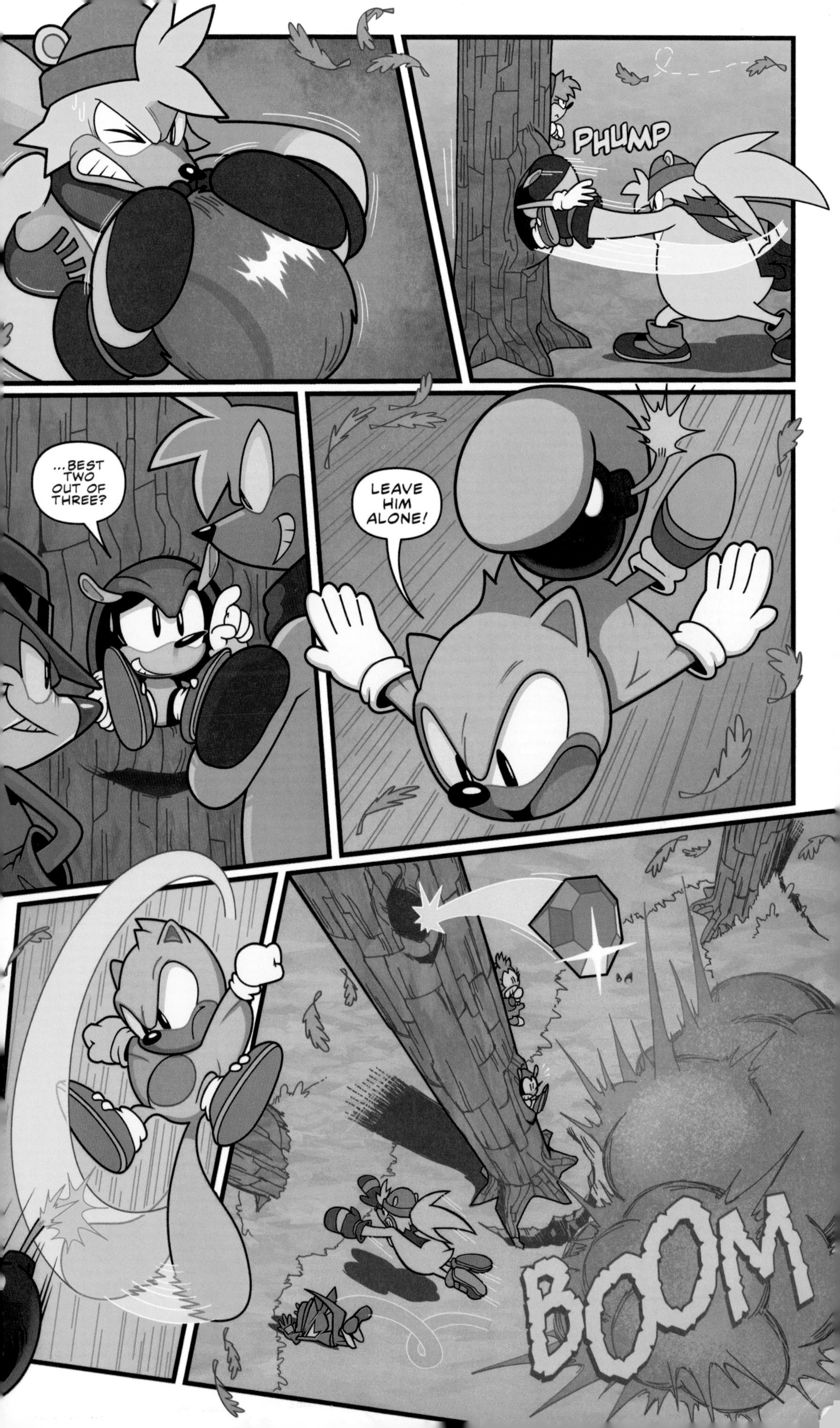
PHUMP
...BEST TWO OUT OF THREE?
LEAVE HIM ALONE!
BOOM

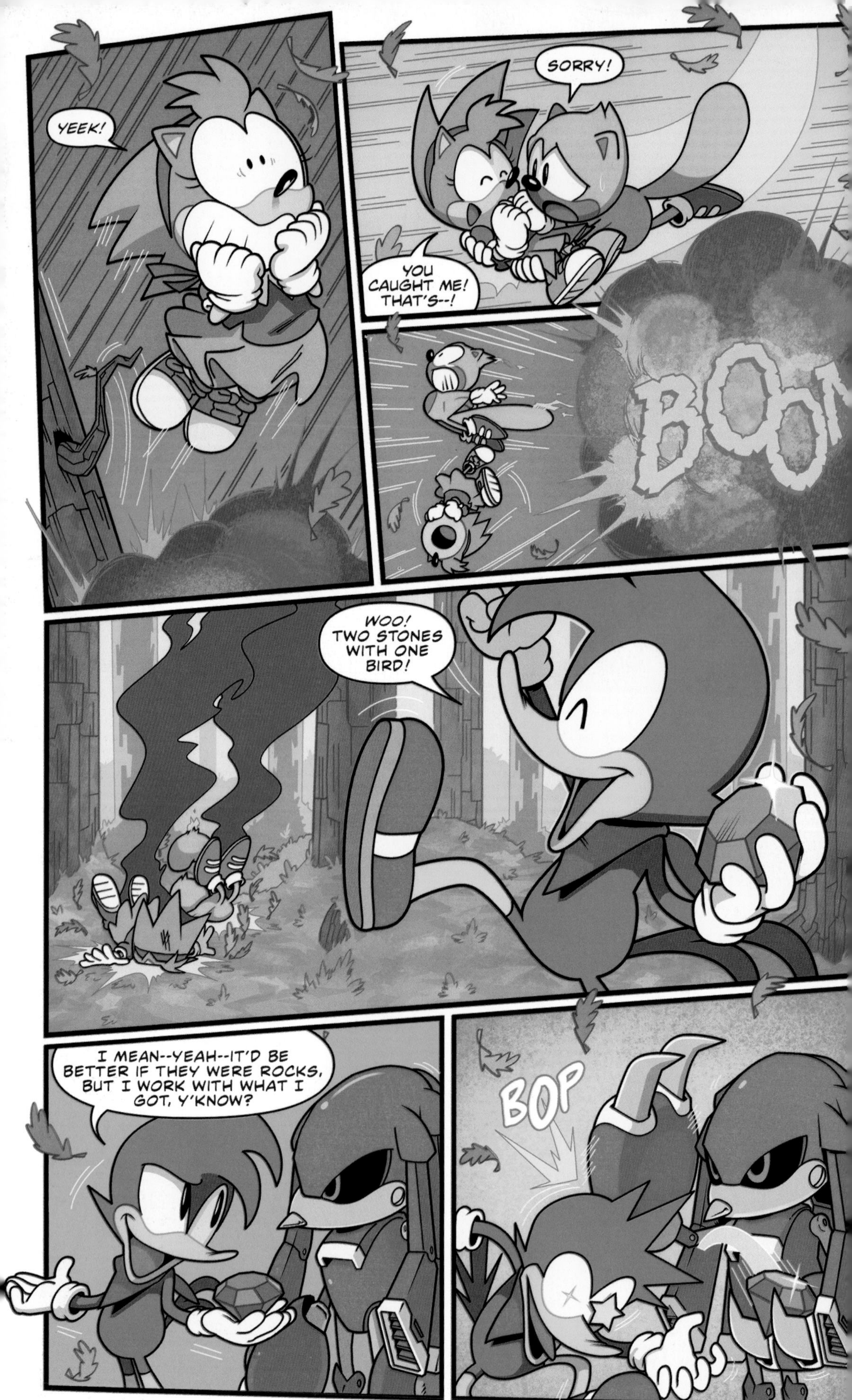
YEEK!
SORRY!
YOU CAUGHT ME! THAT'S--!
BOOM
WOO! TWO STONES WITH ONE BIRD!
I MEAN--YEAH--IT'D BE BETTER IF THEY WERE ROCKS, BUT I WORK WITH WHAT I GOT, Y'KNOW?
BOP

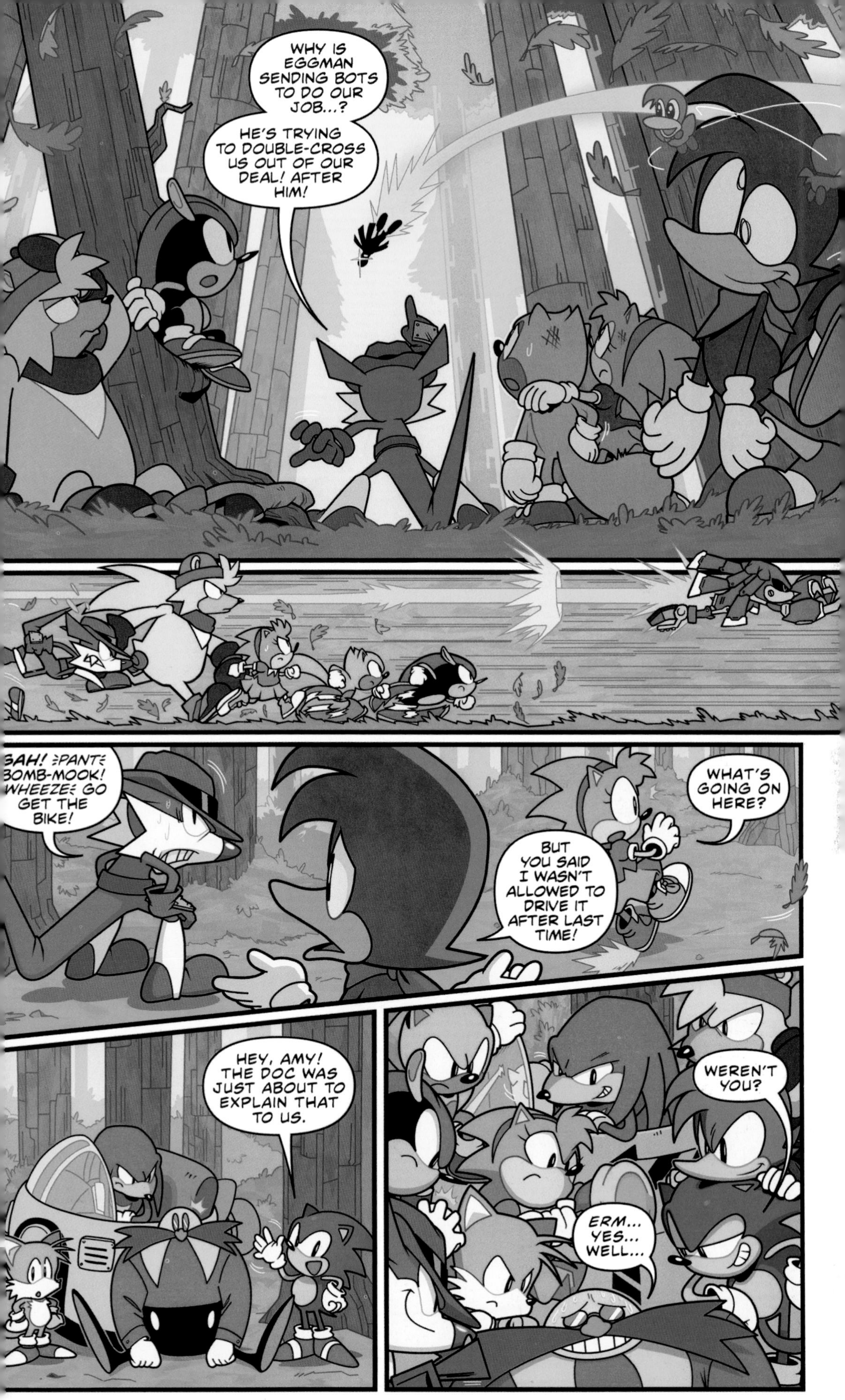
WHY IS EGGMAN SENDING BOTS TO DO OUR JOB...?
HE'S TRYING TO DOUBLE-CROSS US OUT OF OUR DEAL! AFTER HIM!
GAH! =PANT= BOMB-MOOK! =WHEEZE= GO GET THE BIKE!
BUT YOU SAID I WASN'T ALLOWED TO DRIVE IT AFTER LAST TIME!
WHAT'S GOING ON HERE?
HEY, AMY! THE DOC WAS JUST ABOUT TO EXPLAIN THAT TO US.
WEREN'T YOU?
ERM... YES... WELL...

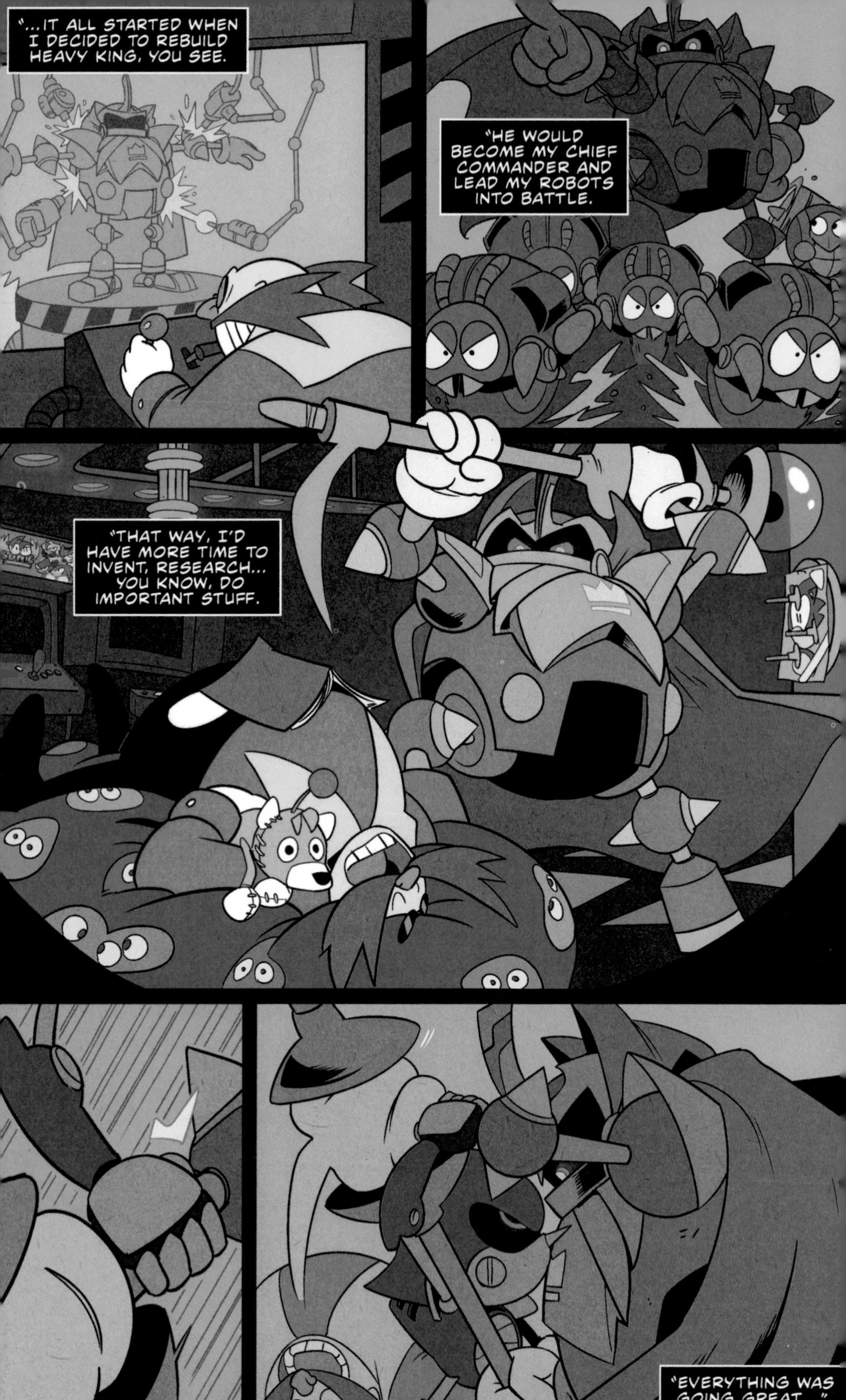
"...IT ALL STARTED WHEN I DECIDED TO REBUILD HEAVY KING, YOU SEE.
"HE WOULD BECOME MY CHIEF COMMANDER AND LEAD MY ROBOTS INTO BATTLE.
"THAT WAY, I'D HAVE MORE TIME TO INVENT, RESEARCH... YOU KNOW, DO IMPORTANT STUFF.
"EVERYTHING WAS GOING GREAT..."

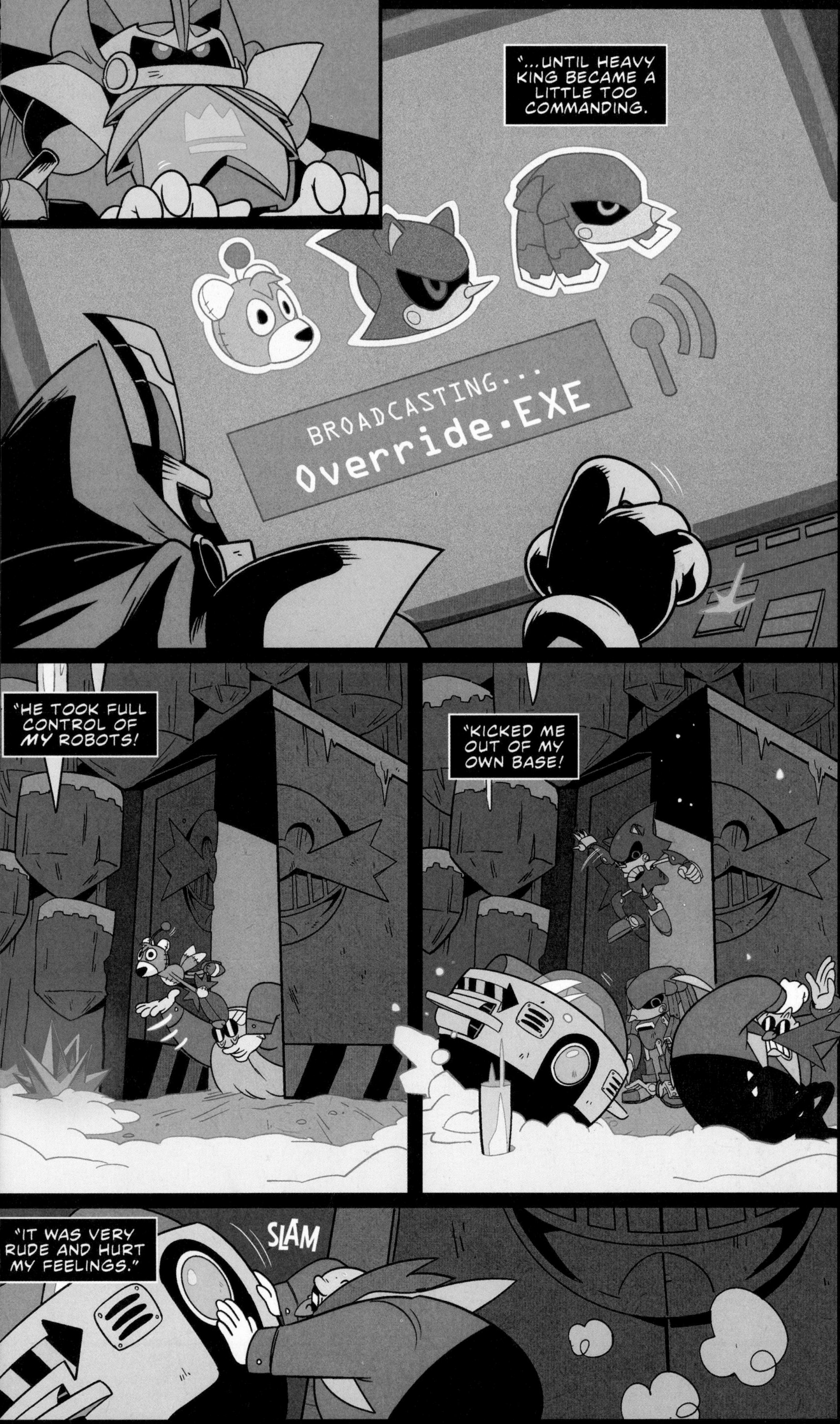
"...UNTIL HEAVY KING BECAME A LITTLE TOO COMMANDING.
BROADCASTING...
Override.EXE
"HE TOOK FULL CONTROL OF MY ROBOTS!
"KICKED ME OUT OF MY OWN BASE!
"IT WAS VERY RUDE AND HURT MY FEELINGS."
SLAM

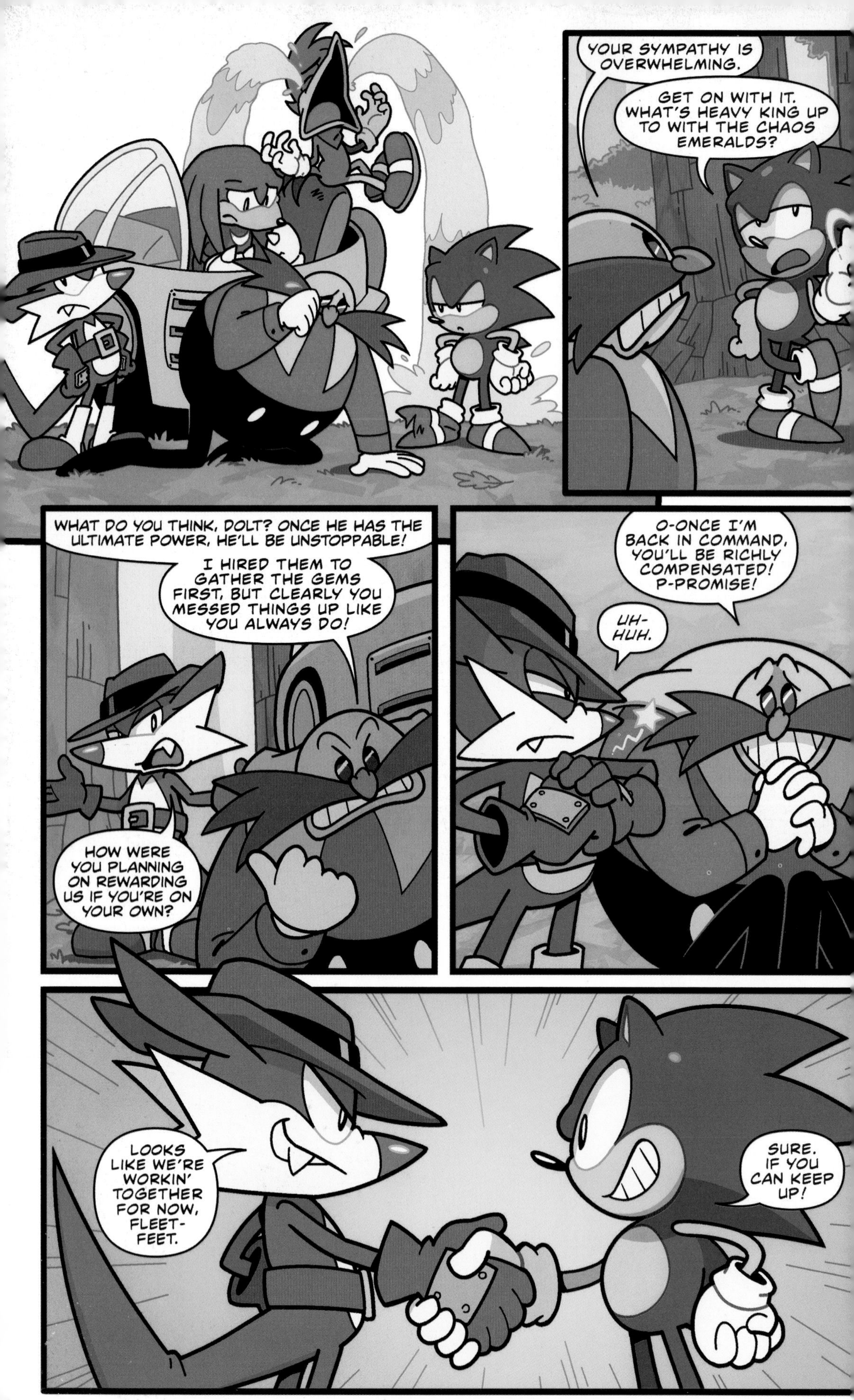
YOUR SYMPATHY IS OVERWHELMING.
GET ON WITH IT. WHAT'S HEAVY KING UP TO WITH THE CHAOS EMERALDS?
WHAT DO YOU THINK, DOLT? ONCE HE HAS THE ULTIMATE POWER, HE'LL BE UNSTOPPABLE!
I HIRED THEM TO GATHER THE GEMS FIRST, BUT CLEARLY YOU MESSED THINGS UP LIKE YOU ALWAYS DO!
HOW WERE YOU PLANNING ON REWARDING US IF YOU'RE ON YOUR OWN?
O-ONCE I'M BACK IN COMMAND, YOU'LL BE RICHLY COMPENSATED! P-PROMISE!
UH-HUH.
LOOKS LIKE WE'RE WORKIN' TOGETHER FOR NOW, FLEET-FEET.
SURE. IF YOU CAN KEEP UP!

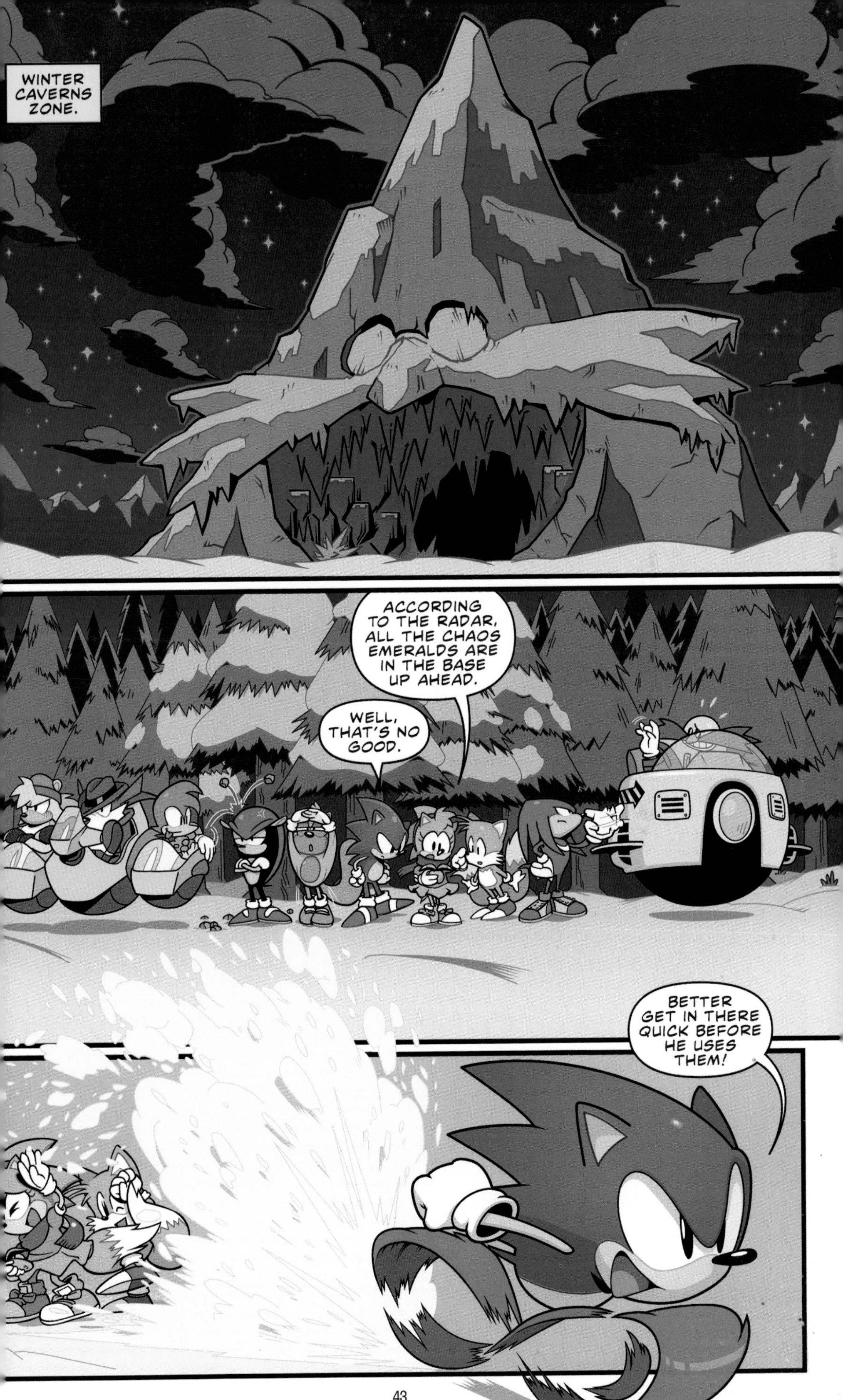
WINTER CAVERNS ZONE.
ACCORDING TO THE RADAR, ALL THE CHAOS EMERALDS ARE IN THE BASE UP AHEAD.
WELL, THAT'S NO GOOD.
BETTER GET IN THERE QUICK BEFORE HE USES THEM!

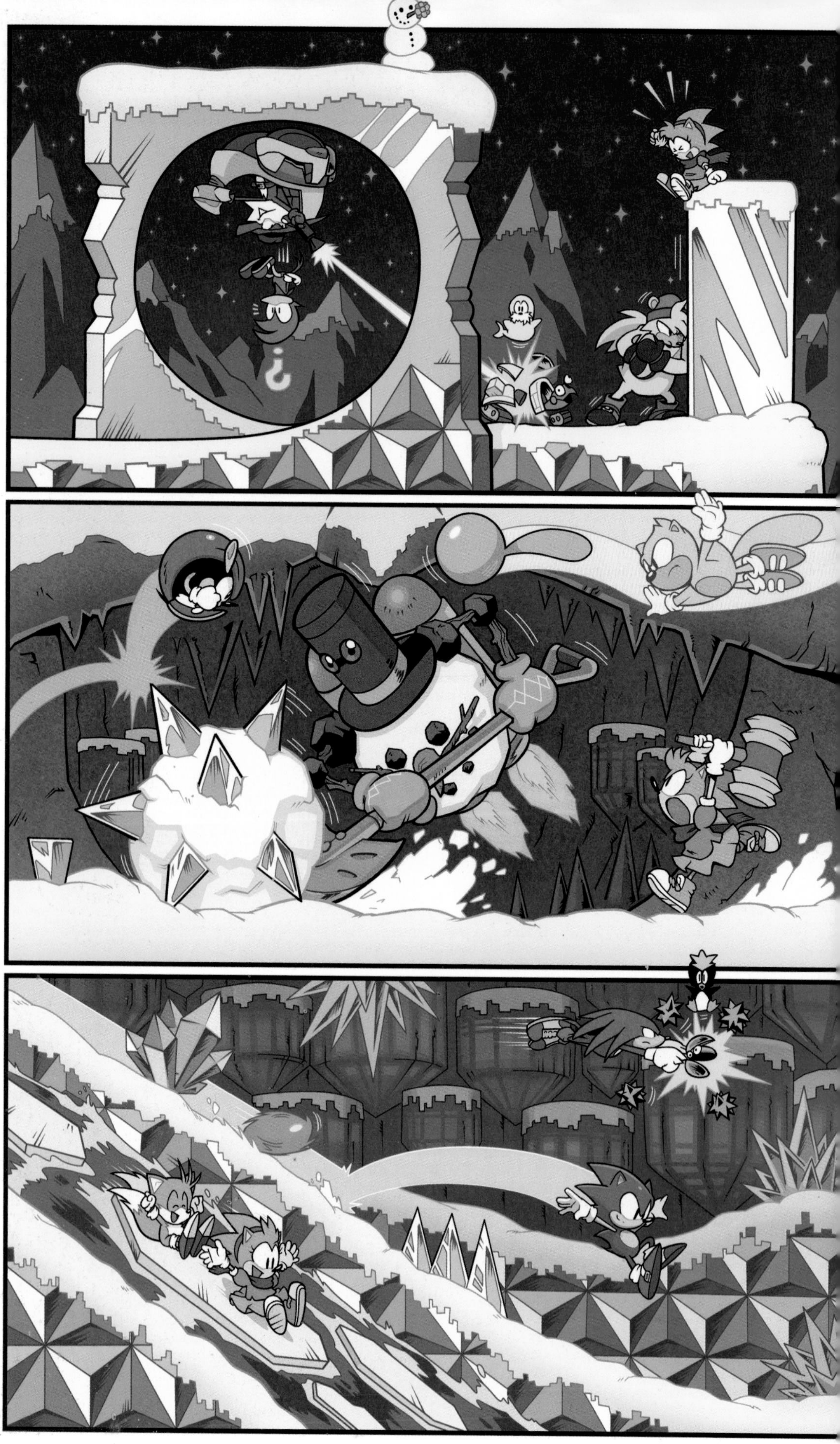

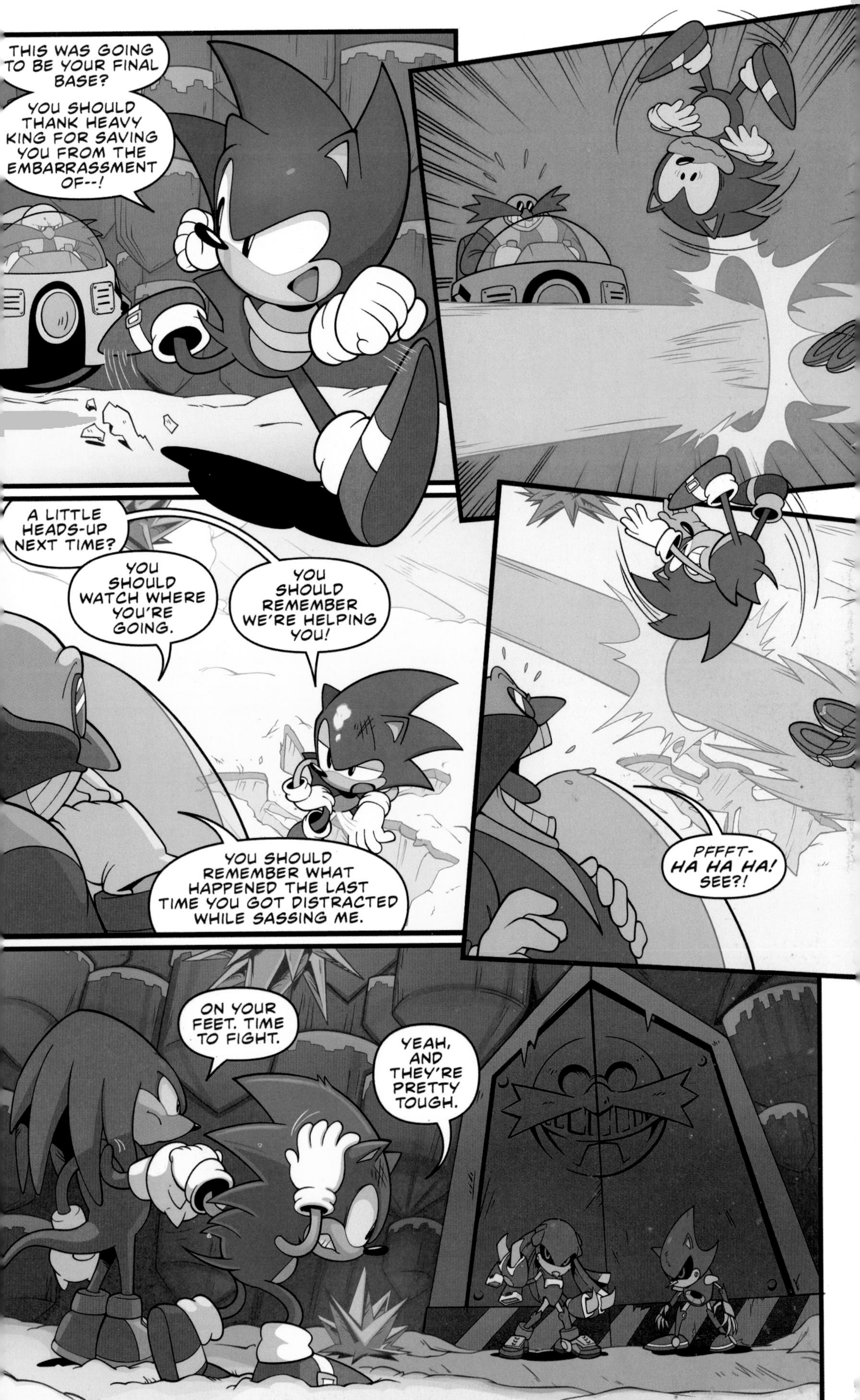
THIS WAS GOING TO BE YOUR FINAL BASE?
YOU SHOULD THANK HEAVY KING FOR SAVING YOU FROM THE EMBARRASSMENT OF--!
A LITTLE HEADS-UP NEXT TIME?
YOU SHOULD WATCH WHERE YOU'RE GOING.
YOU SHOULD REMEMBER WE'RE HELPING YOU!
YOU SHOULD REMEMBER WHAT HAPPENED THE LAST TIME YOU GOT DISTRACTED WHILE SASSING ME.
PFFFT- HA HA HA! SEE?!
ON YOUR FEET. TIME TO FIGHT.
YEAH, AND THEY'RE PRETTY TOUGH.

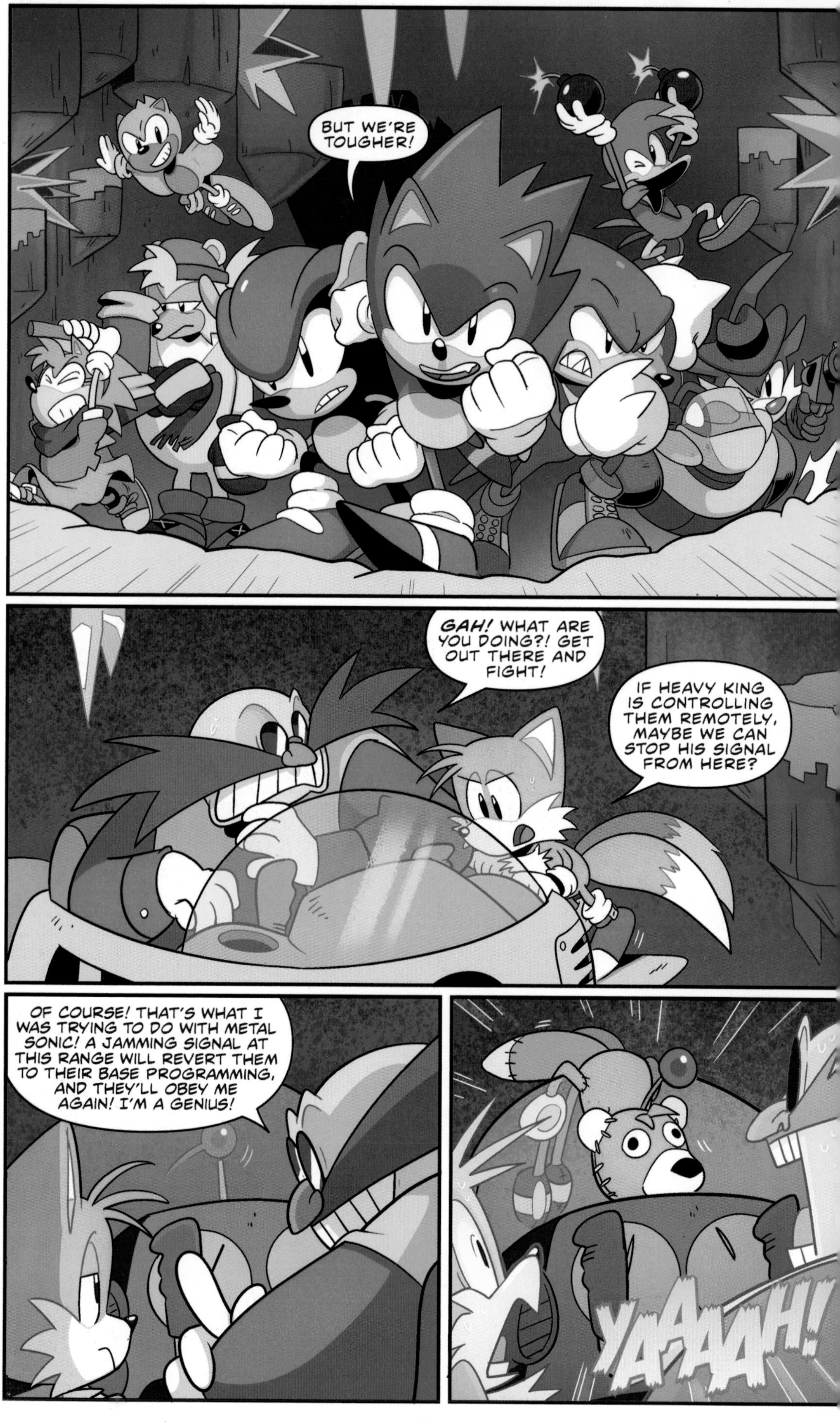
BUT WE'RE TOUGHER!
GAH! WHAT ARE YOU DOING?! GET OUT THERE AND FIGHT!
IF HEAVY KING IS CONTROLLING THEM REMOTELY, MAYBE WE CAN STOP HIS SIGNAL FROM HERE?
OF COURSE! THAT'S WHAT I WAS TRYING TO DO WITH METAL SONIC! A JAMMING SIGNAL AT THIS RANGE WILL REVERT THEM TO THEIR BASE PROGRAMMING, AND THEY'LL OBEY ME AGAIN! I'M A GENIUS!
YAAAAH!

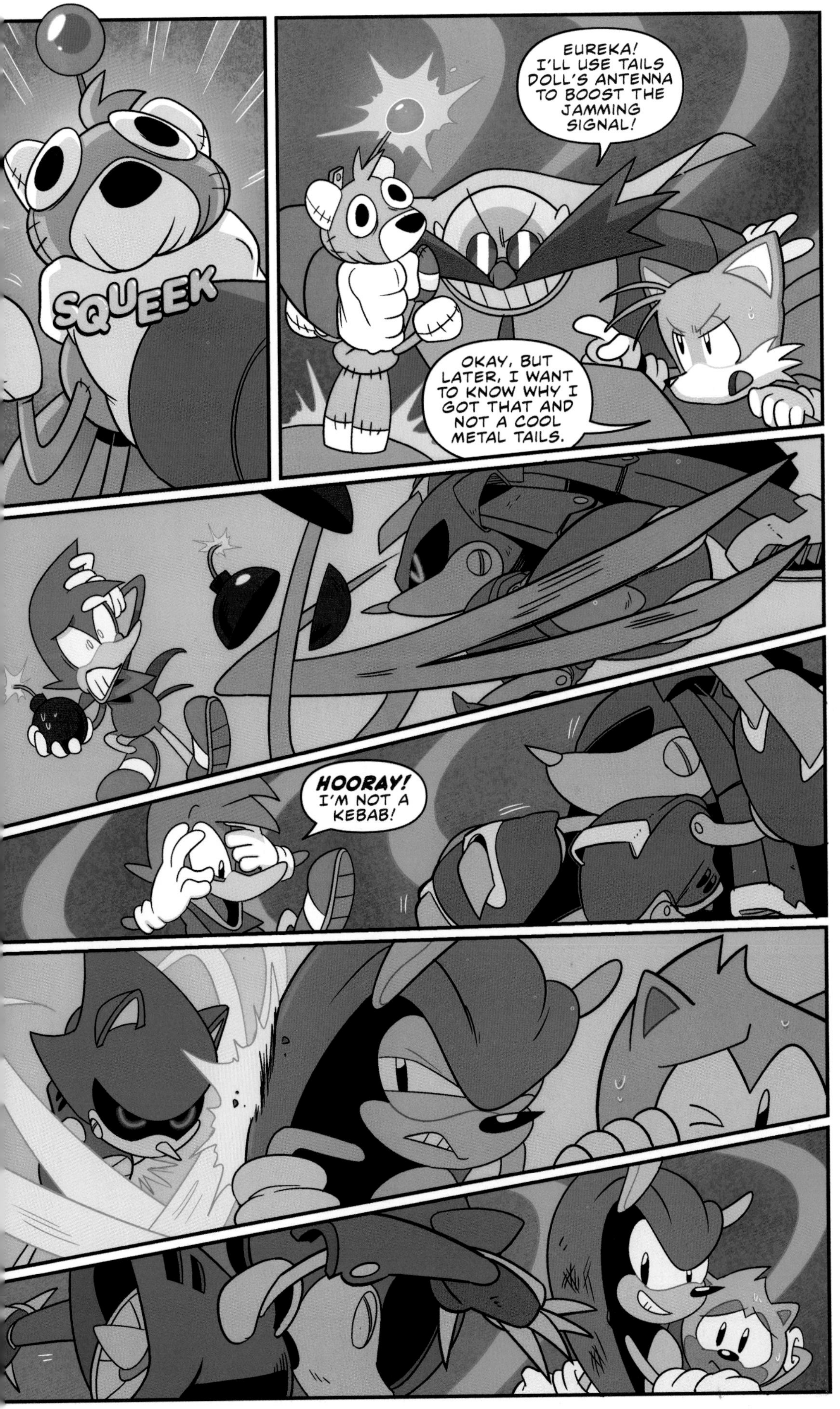
SQUEEK
EUREKA! I'LL USE TAILS DOLL'S ANTENNA TO BOOST THE JAMMING SIGNAL!
OKAY, BUT LATER, I WANT TO KNOW WHY I GOT THAT AND NOT A COOL METAL TAILS.
HOORAY! I'M NOT A KEBAB!

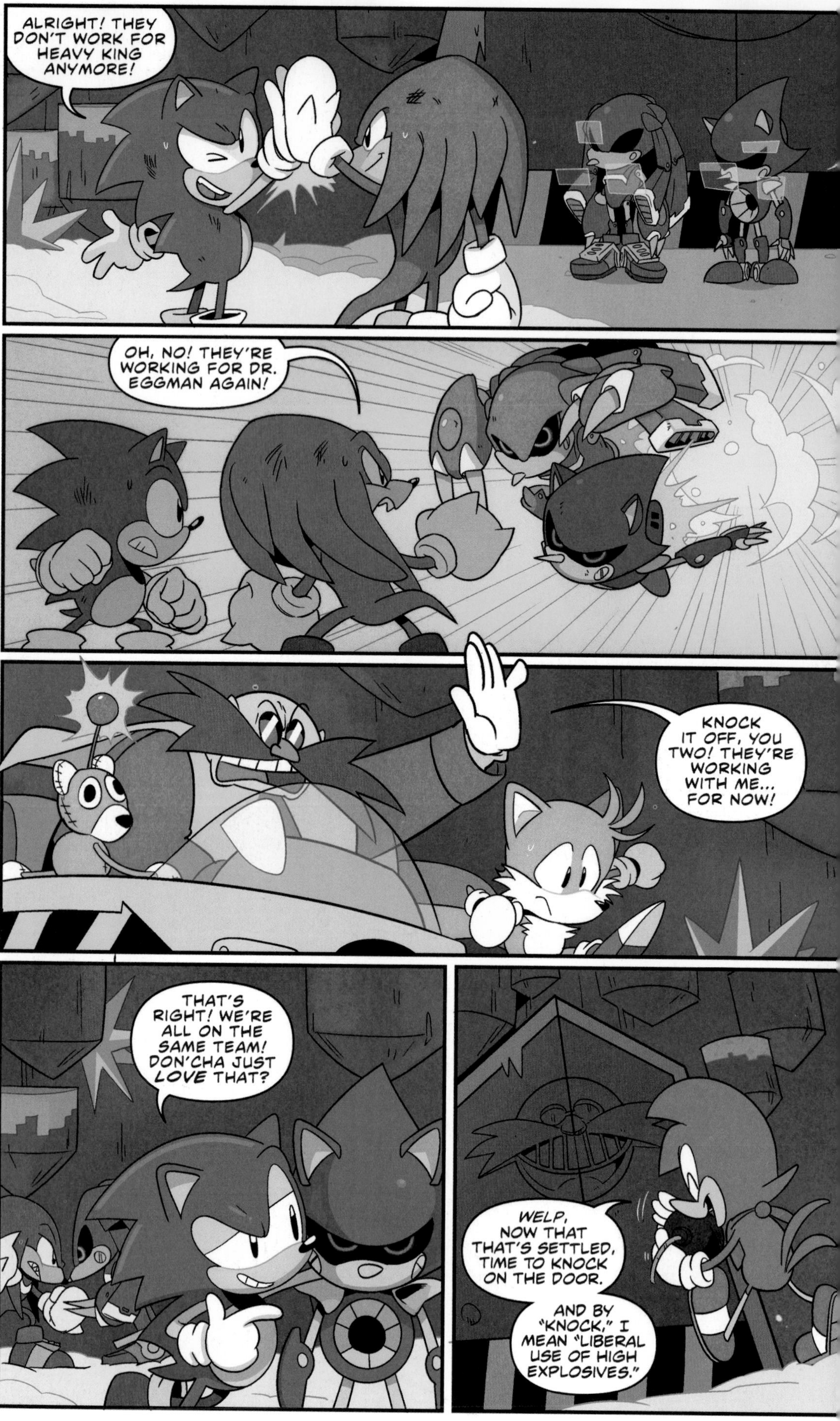
ALRIGHT! THEY DON'T WORK FOR HEAVY KING ANYMORE!
OH, NO! THEY'RE WORKING FOR DR. EGGMAN AGAIN!
KNOCK IT OFF, YOU TWO! THEY'RE WORKING WITH ME... FOR NOW!
THAT'S RIGHT! WE'RE ALL ON THE SAME TEAM! DON'CHA JUST LOVE THAT?
WELP, NOW THAT THAT'S SETTLED, TIME TO KNOCK ON THE DOOR.
AND BY "KNOCK," I MEAN "LIBERAL USE OF HIGH EXPLOSIVES."

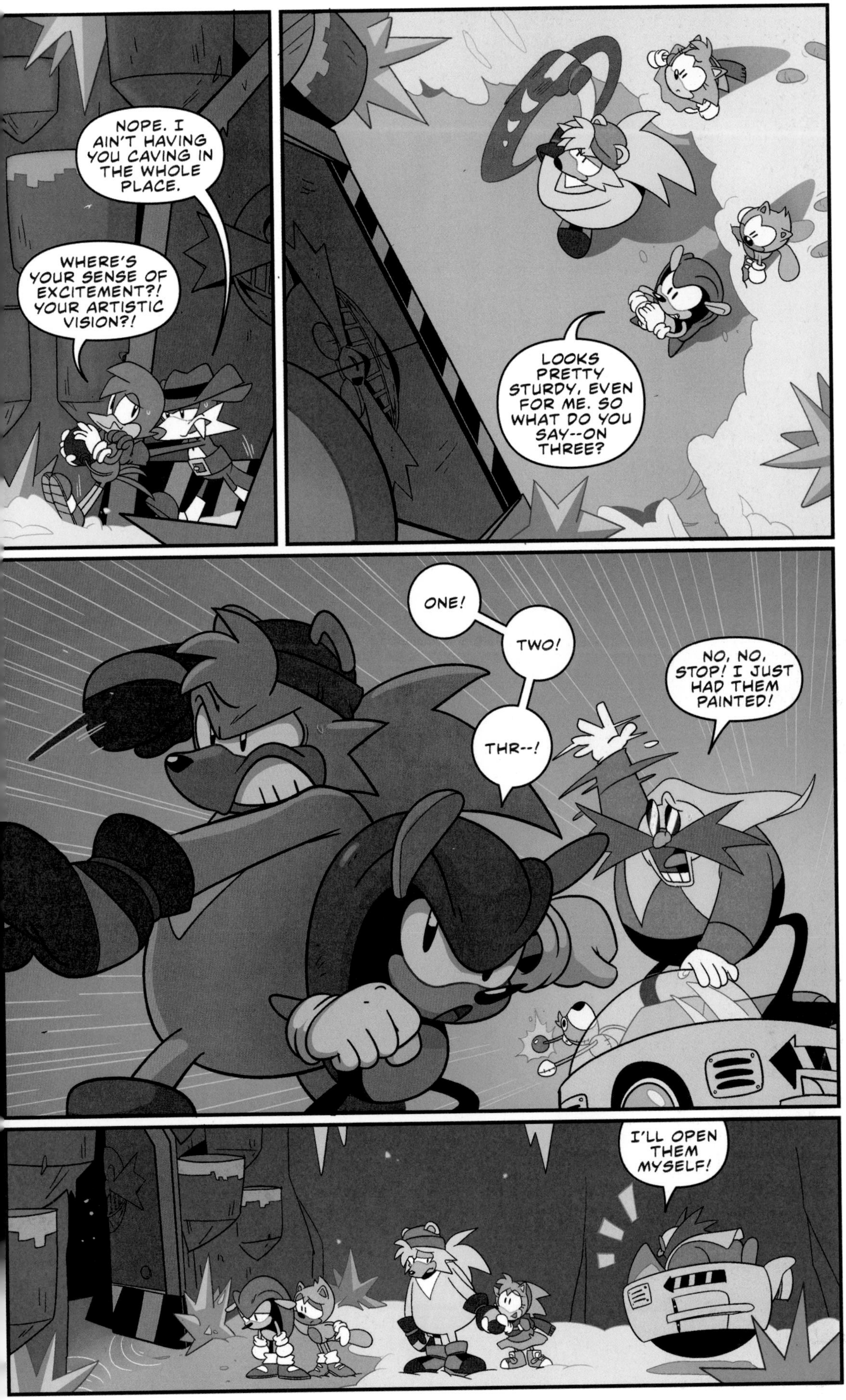
NOPE. I AIN'T HAVING YOU CAVING IN THE WHOLE PLACE.
WHERE'S YOUR SENSE OF EXCITEMENT?! YOUR ARTISTIC VISION?!
LOOKS PRETTY STURDY, EVEN FOR ME. SO WHAT DO YOU SAY--ON THREE?
ONE!
TWO!
THR--!
NO, NO, STOP! I JUST HAD THEM PAINTED!
I'LL OPEN THEM MYSELF!

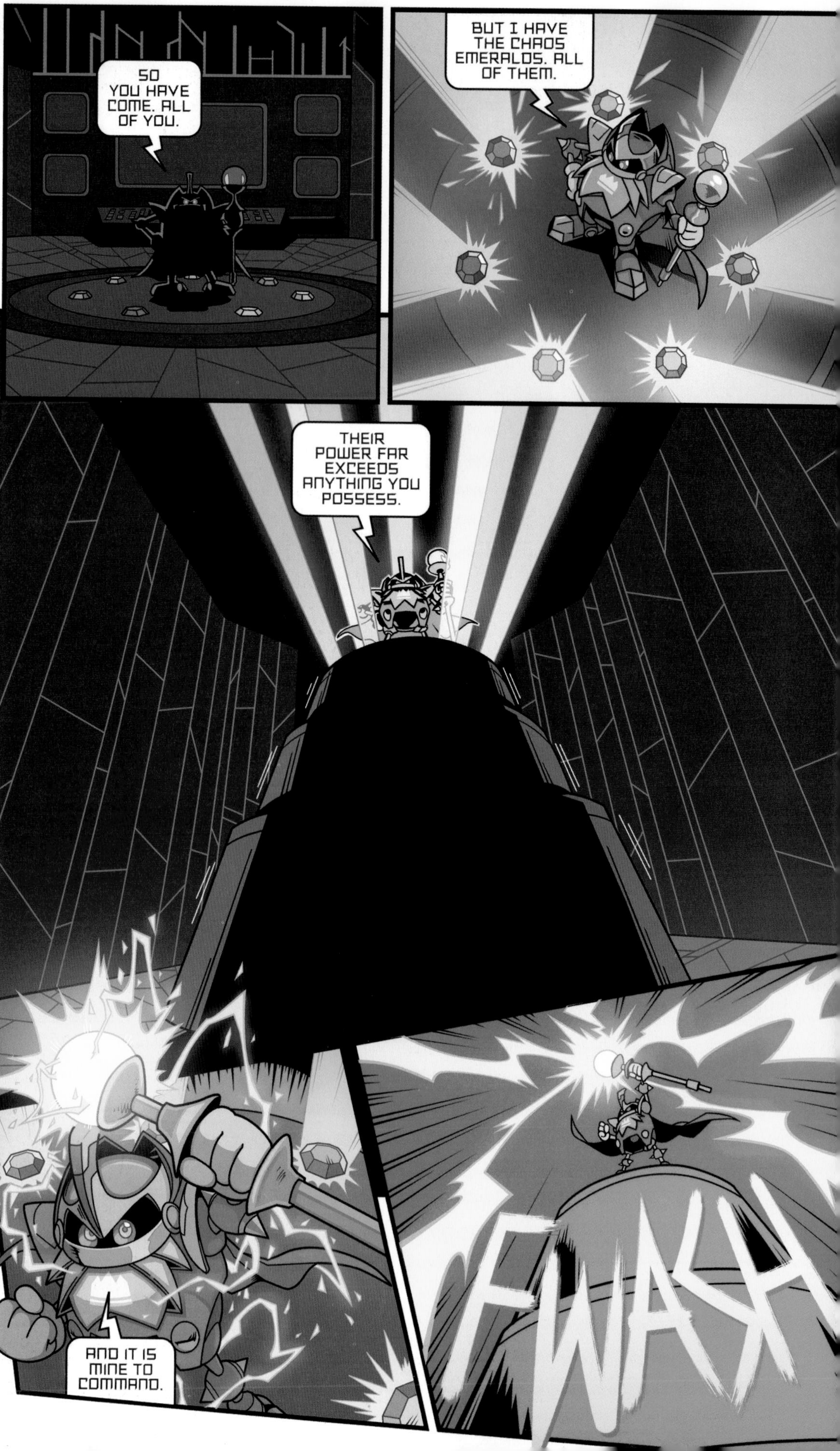
SO YOU HAVE COME. ALL OF YOU.
BUT I HAVE THE CHAOS EMERALDS. ALL OF THEM.
THEIR POWER FAR EXCEEDS ANYTHING YOU POSSESS.
AND IT IS MINE TO COMMAND.
FWASH

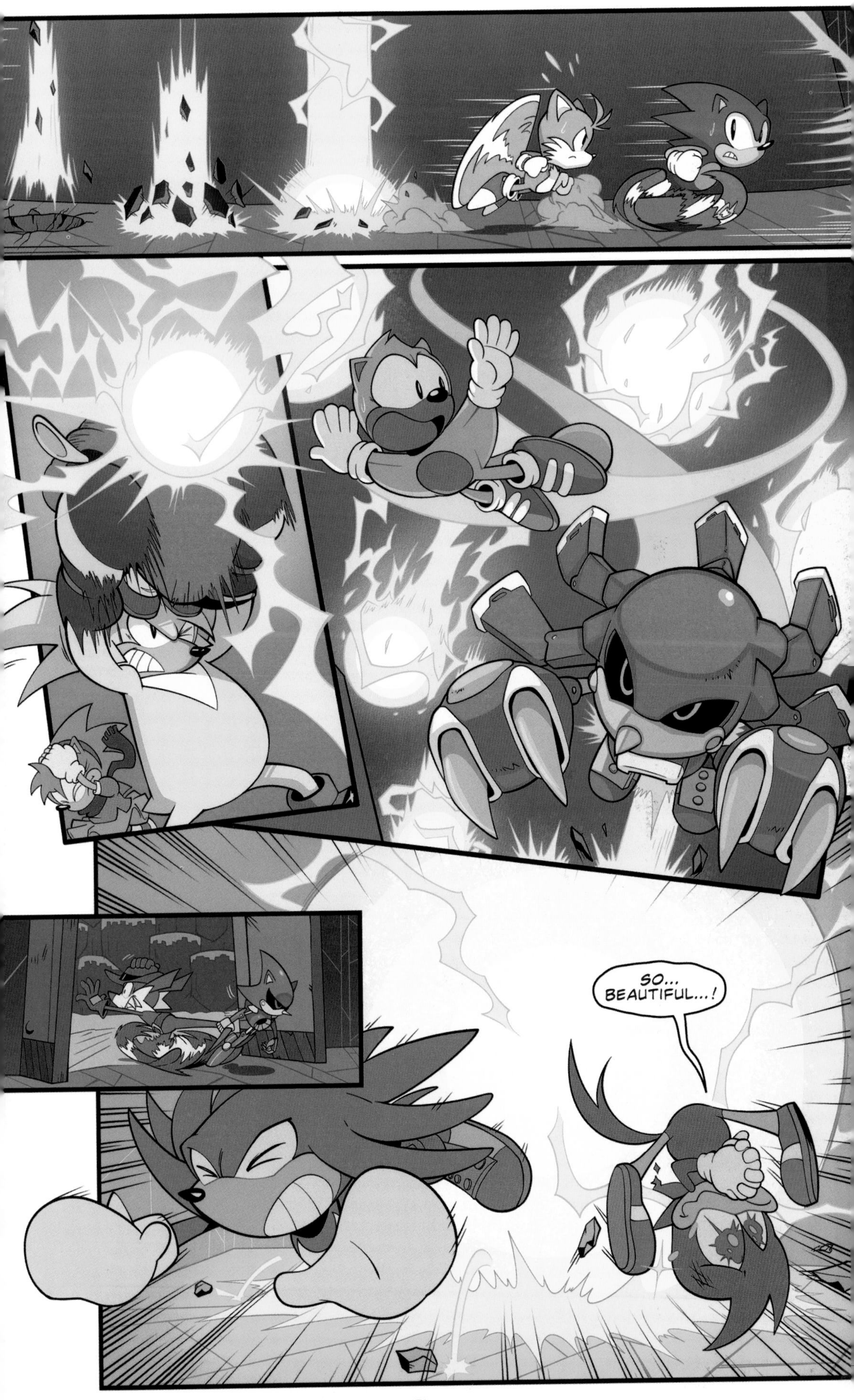
SO... BEAUTIFUL...!

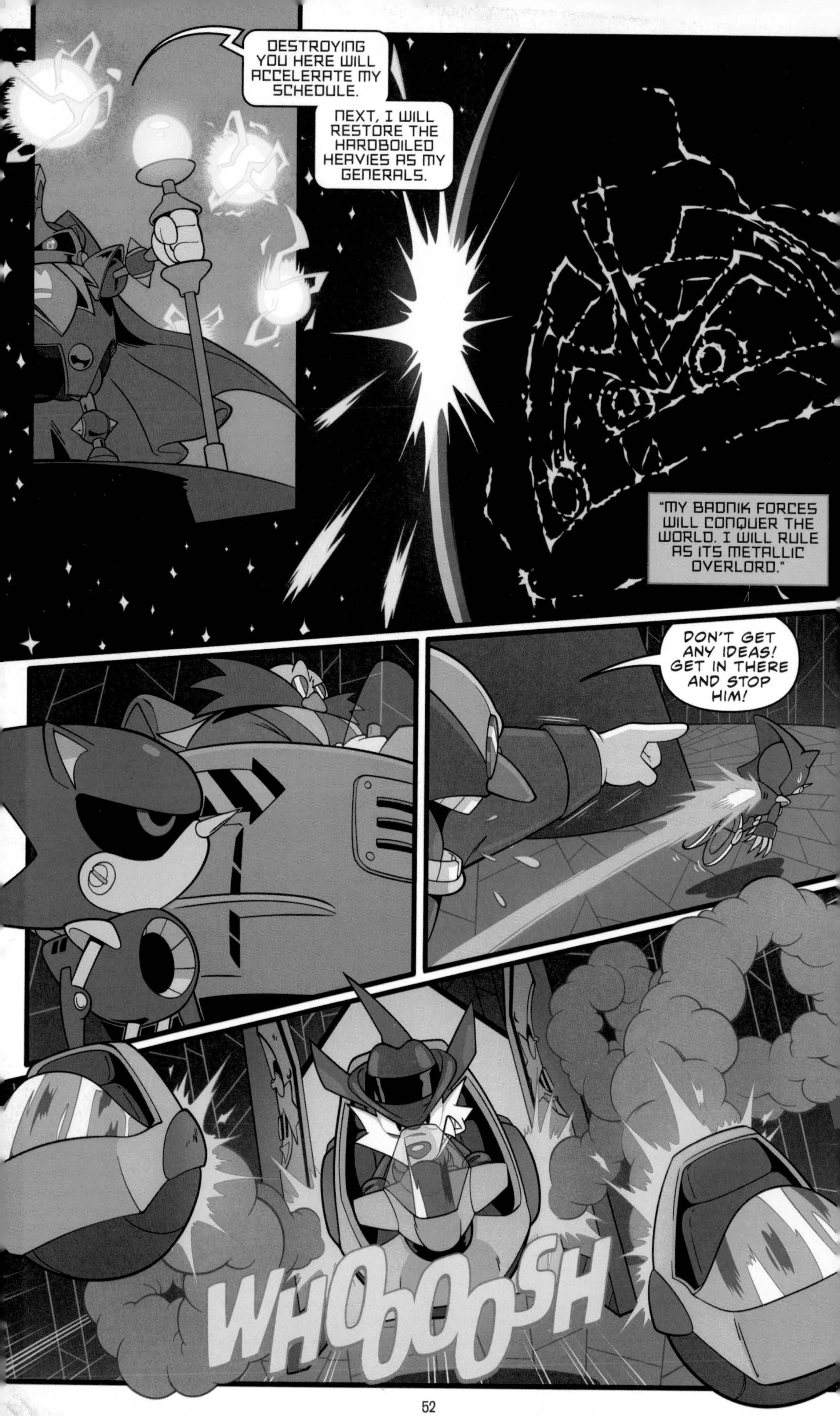
DESTROYING YOU HERE WILL ACCELERATE MY SCHEDULE.
NEXT, I WILL RESTORE THE HARDBOILED HEAVIES AS MY GENERALS.
"MY BADNIK FORCES WILL CONQUER THE WORLD. I WILL RULE AS ITS METALLIC OVERLORD."
DON'T GET ANY IDEAS! GET IN THERE AND STOP HIM!
WHOOOOOSH

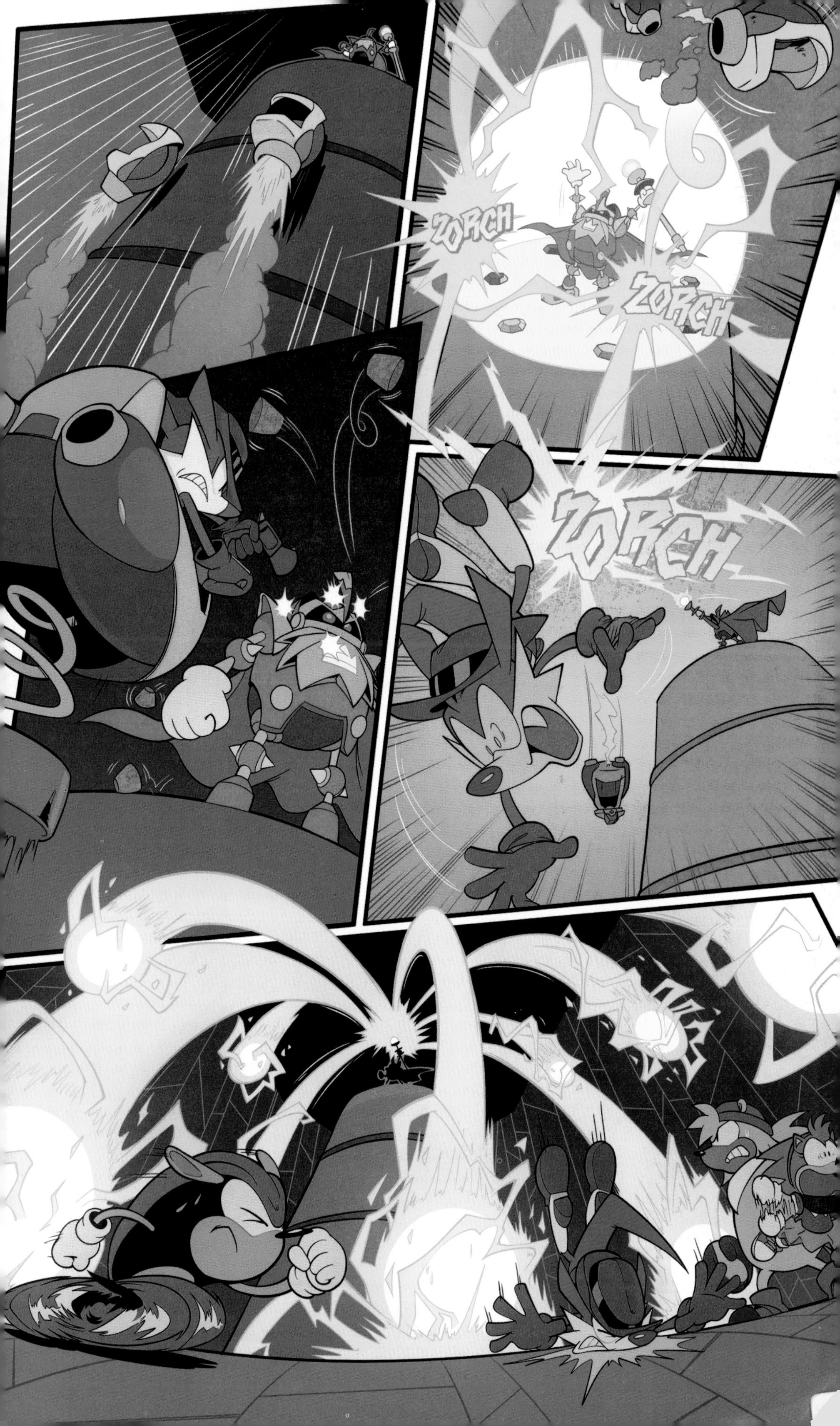
ZORCH
ZORCH
ZORCH

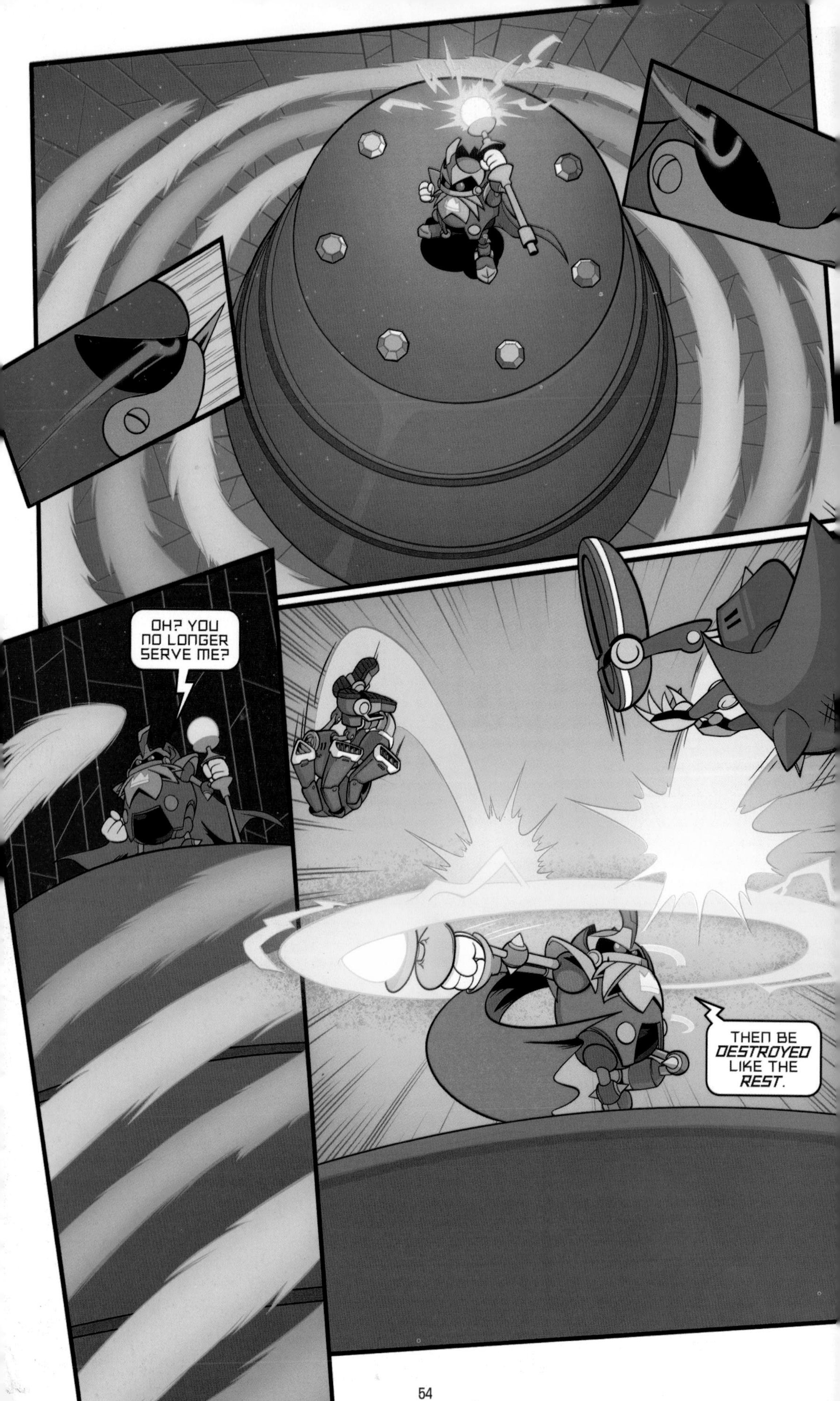
OH? YOU NO LONGER SERVE ME?
THEN BE DESTROYED LIKE THE REST.

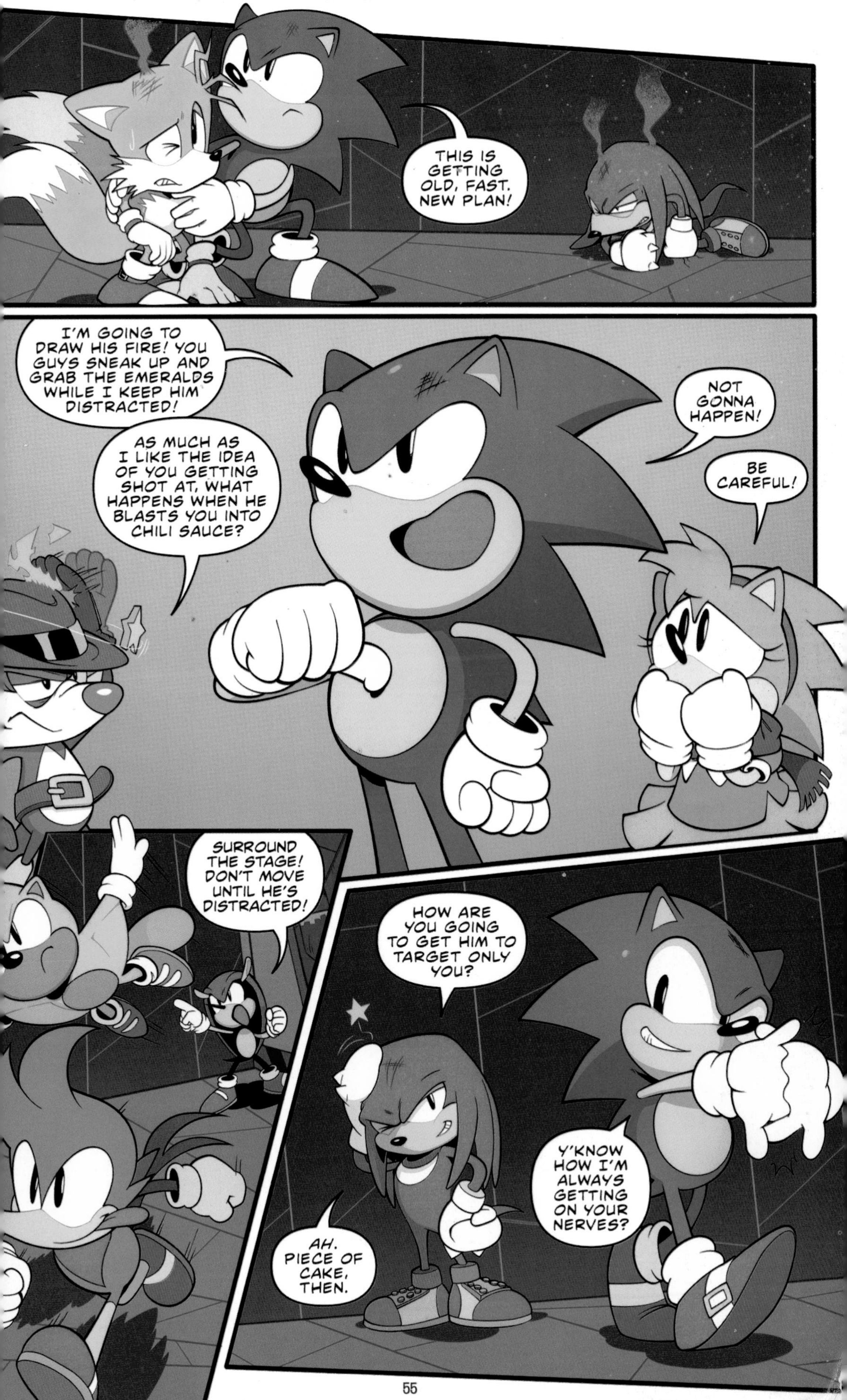
THIS IS GETTING OLD, FAST. NEW PLAN!
I'M GOING TO DRAW HIS FIRE! YOU GUYS SNEAK UP AND GRAB THE EMERALDS WHILE I KEEP HIM DISTRACTED!
AS MUCH AS I LIKE THE IDEA OF YOU GETTING SHOT AT, WHAT HAPPENS WHEN HE BLASTS YOU INTO CHILI SAUCE?
NOT GONNA HAPPEN!
BE CAREFUL!
SURROUND THE STAGE! DON'T MOVE UNTIL HE'S DISTRACTED!
HOW ARE YOU GOING TO GET HIM TO TARGET ONLY YOU?
Y'KNOW HOW I'M ALWAYS GETTING ON YOUR NERVES?
AH. PIECE OF CAKE, THEN.

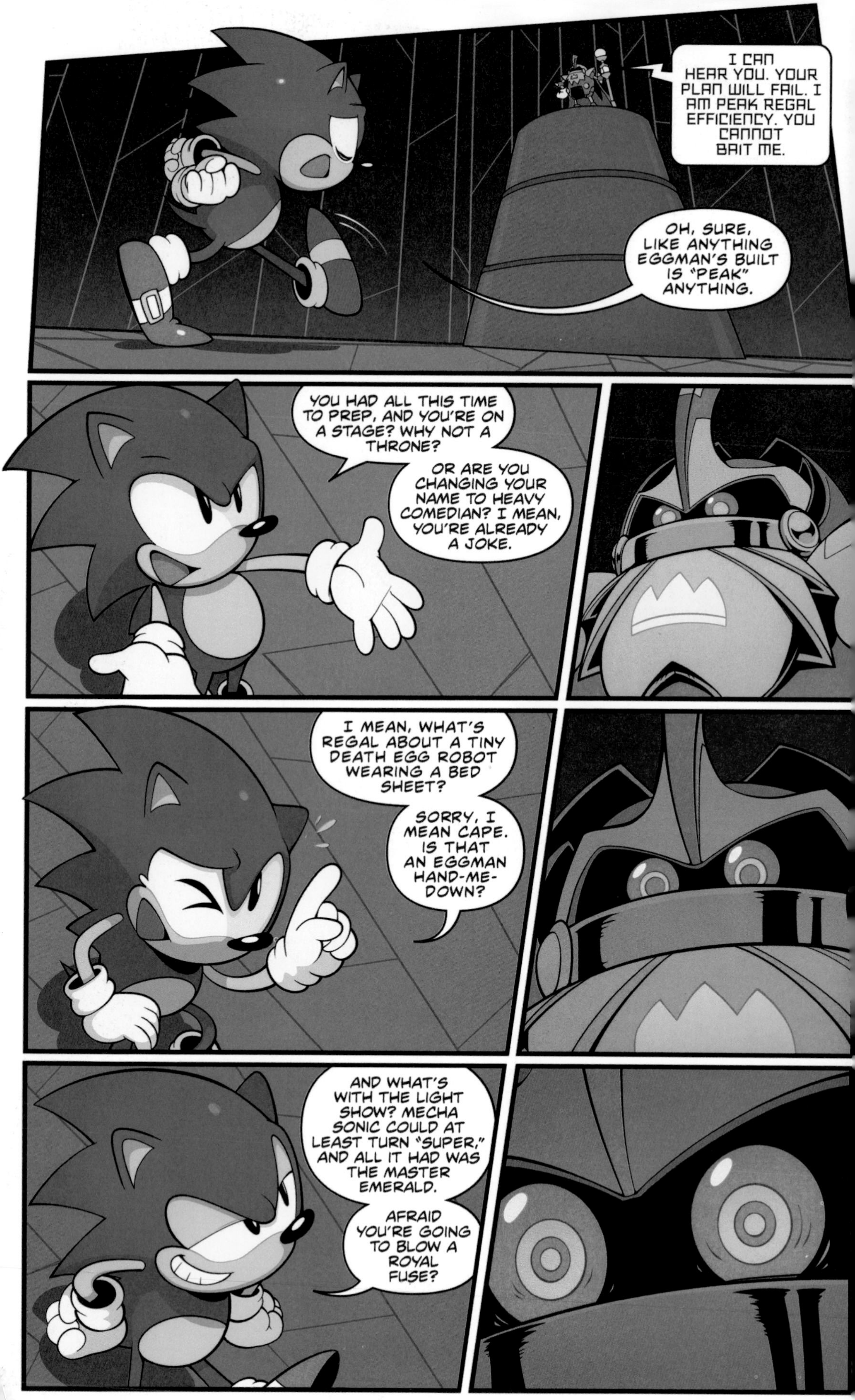
I CAN HEAR YOU. YOUR PLAN WILL FAIL. I AM PEAK REGAL EFFICIENCY. YOU CANNOT BAIT ME.
OH, SURE, LIKE ANYTHING EGGMAN'S BUILT IS "PEAK" ANYTHING.
YOU HAD ALL THIS TIME TO PREP, AND YOU'RE ON A STAGE? WHY NOT A THRONE?
OR ARE YOU CHANGING YOUR NAME TO HEAVY COMEDIAN? I MEAN, YOU'RE ALREADY A JOKE.
I MEAN, WHAT'S REGAL ABOUT A TINY DEATH EGG ROBOT WEARING A BED SHEET?
SORRY, I MEAN CAPE. IS THAT AN EGGMAN HAND-ME-DOWN?
AND WHAT'S WITH THE LIGHT SHOW? MECHA SONIC COULD AT LEAST TURN "SUPER," AND ALL IT HAD WAS THE MASTER EMERALD.
AFRAID YOU'RE GOING TO BLOW A ROYAL FUSE?

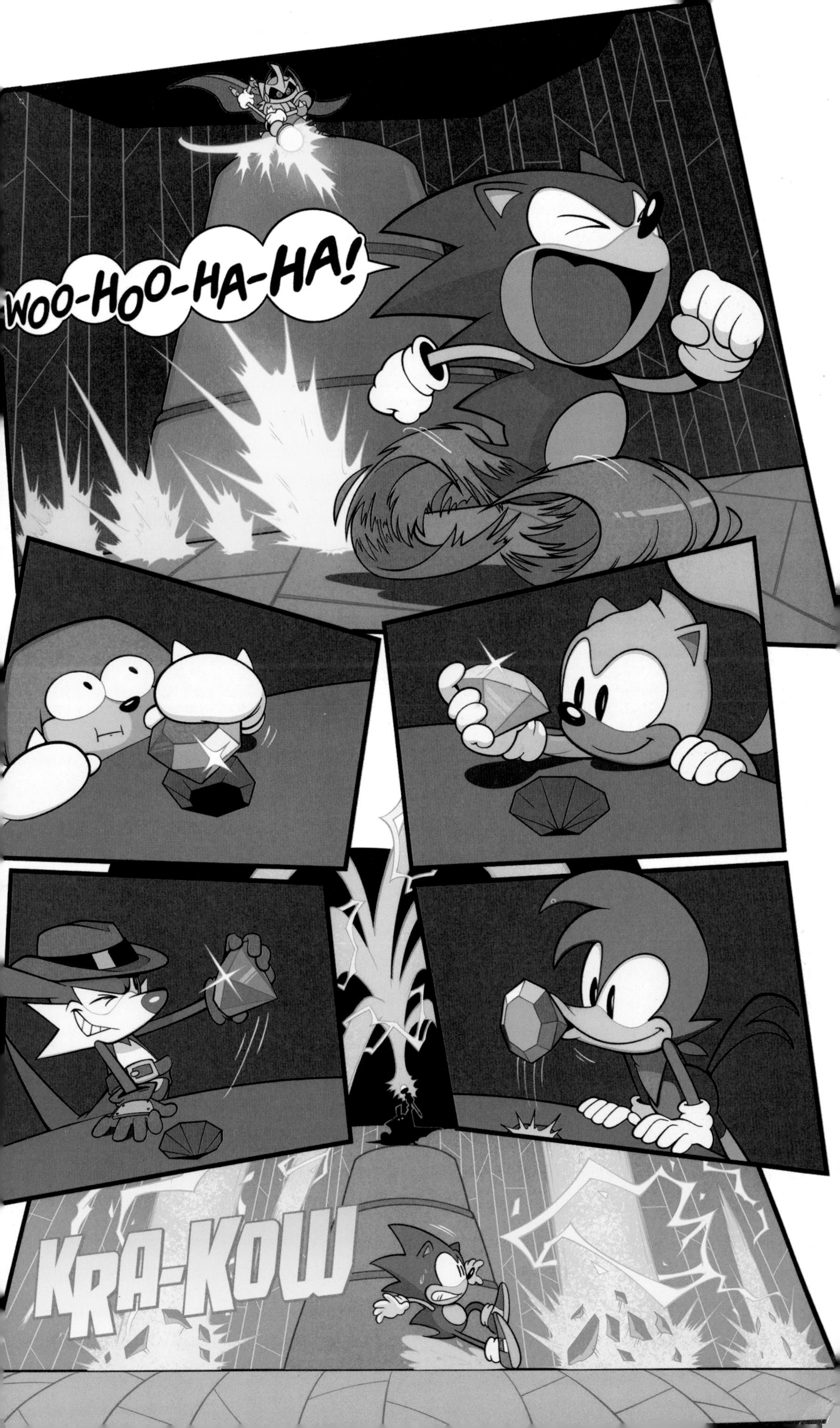
WOO-HOO-HA-HA!
KRA-KOW

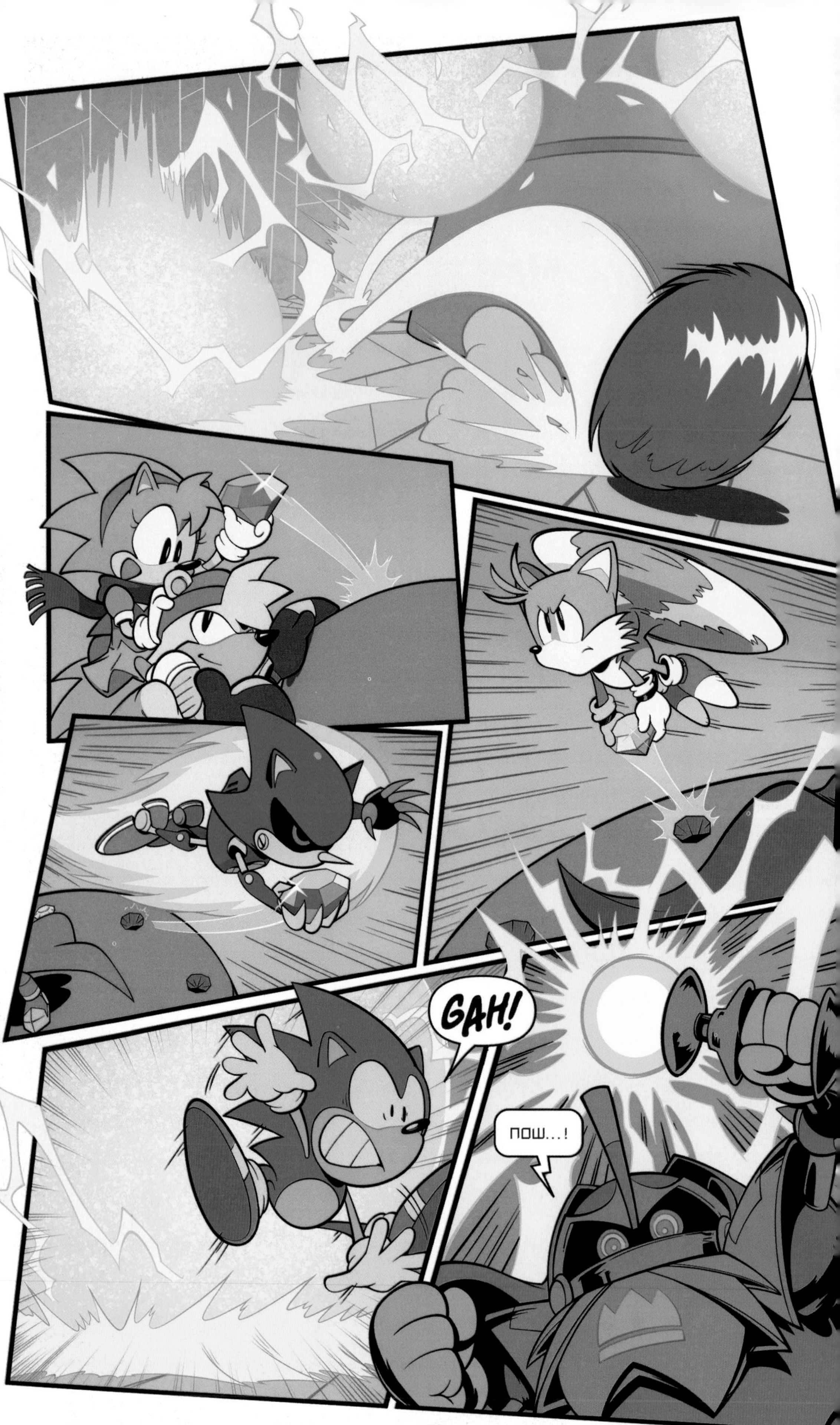
GAH!
NOW...!

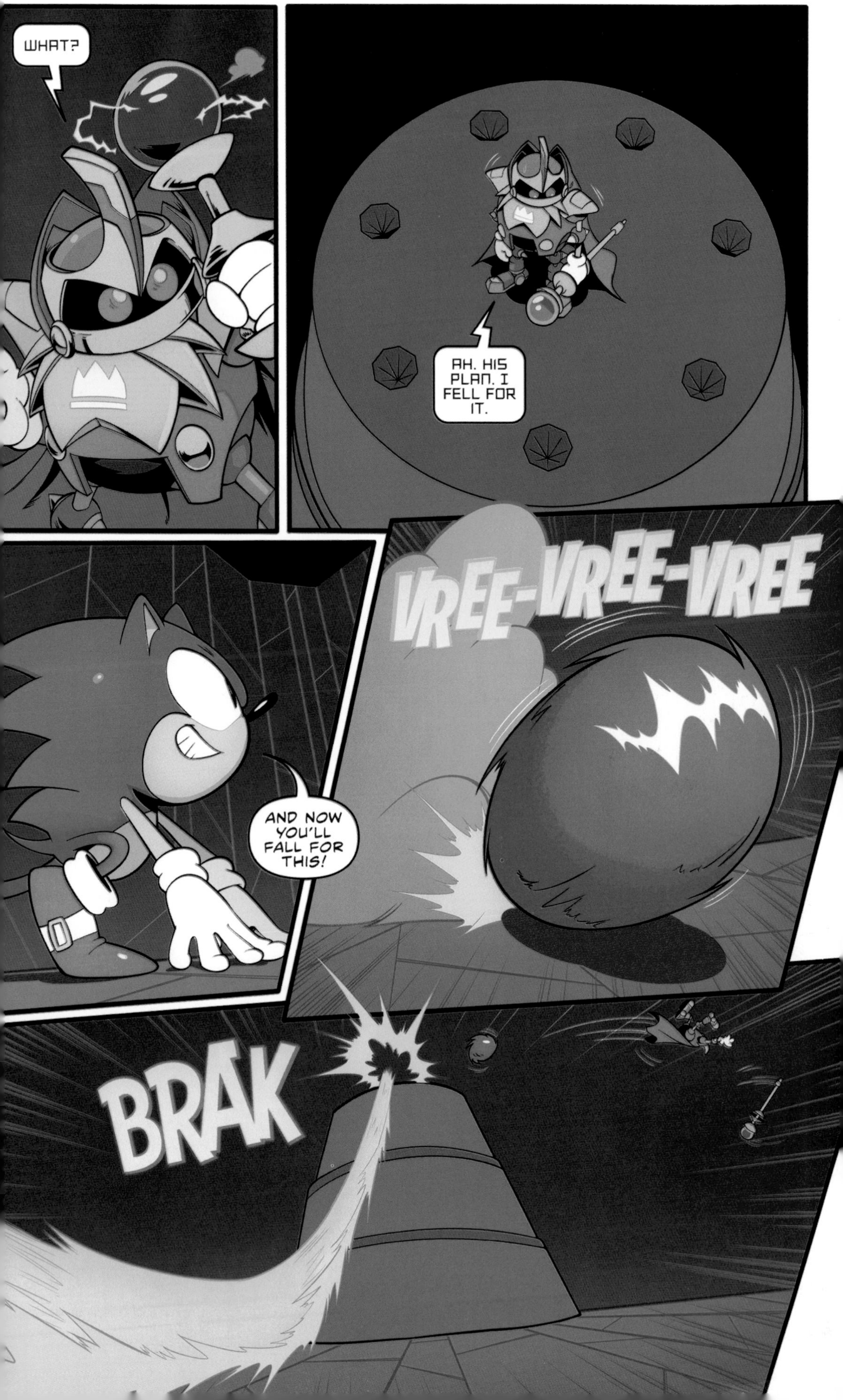
WHAT?
AH. HIS PLAN. I FELL FOR IT.
AND NOW YOU'LL FALL FOR THIS!
VREE-VREE-VREE
BRAK

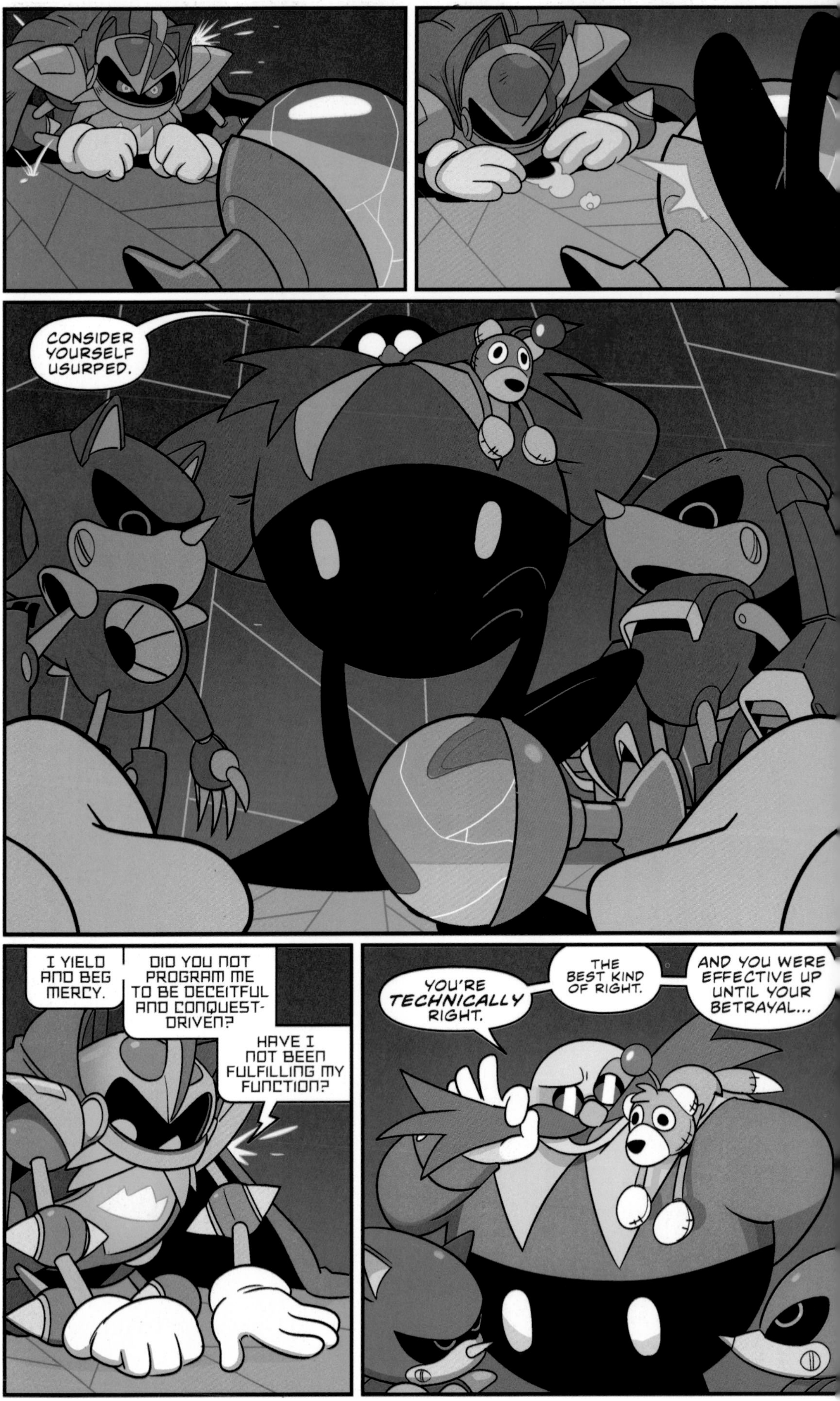
CONSIDER YOURSELF USURPED.
I YIELD AND BEG MERCY.
DID YOU NOT PROGRAM ME TO BE DECEITFUL AND CONQUEST-DRIVEN?
HAVE I NOT BEEN FULFILLING MY FUNCTION?
YOU'RE *TECHNICALLY* RIGHT.
THE BEST KIND OF RIGHT.
AND YOU WERE EFFECTIVE UP UNTIL YOUR BETRAYAL...

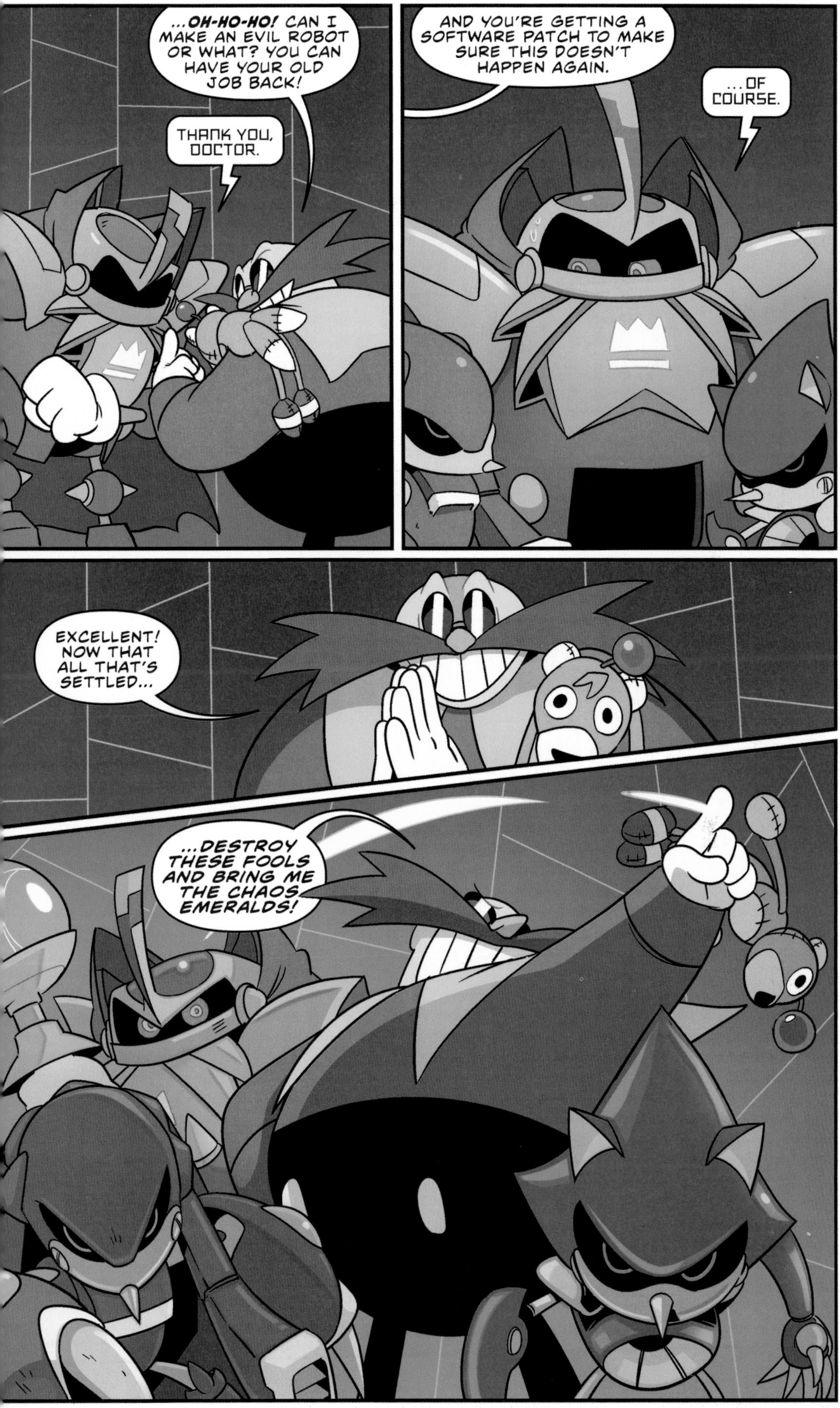

...**OH-HO-HO!** CAN I MAKE AN EVIL ROBOT OR WHAT? YOU CAN HAVE YOUR OLD JOB BACK!
THANK YOU, DOCTOR.
AND YOU'RE GETTING A SOFTWARE PATCH TO MAKE SURE THIS DOESN'T HAPPEN AGAIN.
...OF COURSE.
EXCELLENT! NOW THAT ALL THAT'S SETTLED...
...DESTROY THESE FOOLS AND BRING ME THE CHAOS EMERALDS!

WHERE IS EVERYONE?

APOLOGIES, SIR. THEY MUST HAVE LEFT WHILE YOU WERE THREATENING ME.

WELL THEN MARSHAL MY FORCES AND TRACK THEM DOWN! THEY CAN'T HAVE GOTTEN FAR!

APOLOGIES, SIR. YOU HAD THEM DESTROY ALL THE BADNIKS WHILE INVADING MY BASE. YOUR BASE.

METAL SONIC! METAL KNUCKLES! CHASE THEM DOWN AND--EH?!

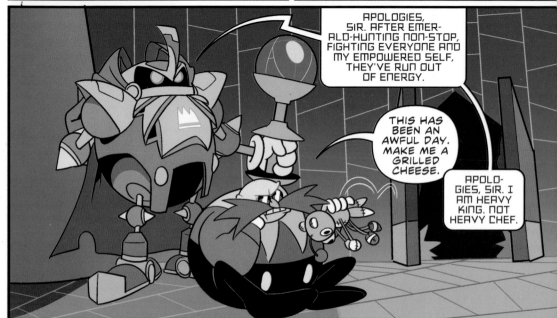

APOLOGIES, SIR. AFTER EMER-ALD-HUNTING NON-STOP, FIGHTING EVERYONE AND MY EMPOWERED SELF, THEY'VE RUN OUT OF ENERGY.

THIS HAS BEEN AN AWFUL DAY. MAKE ME A GRILLED CHEESE.

APOLO-GIES, SIR. I AM HEAVY KING, NOT HEAVY CHEF.

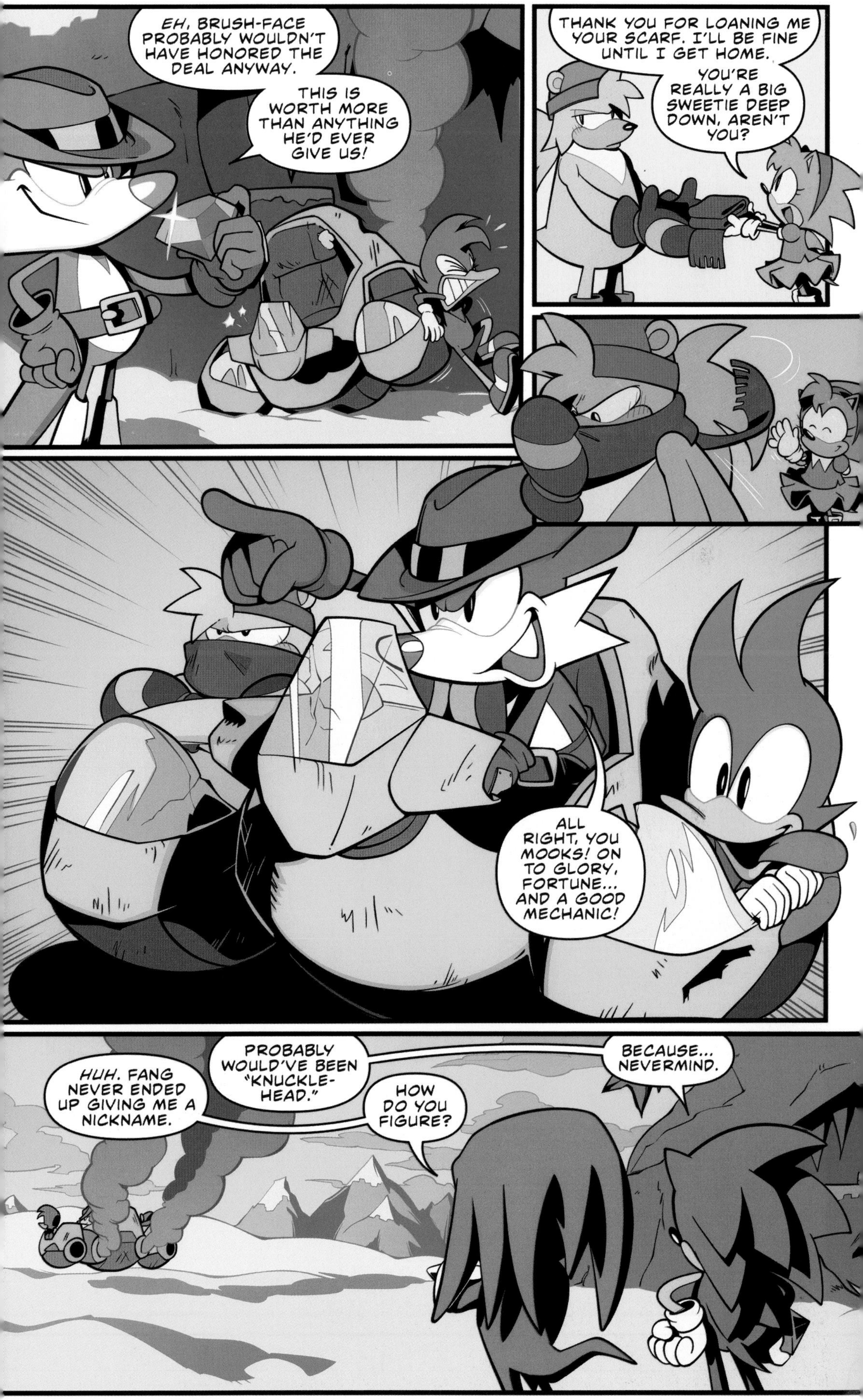
EH, BRUSH-FACE PROBABLY WOULDN'T HAVE HONORED THE DEAL ANYWAY.
THIS IS WORTH MORE THAN ANYTHING HE'D EVER GIVE US!
THANK YOU FOR LOANING ME YOUR SCARF. I'LL BE FINE UNTIL I GET HOME.
YOU'RE REALLY A BIG SWEETIE DEEP DOWN, AREN'T YOU?
ALL RIGHT, YOU MOOKS! ON TO GLORY, FORTUNE... AND A GOOD MECHANIC!
HUH. FANG NEVER ENDED UP GIVING ME A NICKNAME.
PROBABLY WOULD'VE BEEN "KNUCKLE-HEAD."
HOW DO YOU FIGURE?
BECAUSE... NEVERMIND.

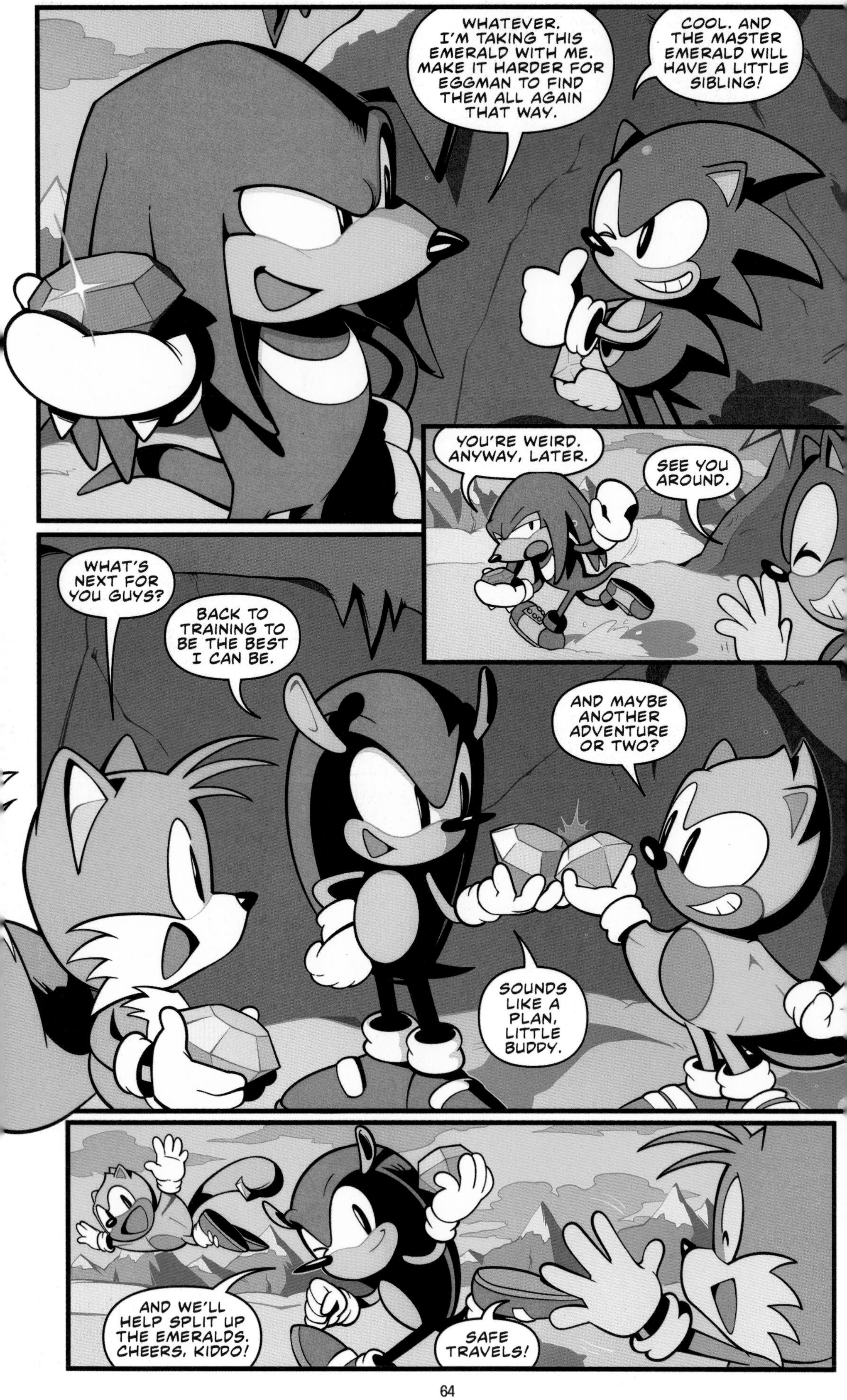
WHATEVER. I'M TAKING THIS EMERALD WITH ME. MAKE IT HARDER FOR EGGMAN TO FIND THEM ALL AGAIN THAT WAY.
COOL. AND THE MASTER EMERALD WILL HAVE A LITTLE SIBLING!
YOU'RE WEIRD. ANYWAY, LATER.
SEE YOU AROUND.
WHAT'S NEXT FOR YOU GUYS?
BACK TO TRAINING TO BE THE BEST I CAN BE.
AND MAYBE ANOTHER ADVENTURE OR TWO?
SOUNDS LIKE A PLAN, LITTLE BUDDY.
AND WE'LL HELP SPLIT UP THE EMERALDS. CHEERS, KIDDO!
SAFE TRAVELS!

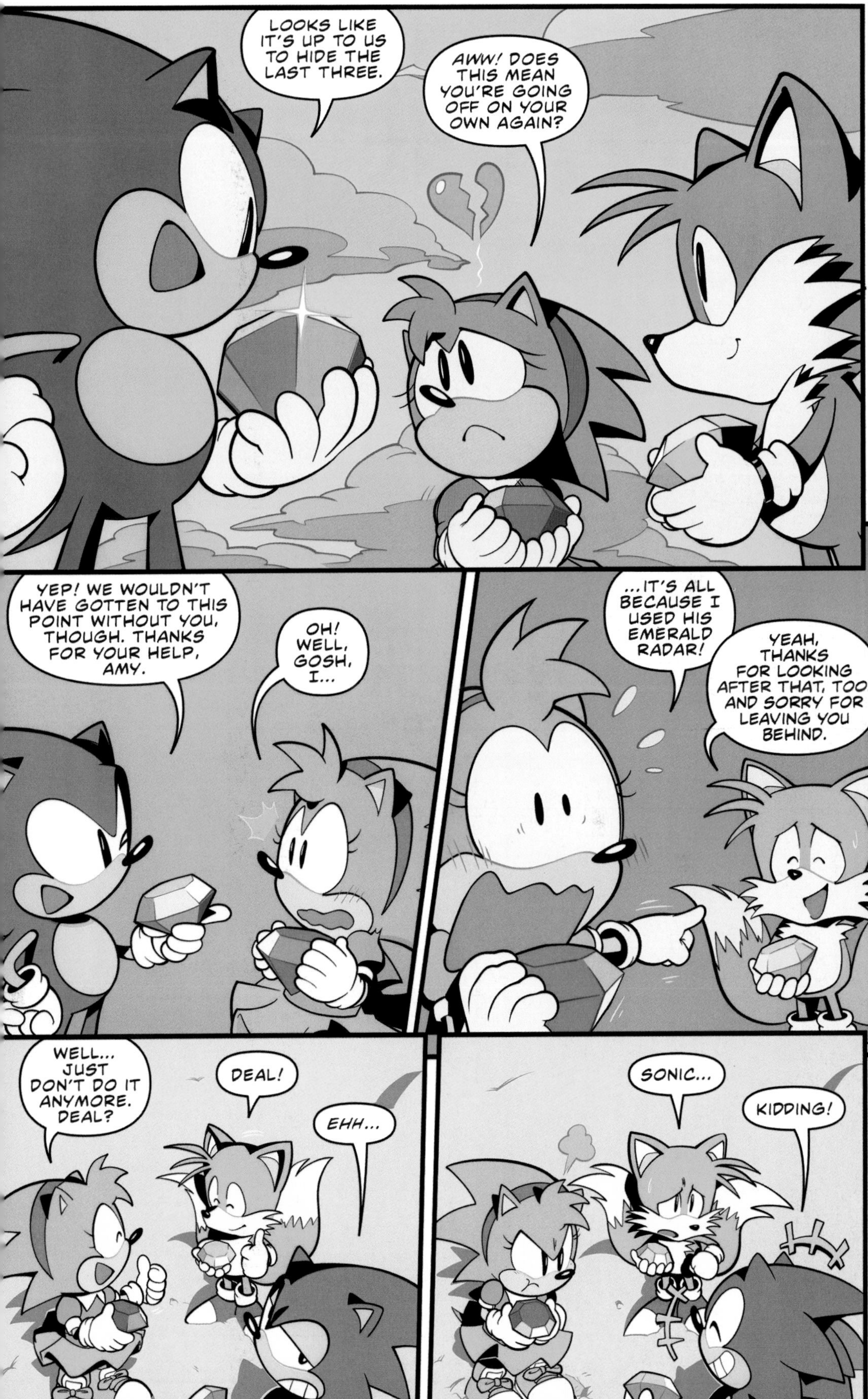
LOOKS LIKE IT'S UP TO US TO HIDE THE LAST THREE.
AWW! DOES THIS MEAN YOU'RE GOING OFF ON YOUR OWN AGAIN?
YEP! WE WOULDN'T HAVE GOTTEN TO THIS POINT WITHOUT YOU, THOUGH. THANKS FOR YOUR HELP, AMY.
OH! WELL, GOSH, I...
...IT'S ALL BECAUSE I USED HIS EMERALD RADAR!
YEAH, THANKS FOR LOOKING AFTER THAT, TOO. AND SORRY FOR LEAVING YOU BEHIND.
WELL... JUST DON'T DO IT ANYMORE. DEAL?
DEAL!
EHH...
SONIC...
KIDDING!

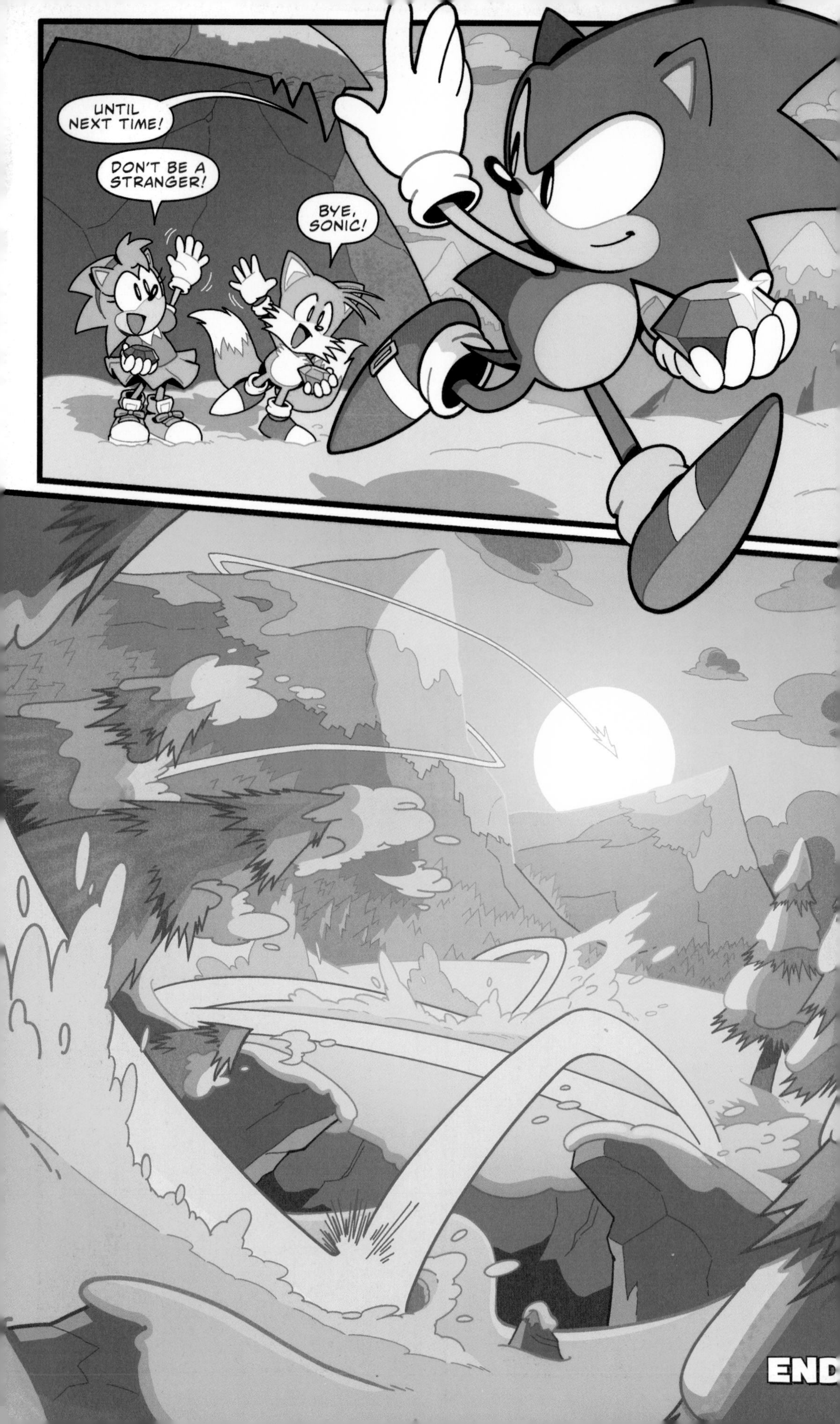
UNTIL NEXT TIME!
DON'T BE A STRANGER!
BYE, SONIC!
END

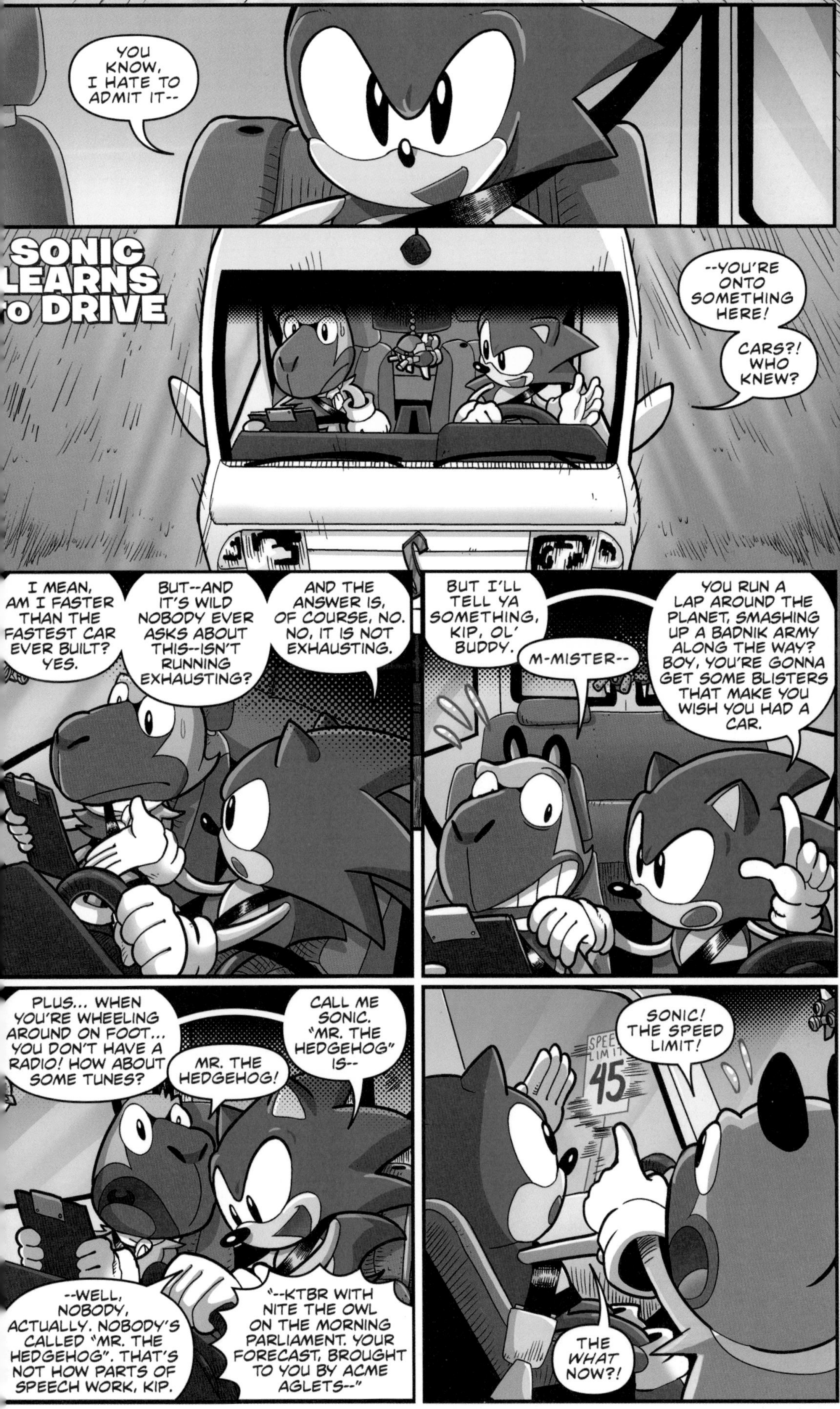

YOU KNOW, I HATE TO ADMIT IT--
SONIC LEARNS TO DRIVE
--YOU'RE ONTO SOMETHING HERE!
CARS?! WHO KNEW?
I MEAN, AM I FASTER THAN THE FASTEST CAR EVER BUILT? YES.
BUT--AND IT'S WILD NOBODY EVER ASKS ABOUT THIS--ISN'T RUNNING EXHAUSTING?
AND THE ANSWER IS, OF COURSE, NO. NO, IT IS NOT EXHAUSTING.
BUT I'LL TELL YA SOMETHING, KIP, OL' BUDDY.
M-MISTER--
YOU RUN A LAP AROUND THE PLANET, SMASHING UP A BADNIK ARMY ALONG THE WAY? BOY, YOU'RE GONNA GET SOME BLISTERS THAT MAKE YOU WISH YOU HAD A CAR.
PLUS... WHEN YOU'RE WHEELING AROUND ON FOOT... YOU DON'T HAVE A RADIO! HOW ABOUT SOME TUNES?
MR. THE HEDGEHOG!
CALL ME SONIC. "MR. THE HEDGEHOG" IS--
--WELL, NOBODY, ACTUALLY. NOBODY'S CALLED "MR. THE HEDGEHOG". THAT'S NOT HOW PARTS OF SPEECH WORK, KIP.
"--KTBR WITH NITE THE OWL ON THE MORNING PARLIAMENT. YOUR FORECAST, BROUGHT TO YOU BY ACME AGLETS--"
SONIC! THE SPEED LIMIT!
45
THE WHAT NOW?!

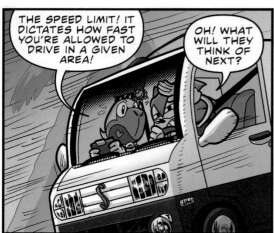

THE SPEED LIMIT! IT DICTATES HOW FAST YOU'RE ALLOWED TO DRIVE IN A GIVEN AREA!

OH! WHAT WILL THEY THINK OF NEXT?

GUESS I'LL... STOP... HITTING THE GAS SO MUCH?

AND THE CAR WILL EVENTUALLY... NOT BE FAST, ANYMORE?!

SORRY, KIP. WE'RE IN UNCHARTED WATERS HERE.

THE BRAKES, SONIC.

THE BRAKES MAKE THE CAR STOP.

OH, WOW! OKAY! I THOUGHT THAT WAS THE TURBO PEDAL OR SOMETHING!

THERE'S... THERE'S NO TURBO PEDAL, SONIC.

WE'RE IN A NORMAL CAR.

MY NORMAL CAR.

RIGHT, YEAH! NO, I GET IT NOW, TOTALLY.

HERE WE GO.

TIME TO SLOW THINGS RIGHT ON DOWN.

YES. PLEASE.

YOU'RE... GOING TO HAVE TO PRESS HARDER THAN THAT.

HERE'S THE WEIRD THING, KIP, I'M TRYING TO. I SWEAR.

SHOULD TOUCHING IT MAKE ME SICK?

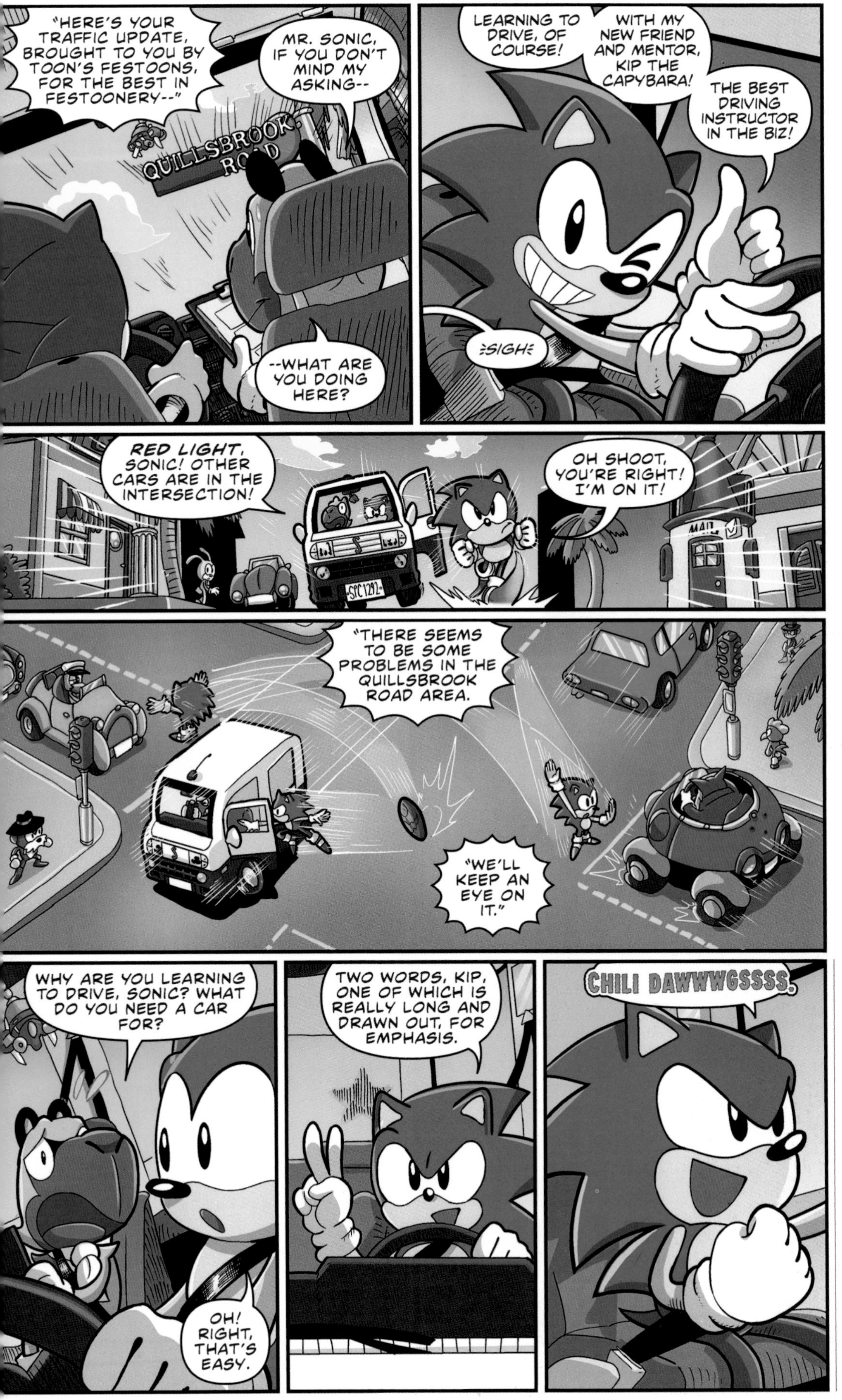
"HERE'S YOUR TRAFFIC UPDATE, BROUGHT TO YOU BY TOON'S FESTOONS, FOR THE BEST IN FESTOONERY--"
MR. SONIC, IF YOU DON'T MIND MY ASKING--
QUILLSBROOK ROAD
--WHAT ARE YOU DOING HERE?
LEARNING TO DRIVE, OF COURSE!
WITH MY NEW FRIEND AND MENTOR, KIP THE CAPYBARA!
THE BEST DRIVING INSTRUCTOR IN THE BIZ!
SIGH
RED LIGHT, SONIC! OTHER CARS ARE IN THE INTERSECTION!
OH SHOOT, YOU'RE RIGHT! I'M ON IT!
MAIL
SPC1292
"THERE SEEMS TO BE SOME PROBLEMS IN THE QUILLSBROOK ROAD AREA.
"WE'LL KEEP AN EYE ON IT."
WHY ARE YOU LEARNING TO DRIVE, SONIC? WHAT DO YOU NEED A CAR FOR?
OH! RIGHT, THAT'S EASY.
TWO WORDS, KIP, ONE OF WHICH IS REALLY LONG AND DRAWN OUT, FOR EMPHASIS.
CHILI DAWWWGSSSS.

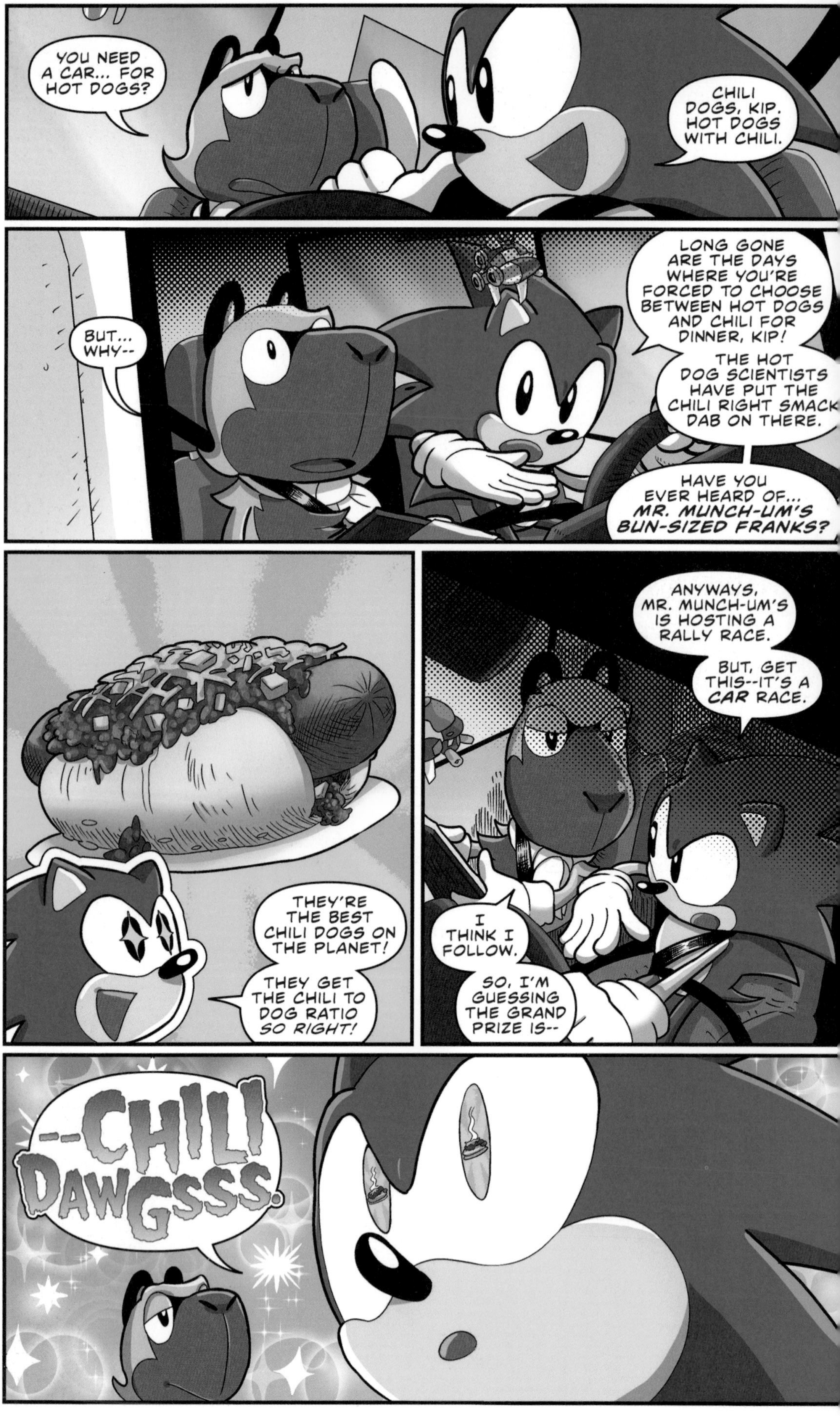
YOU NEED A CAR... FOR HOT DOGS?
CHILI DOGS, KIP. HOT DOGS WITH CHILI.
BUT... WHY--
LONG GONE ARE THE DAYS WHERE YOU'RE FORCED TO CHOOSE BETWEEN HOT DOGS AND CHILI FOR DINNER, KIP!
THE HOT DOG SCIENTISTS HAVE PUT THE CHILI RIGHT SMACK DAB ON THERE.
HAVE YOU EVER HEARD OF... MR. MUNCH-UM'S BUN-SIZED FRANKS?
THEY'RE THE BEST CHILI DOGS ON THE PLANET!
THEY GET THE CHILI TO DOG RATIO SO RIGHT!
ANYWAYS, MR. MUNCH-UM'S IS HOSTING A RALLY RACE.
BUT, GET THIS--IT'S A CAR RACE.
I THINK I FOLLOW.
SO, I'M GUESSING THE GRAND PRIZE IS--
--CHILI DAWGSSS.

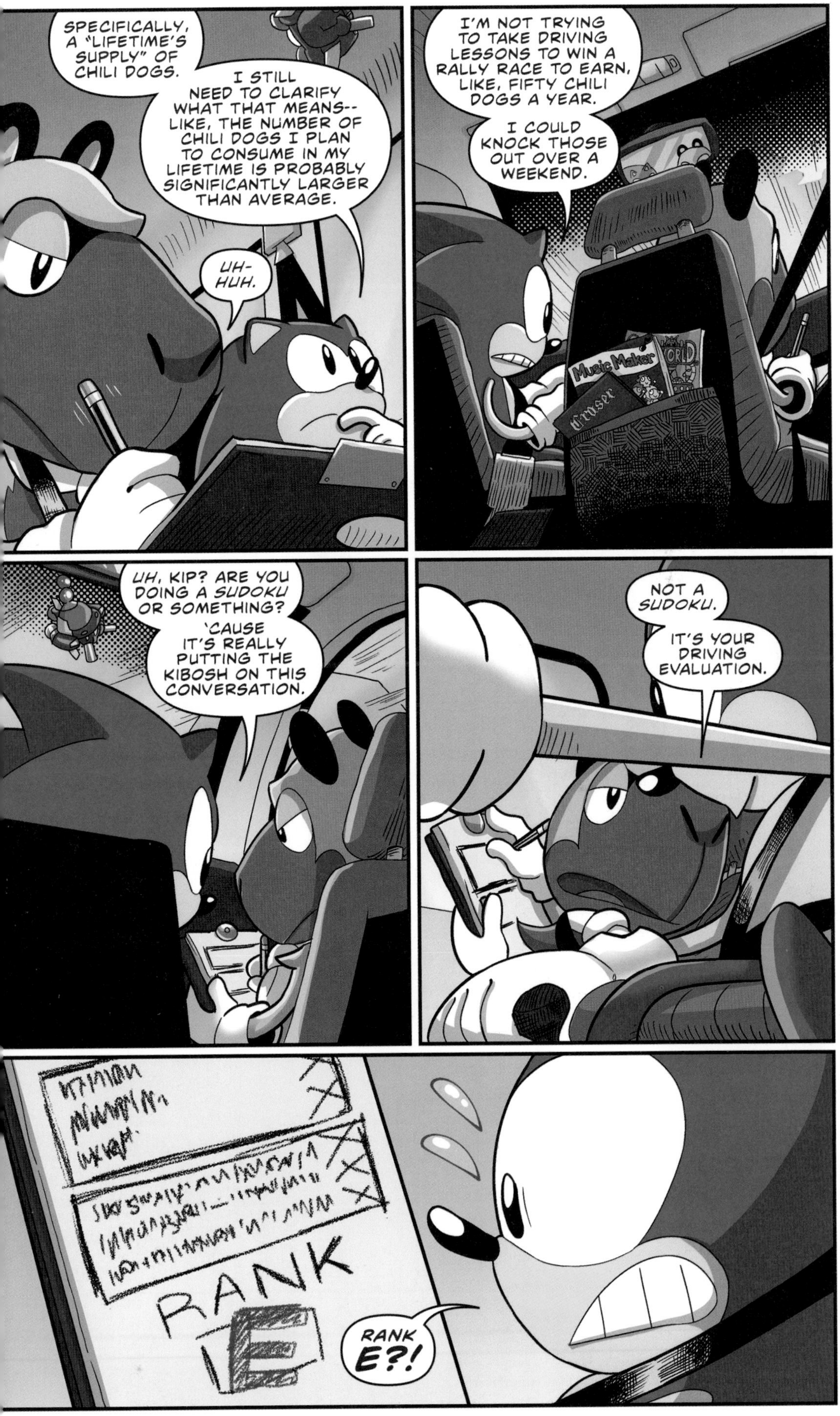
SPECIFICALLY, A "LIFETIME'S SUPPLY" OF CHILI DOGS.
I STILL NEED TO CLARIFY WHAT THAT MEANS-- LIKE, THE NUMBER OF CHILI DOGS I PLAN TO CONSUME IN MY LIFETIME IS PROBABLY SIGNIFICANTLY LARGER THAN AVERAGE.
UH-HUH.
I'M NOT TRYING TO TAKE DRIVING LESSONS TO WIN A RALLY RACE TO EARN, LIKE, FIFTY CHILI DOGS A YEAR.
I COULD KNOCK THOSE OUT OVER A WEEKEND.
Music Maker
Eraser
UH, KIP? ARE YOU DOING A *SUDOKU* OR SOMETHING?
'CAUSE IT'S REALLY PUTTING THE KIBOSH ON THIS CONVERSATION.
NOT A *SUDOKU*.
IT'S YOUR DRIVING EVALUATION.
RANK E
RANK E?!

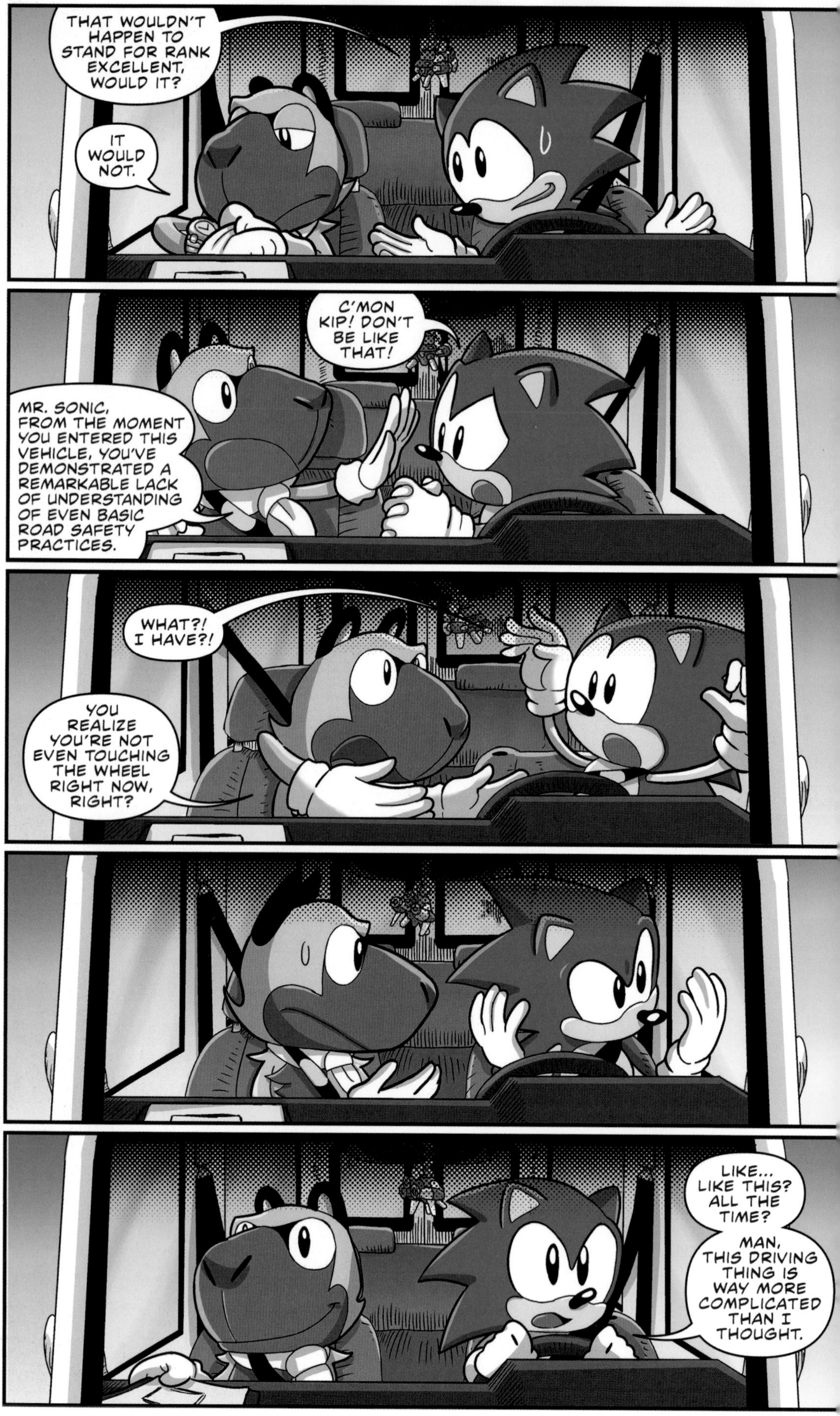
THAT WOULDN'T HAPPEN TO STAND FOR RANK EXCELLENT, WOULD IT?
IT WOULD NOT.
C'MON KIP! DON'T BE LIKE THAT!
MR. SONIC, FROM THE MOMENT YOU ENTERED THIS VEHICLE, YOU'VE DEMONSTRATED A REMARKABLE LACK OF UNDERSTANDING OF EVEN BASIC ROAD SAFETY PRACTICES.
WHAT?! I HAVE?!
YOU REALIZE YOU'RE NOT EVEN TOUCHING THE WHEEL RIGHT NOW, RIGHT?
LIKE... LIKE THIS? ALL THE TIME?
MAN, THIS DRIVING THING IS WAY MORE COMPLICATED THAN I THOUGHT.

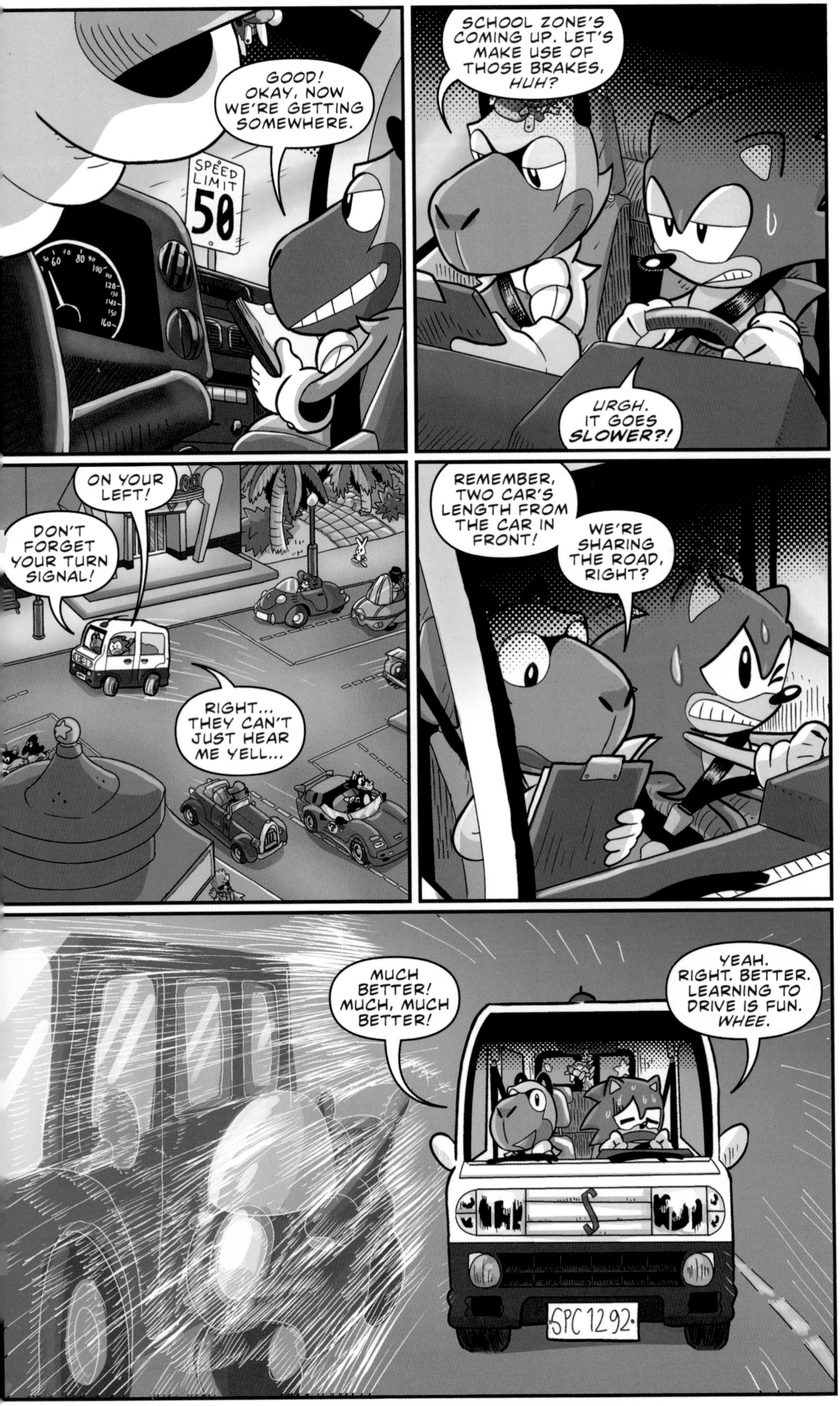
GOOD! OKAY, NOW WE'RE GETTING SOMEWHERE.
SPEED LIMIT 50
SCHOOL ZONE'S COMING UP. LET'S MAKE USE OF THOSE BRAKES, HUH?
URGH. IT GOES SLOWER?!
ON YOUR LEFT!
DON'T FORGET YOUR TURN SIGNAL!
RIGHT... THEY CAN'T JUST HEAR ME YELL...
REMEMBER, TWO CAR'S LENGTH FROM THE CAR IN FRONT!
WE'RE SHARING THE ROAD, RIGHT?
MUCH BETTER! MUCH, MUCH BETTER!
YEAH. RIGHT. BETTER. LEARNING TO DRIVE IS FUN. WHEE.
SPC 1292

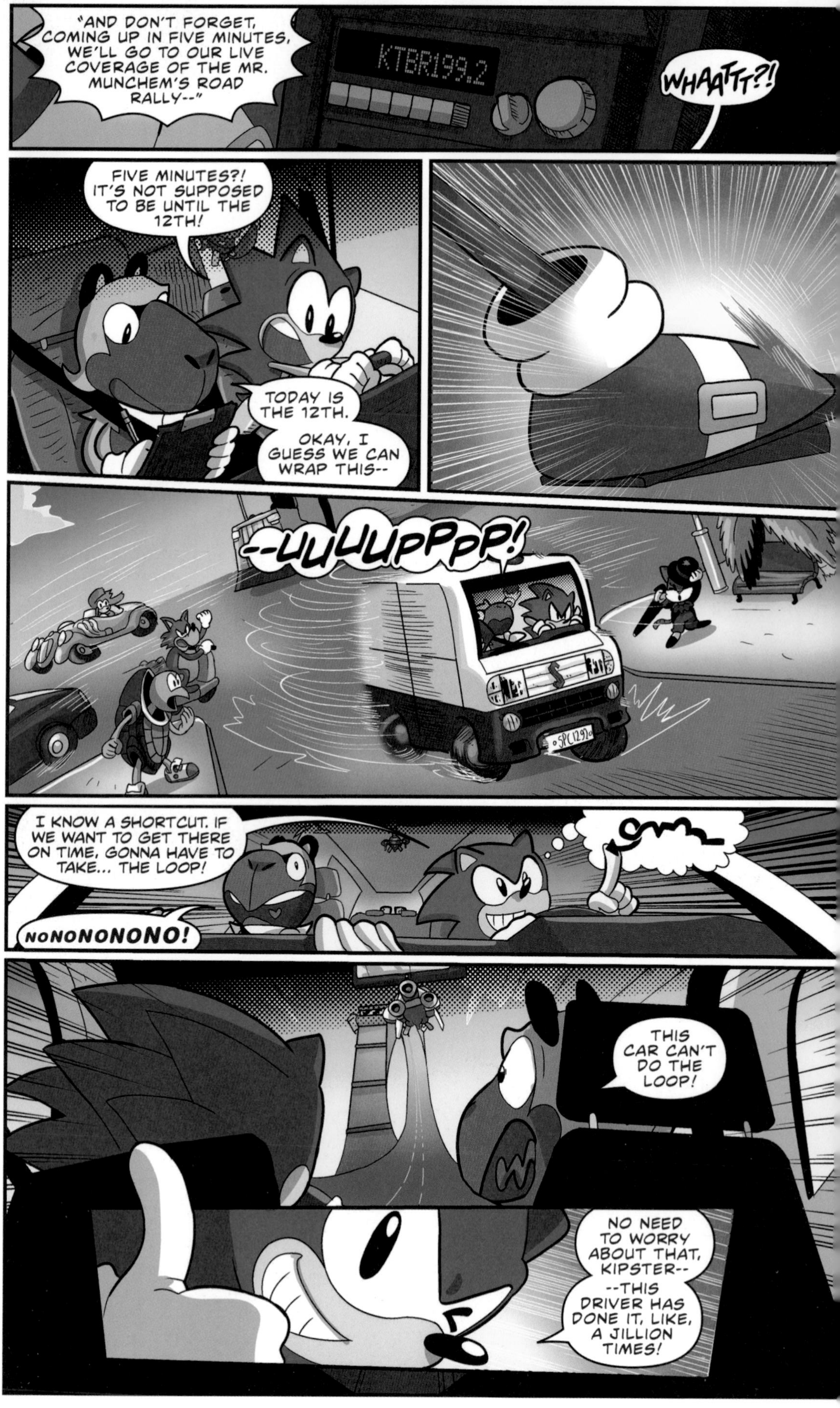
"AND DON'T FORGET, COMING UP IN FIVE MINUTES, WE'LL GO TO OUR LIVE COVERAGE OF THE MR. MUNCHEM'S ROAD RALLY--"
KTBR199.2
WHAATTT?!
FIVE MINUTES?! IT'S NOT SUPPOSED TO BE UNTIL THE 12TH!
TODAY IS THE 12TH.
OKAY, I GUESS WE CAN WRAP THIS--
--UUUUPPPP!
SPC129
I KNOW A SHORTCUT. IF WE WANT TO GET THERE ON TIME, GONNA HAVE TO TAKE... THE LOOP!
NONONONONO!
THIS CAR CAN'T DO THE LOOP!
NO NEED TO WORRY ABOUT THAT, KIPSTER--
--THIS DRIVER HAS DONE IT, LIKE, A JILLION TIMES!

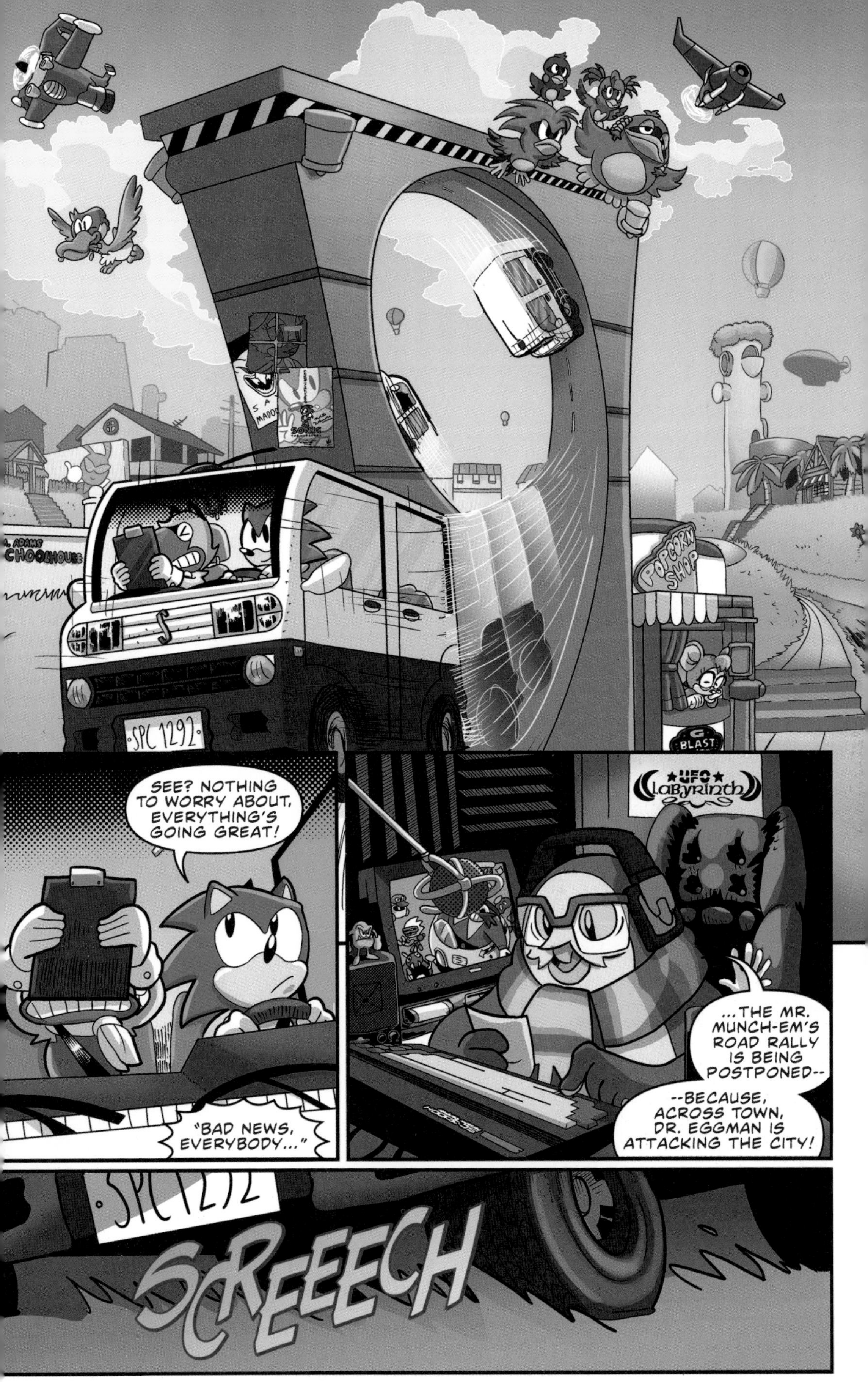
POPCORN SHOP
SPC 1292
SEE? NOTHING TO WORRY ABOUT, EVERYTHING'S GOING GREAT!
"BAD NEWS, EVERYBODY..."
UFO LABYRINTH
...THE MR. MUNCH-EM'S ROAD RALLY IS BEING POSTPONED--
--BECAUSE, ACROSS TOWN, DR. EGGMAN IS ATTACKING THE CITY!
SCREEECH

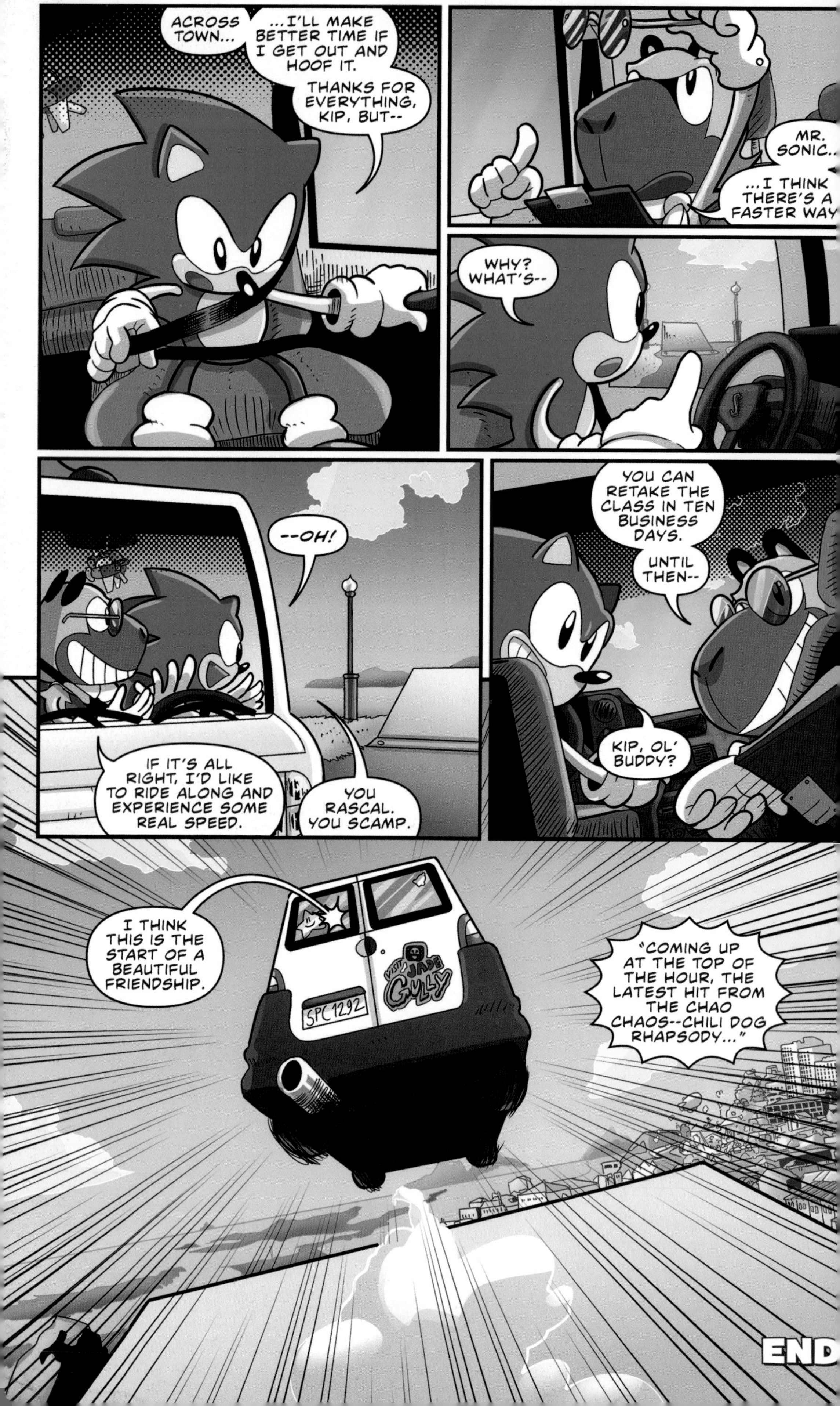
ACROSS TOWN...
...I'LL MAKE BETTER TIME IF I GET OUT AND HOOF IT.
THANKS FOR EVERYTHING, KIP, BUT--
MR. SONIC...
...I THINK THERE'S A FASTER WAY
WHY? WHAT'S--
--OH!
IF IT'S ALL RIGHT, I'D LIKE TO RIDE ALONG AND EXPERIENCE SOME REAL SPEED.
YOU RASCAL. YOU SCAMP.
YOU CAN RETAKE THE CLASS IN TEN BUSINESS DAYS.
UNTIL THEN--
KIP, OL' BUDDY?
I THINK THIS IS THE START OF A BEAUTIFUL FRIENDSHIP.
VISIT JADE GULLY
SPC 1292
"COMING UP AT THE TOP OF THE HOUR, THE LATEST HIT FROM THE CHAO CHAOS--CHILI DOG RHAPSODY..."
END

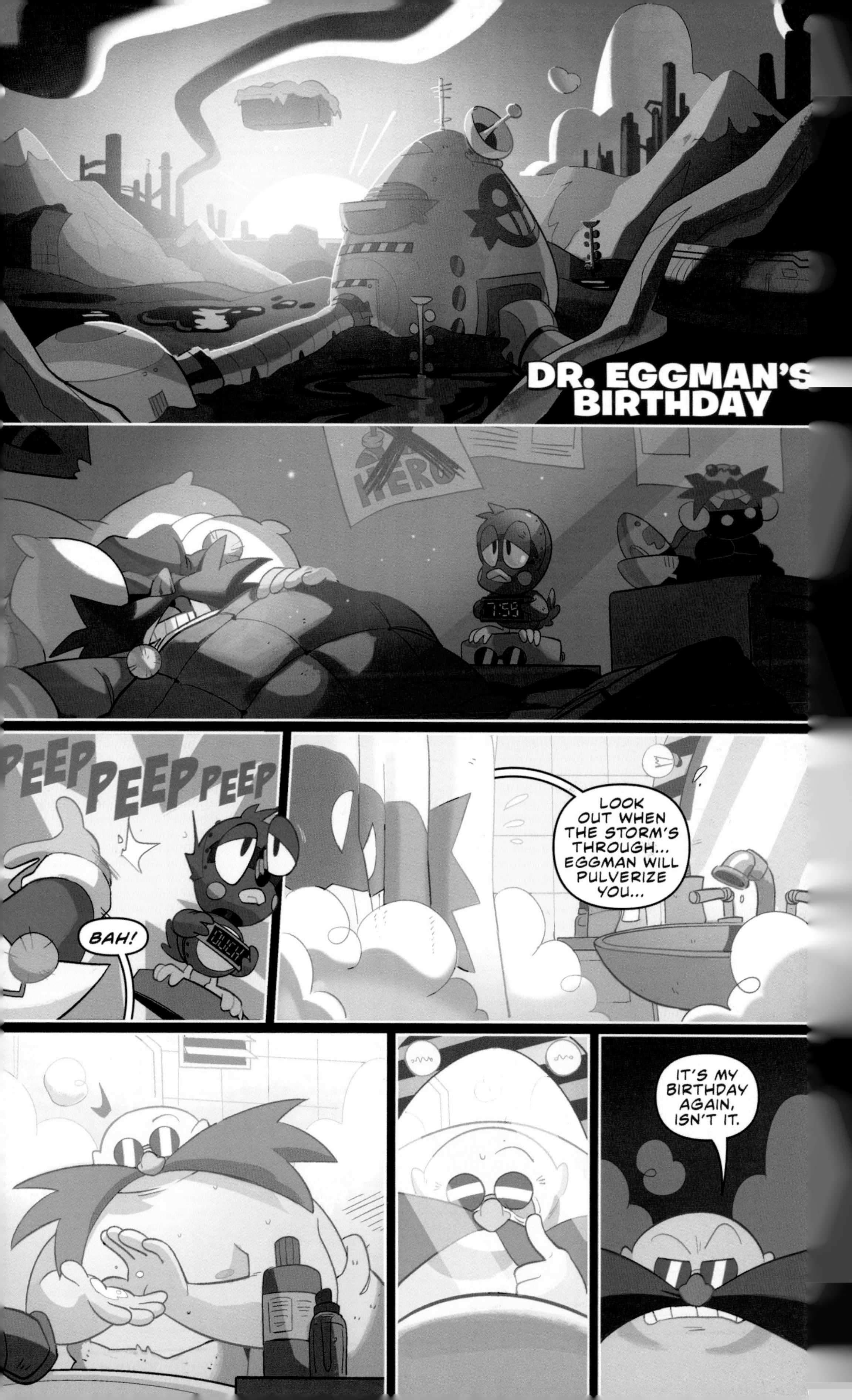
DR. EGGMAN'S BIRTHDAY
HERO
7:59
PEEP PEEP PEEP
BAH!
OUCH
LOOK OUT WHEN THE STORM'S THROUGH... EGGMAN WILL PULVERIZE YOU...
IT'S MY BIRTHDAY AGAIN, ISN'T IT.

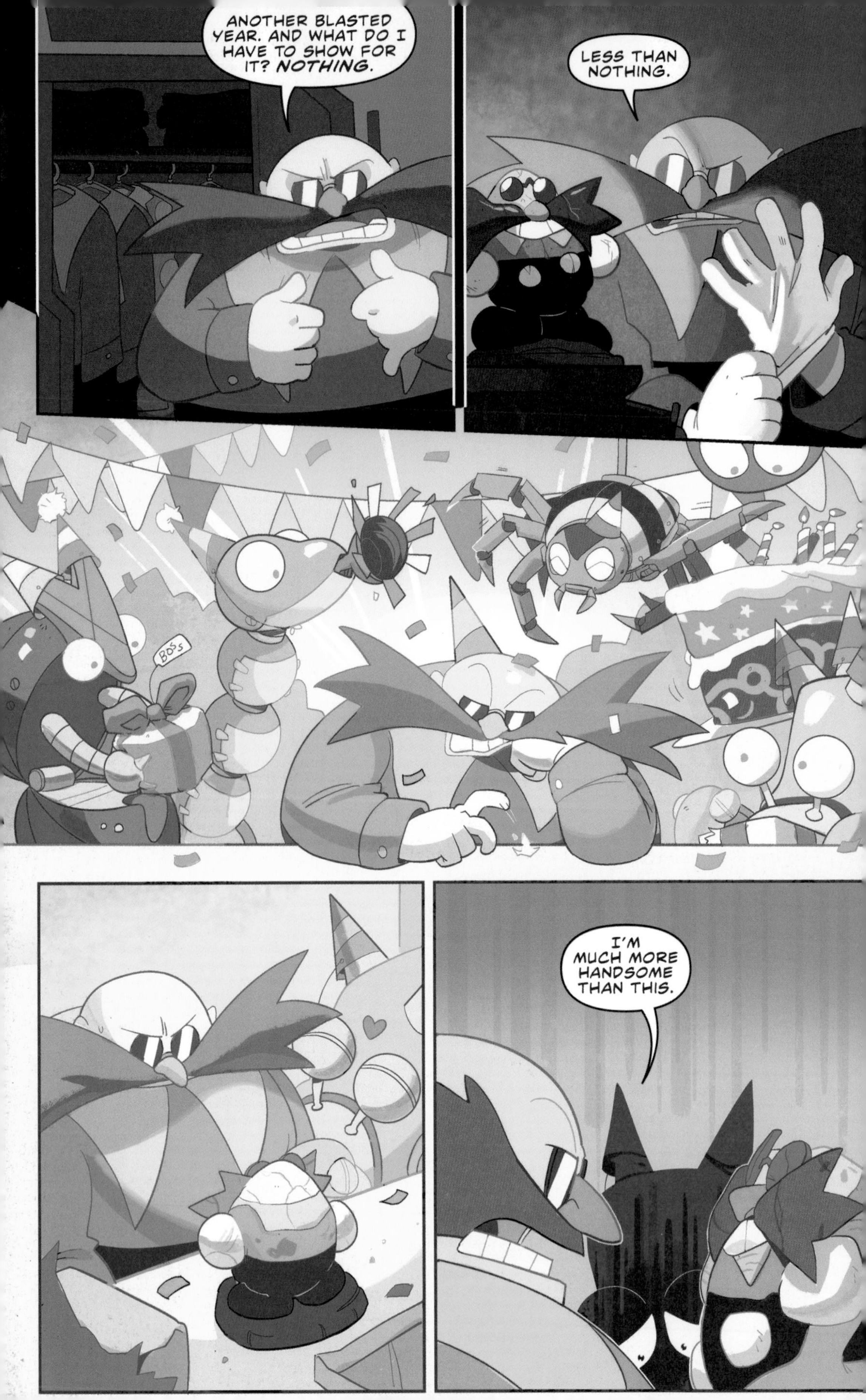
ANOTHER BLASTED YEAR. AND WHAT DO I HAVE TO SHOW FOR IT? *NOTHING*.
LESS THAN NOTHING.
BOSS
I'M MUCH MORE HANDSOME THAN THIS.

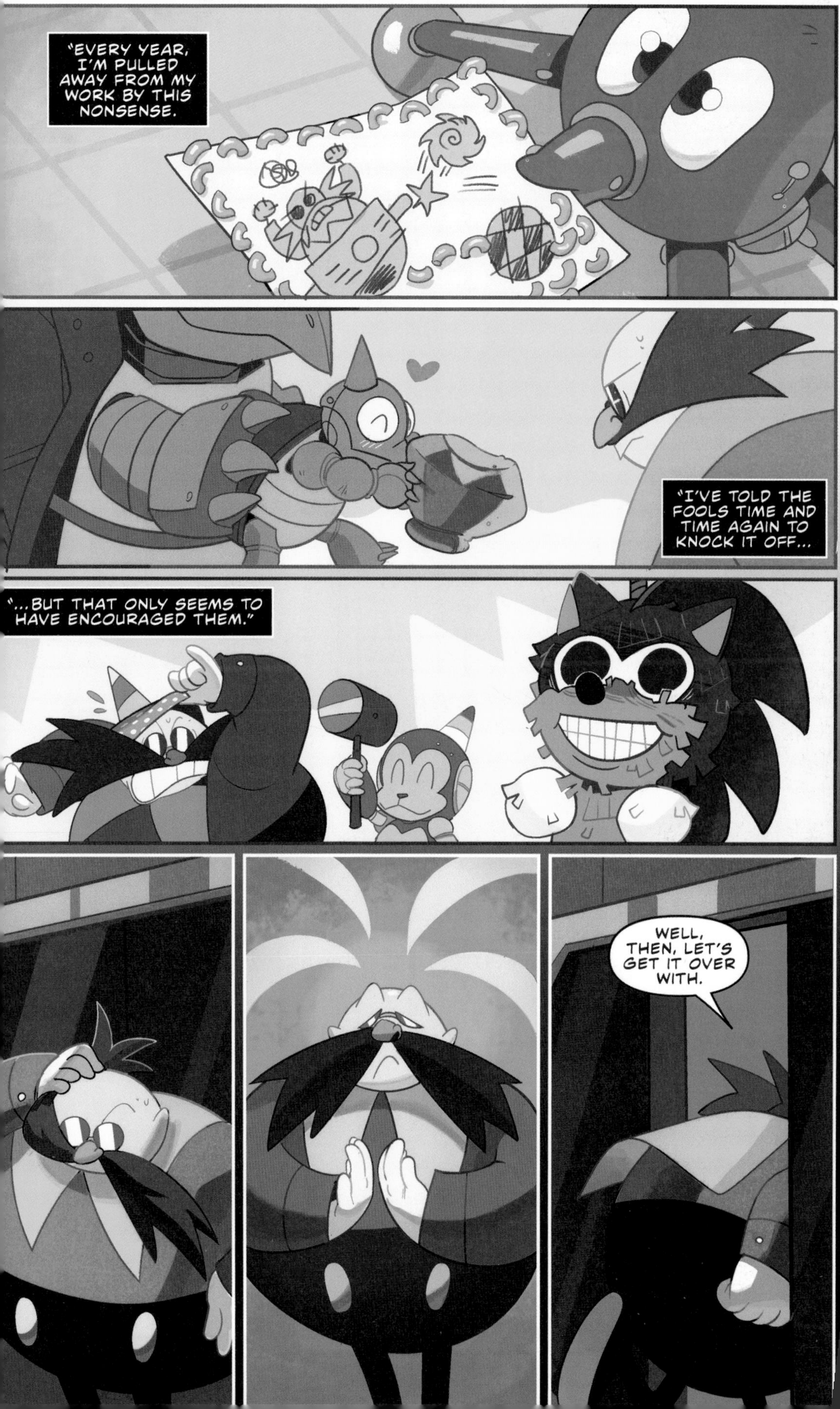
"EVERY YEAR, I'M PULLED AWAY FROM MY WORK BY THIS NONSENSE.
"I'VE TOLD THE FOOLS TIME AND TIME AGAIN TO KNOCK IT OFF...
"...BUT THAT ONLY SEEMS TO HAVE ENCOURAGED THEM."
WELL, THEN, LET'S GET IT OVER WITH.

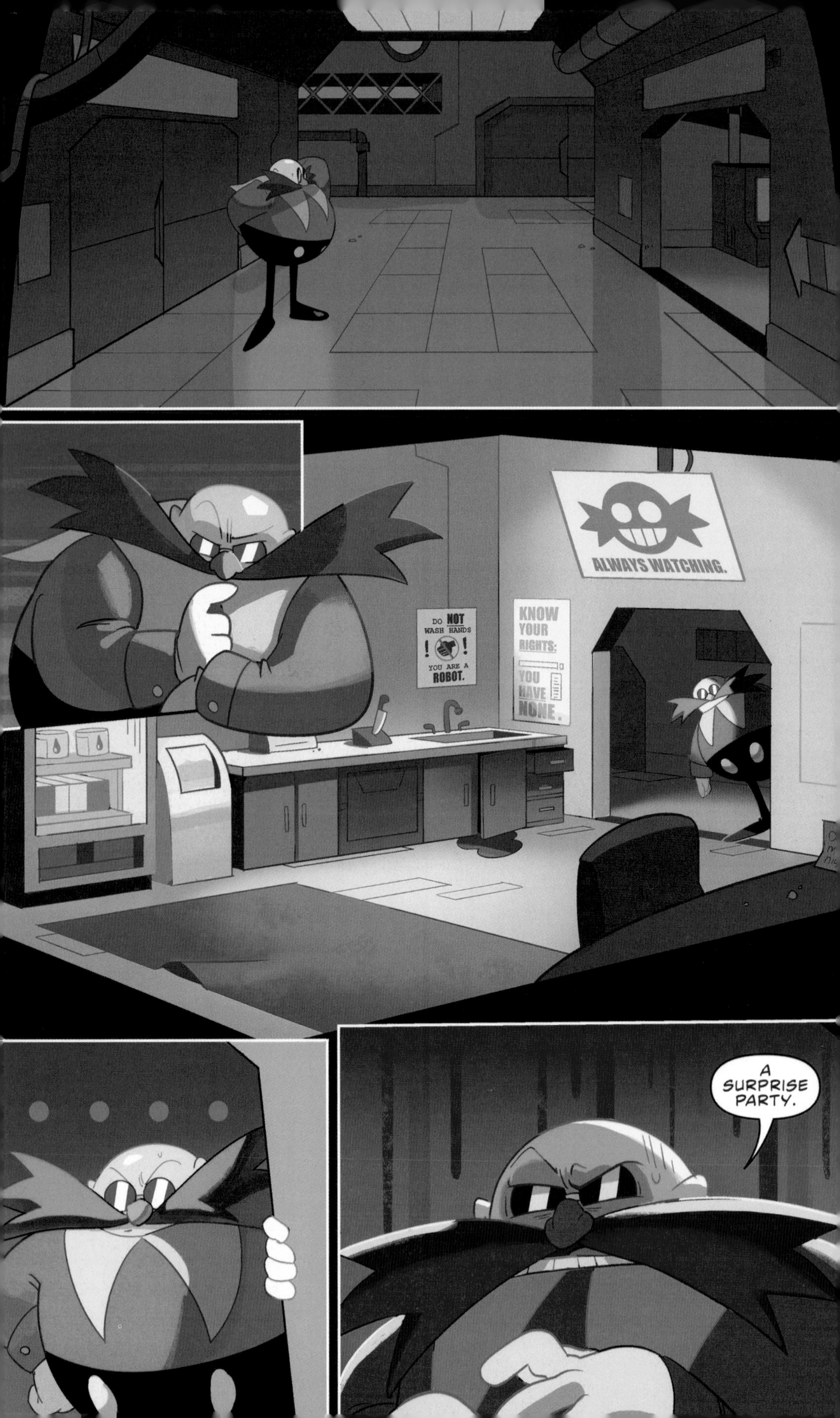
ALWAYS WATCHING.
DO NOT WASH HANDS
! !
YOU ARE A ROBOT.
KNOW YOUR RIGHTS:
YOU HAVE NONE.
A SURPRISE PARTY.

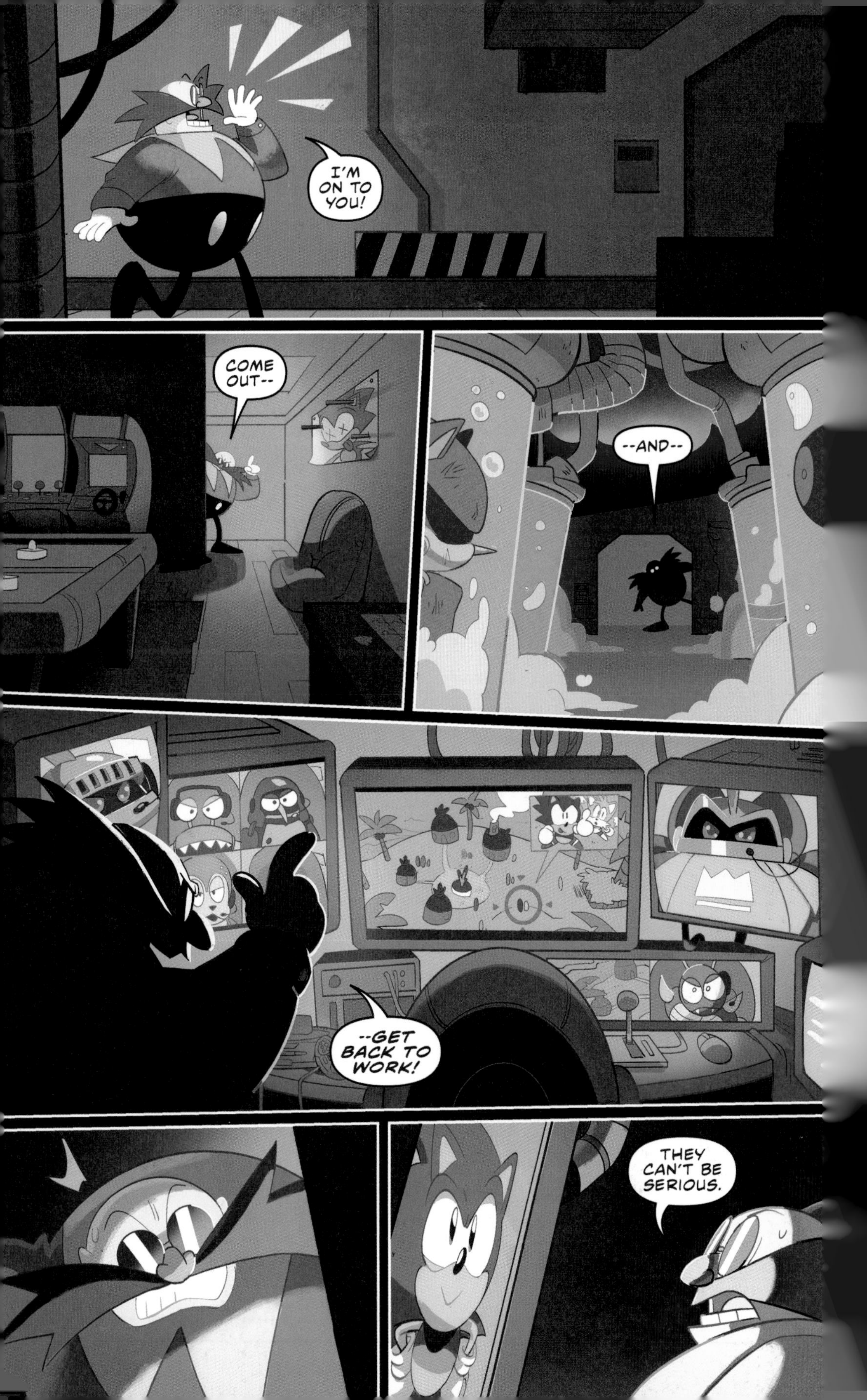
I'M ON TO YOU!
COME OUT--
--AND--
--GET BACK TO WORK!
THEY CAN'T BE SERIOUS.

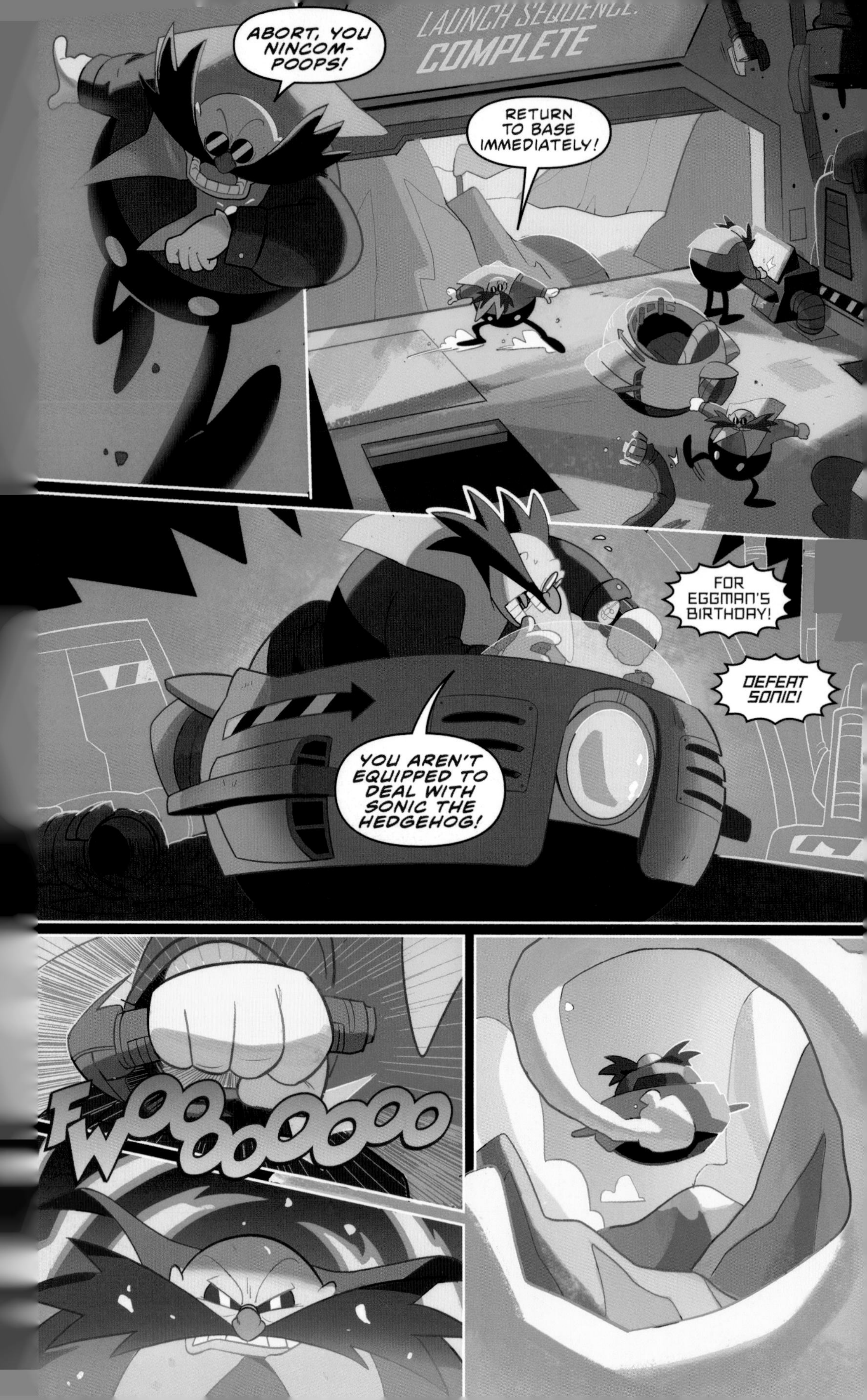
LAUNCH SEQUENCE:
COMPLETE
ABORT, YOU NINCOMPOOPS!
RETURN TO BASE IMMEDIATELY!
FOR EGGMAN'S BIRTHDAY!
DEFEAT SONIC!
YOU AREN'T EQUIPPED TO DEAL WITH SONIC THE HEDGEHOG!
FWOOOOOOOOO

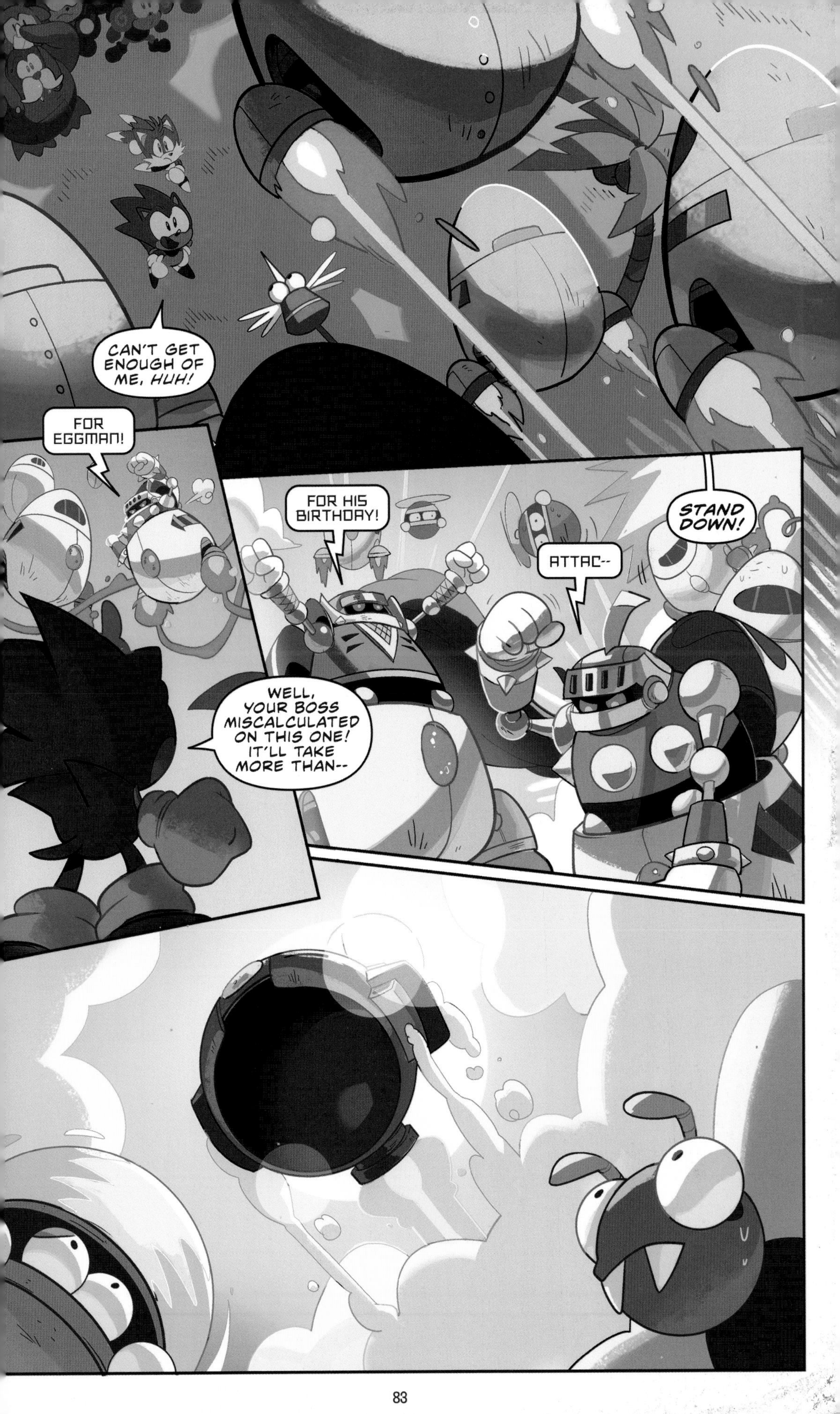
CAN'T GET ENOUGH OF ME, HUH!
FOR EGGMAN!
FOR HIS BIRTHDAY!
ATTAC--
STAND DOWN!
WELL, YOUR BOSS MISCALCULATED ON THIS ONE! IT'LL TAKE MORE THAN--

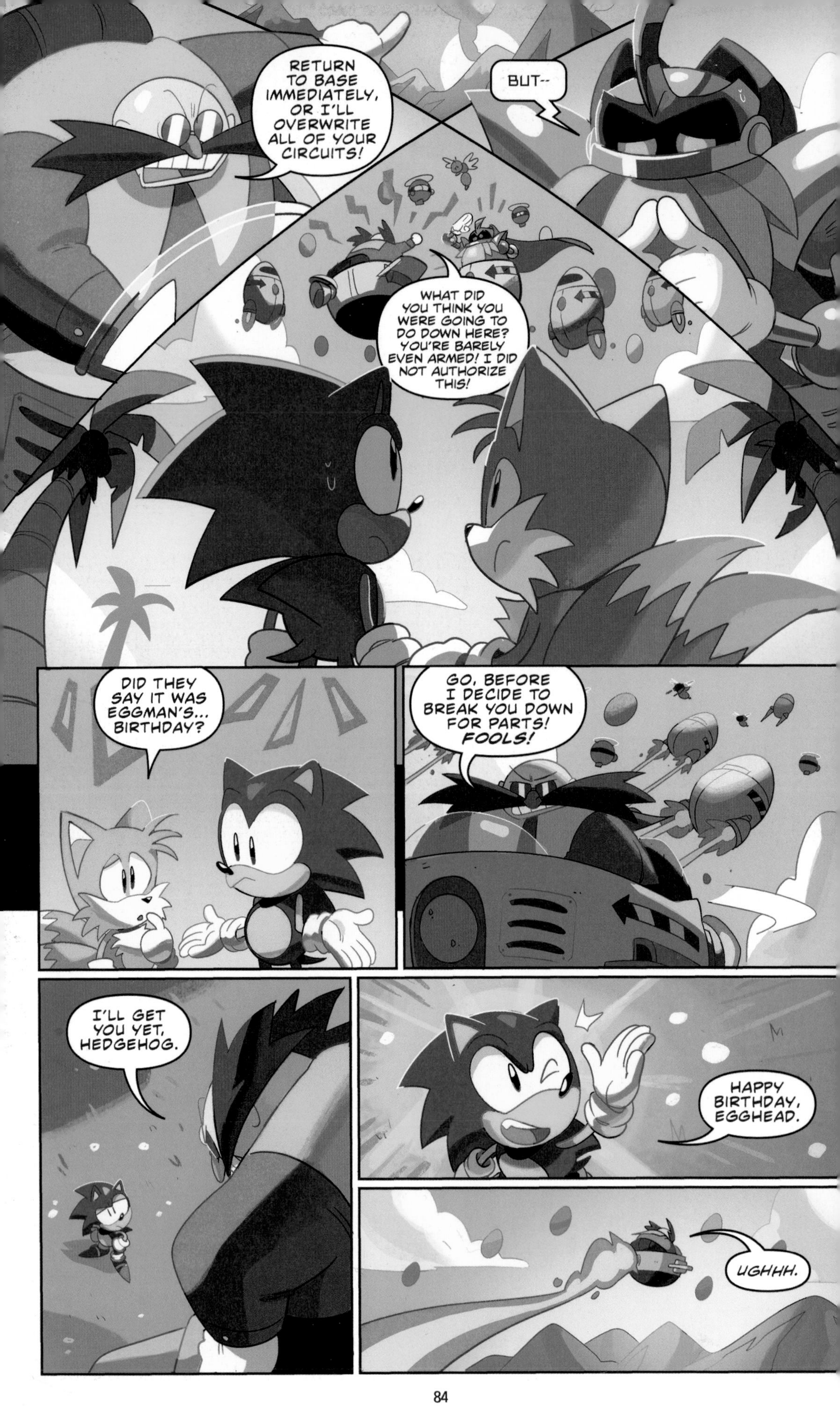
RETURN TO BASE IMMEDIATELY, OR I'LL OVERWRITE ALL OF YOUR CIRCUITS!
BUT--
WHAT DID YOU THINK YOU WERE GOING TO DO DOWN HERE? YOU'RE BARELY EVEN ARMED! I DID NOT AUTHORIZE THIS!
DID THEY SAY IT WAS EGGMAN'S... BIRTHDAY?
GO, BEFORE I DECIDE TO BREAK YOU DOWN FOR PARTS! FOOLS!
I'LL GET YOU YET, HEDGEHOG.
HAPPY BIRTHDAY, EGGHEAD.
UGHHH.

USE THE HEADS I GAVE YOU FOR ONE MOMENT!

I'M NOT SAYING IT WOULDN'T BE EASY TO REPLACE YOU, BUT THAT DOESN'T MEAN IT WOULDN'T BE A HASSLE!

DO YOU UNDERSTAND?!

I SAID, DO YOU UNDERSTAND?!

WE JUST WANTED TO DO SOMETHING NICE FOR YOUR BIRTHDAY, SIR.

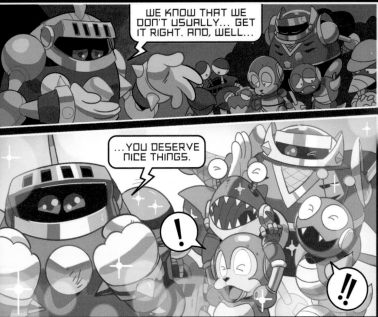

WE KNOW THAT WE DON'T USUALLY... GET IT RIGHT. AND, WELL...

...YOU DESERVE NICE THINGS.

!

!!

I...

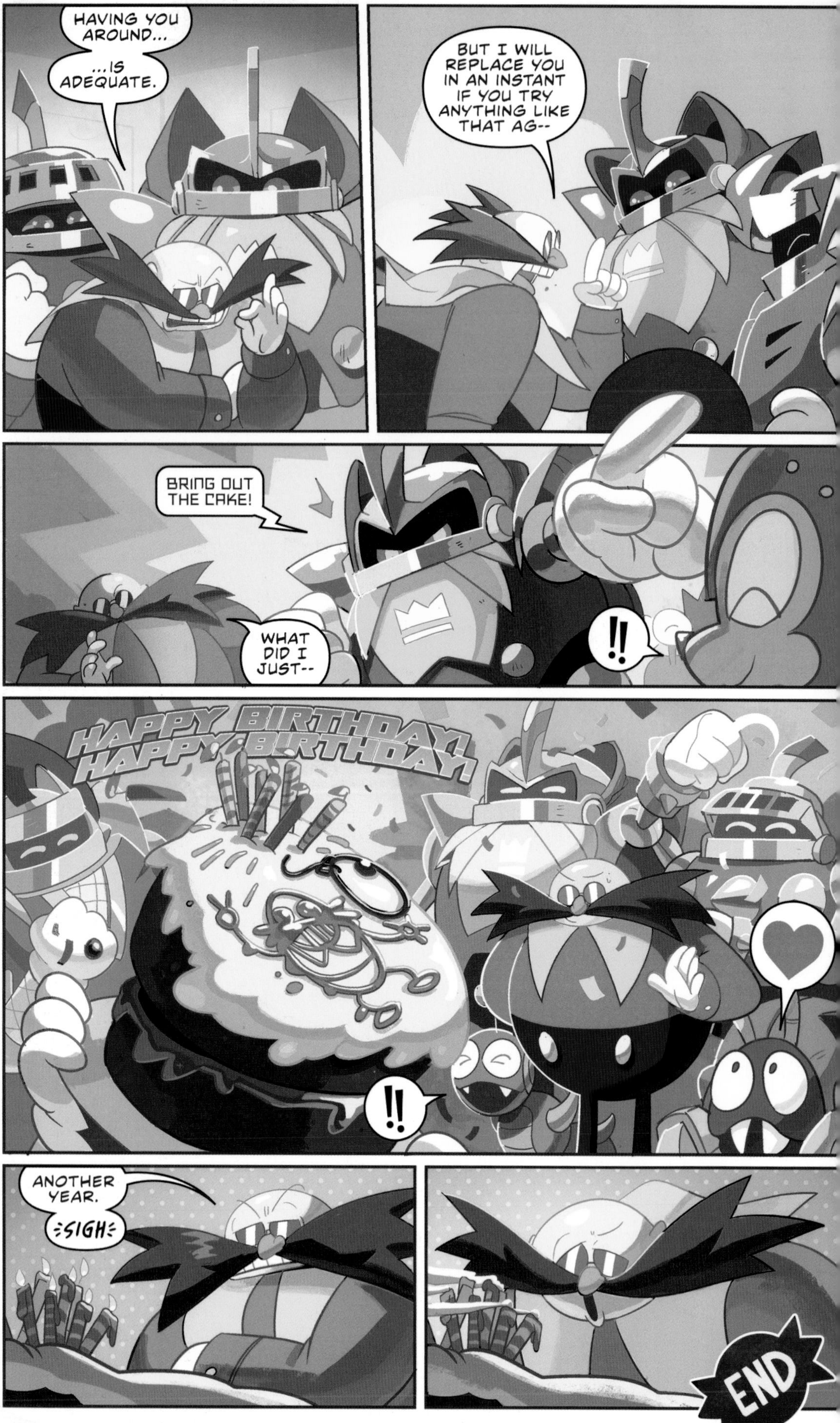
HAVING YOU AROUND...
...IS ADEQUATE.
BUT I WILL REPLACE YOU IN AN INSTANT IF YOU TRY ANYTHING LIKE THAT AG--
BRING OUT THE CAKE!
WHAT DID I JUST--
!!
HAPPY BIRTHDAY! HAPPY BIRTHDAY!
!!
ANOTHER YEAR.
SIGH
END

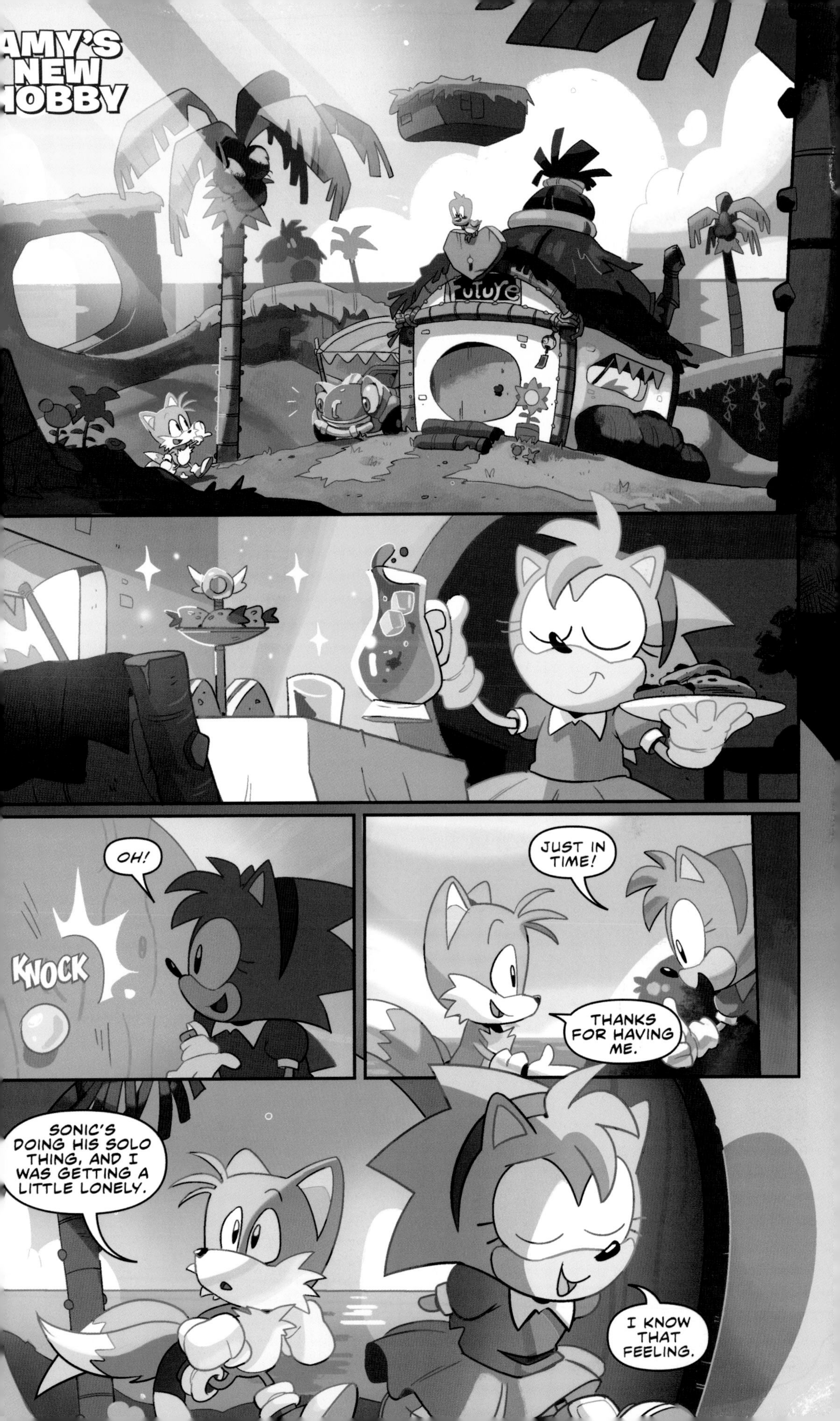
AMY'S NEW HOBBY
FUTURE
OH!
KNOCK
JUST IN TIME!
THANKS FOR HAVING ME.
SONIC'S DOING HIS SOLO THING, AND I WAS GETTING A LITTLE LONELY.
I KNOW THAT FEELING.

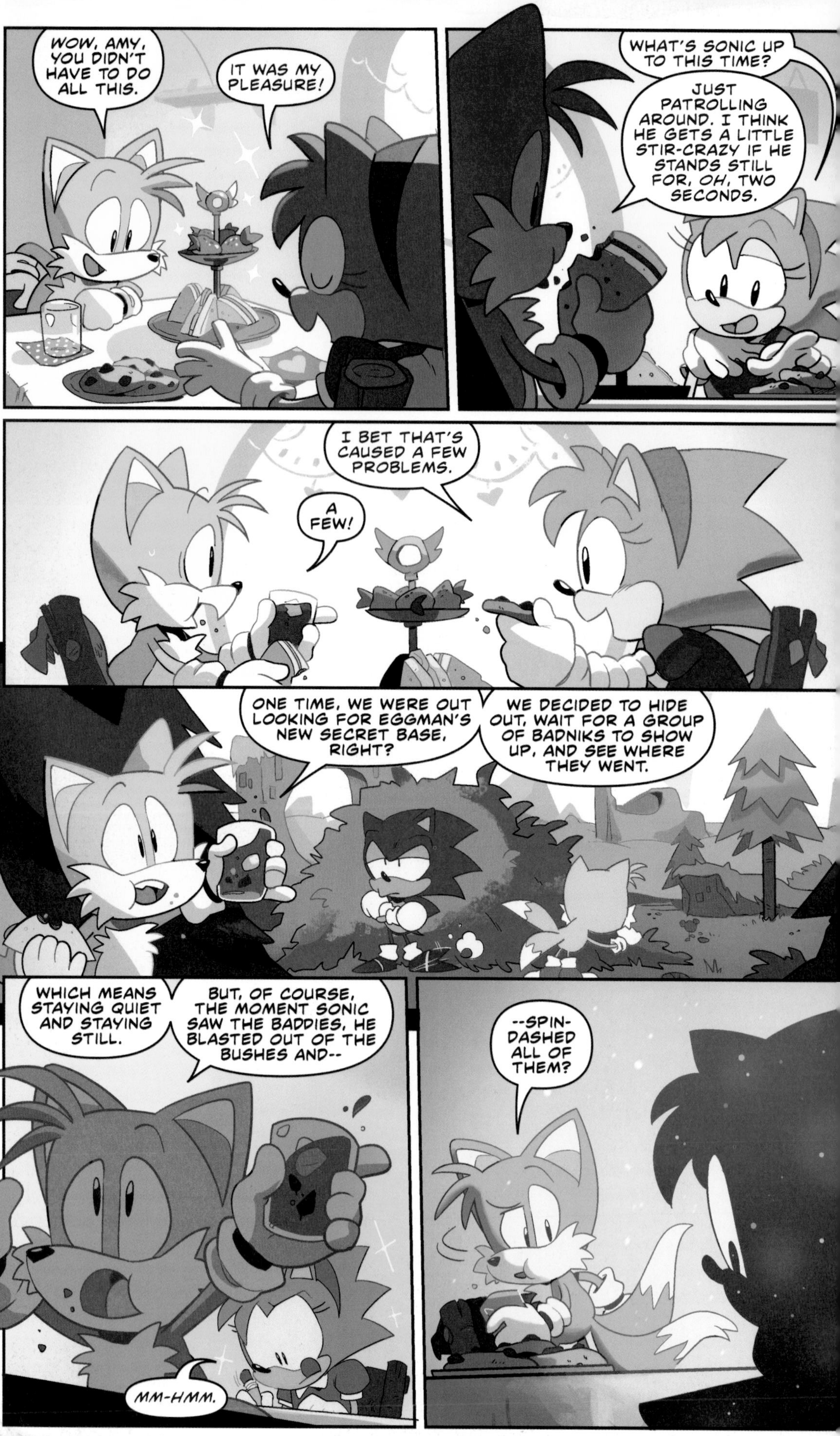
WOW, AMY, YOU DIDN'T HAVE TO DO ALL THIS.
IT WAS MY PLEASURE!
WHAT'S SONIC UP TO THIS TIME?
JUST PATROLLING AROUND. I THINK HE GETS A LITTLE STIR-CRAZY IF HE STANDS STILL FOR, OH, TWO SECONDS.
I BET THAT'S CAUSED A FEW PROBLEMS.
A FEW!
ONE TIME, WE WERE OUT LOOKING FOR EGGMAN'S NEW SECRET BASE, RIGHT?
WE DECIDED TO HIDE OUT, WAIT FOR A GROUP OF BADNIKS TO SHOW UP, AND SEE WHERE THEY WENT.
WHICH MEANS STAYING QUIET AND STAYING STILL.
BUT, OF COURSE, THE MOMENT SONIC SAW THE BADDIES, HE BLASTED OUT OF THE BUSHES AND--
MM-HMM.
--SPIN-DASHED ALL OF THEM?

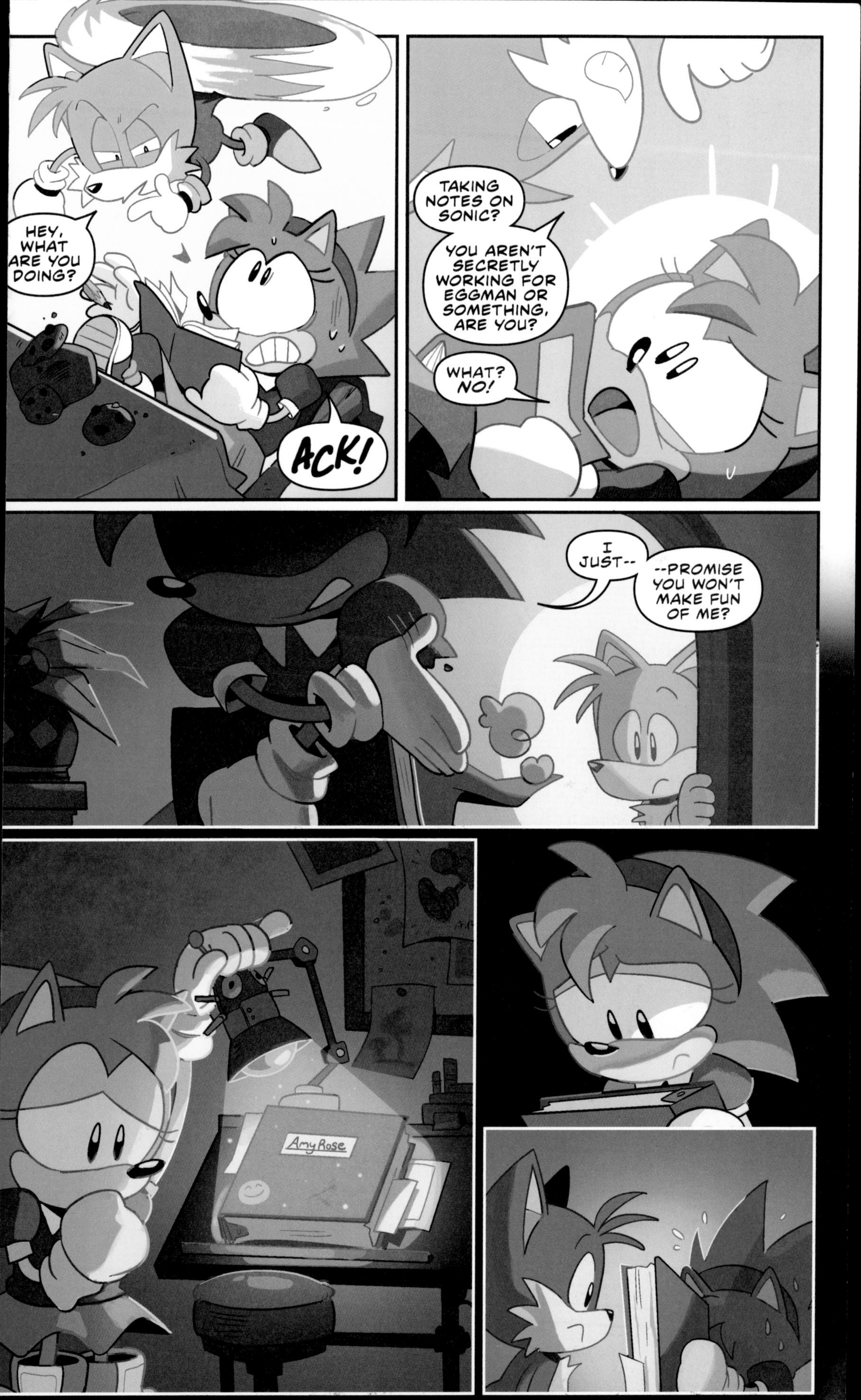
HEY, WHAT ARE YOU DOING?
ACK!
TAKING NOTES ON SONIC?
YOU AREN'T SECRETLY WORKING FOR EGGMAN OR SOMETHING, ARE YOU?
WHAT? NO!
I JUST--
--PROMISE YOU WON'T MAKE FUN OF ME?
Amy Rose

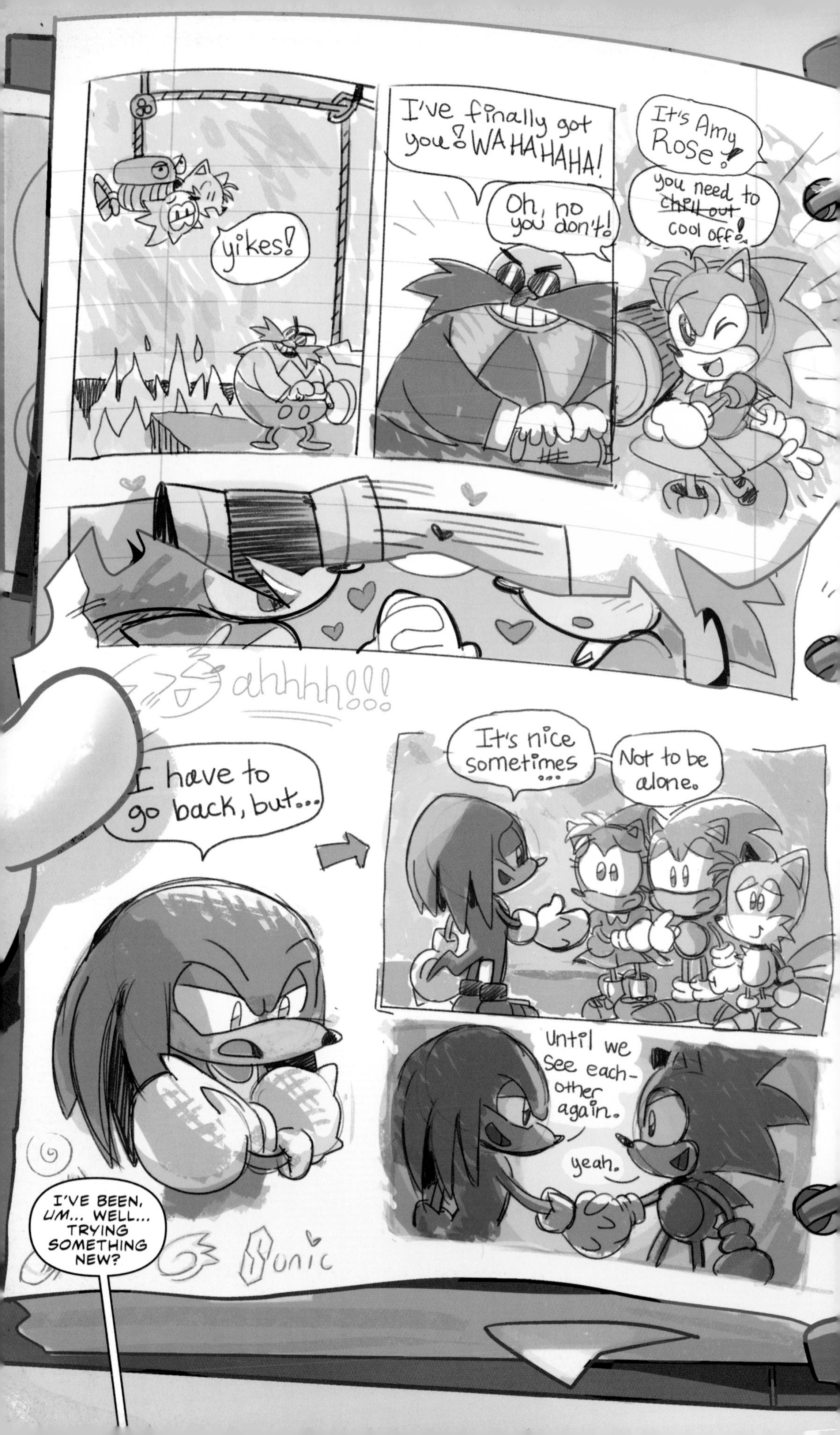

yikes!
I've finally got you! WAHAHAHAHA!
Oh, no you don't!
It's Amy Rose!
you need to ~~chill out~~ cool off!
ahhhh!!!
I have to go back, but...
It's nice sometimes...
Not to be alone.
Until we see each-other again.
yeah.
I'VE BEEN, UM... WELL... TRYING SOMETHING NEW?
Sonic

'The Last Stand'
NEW
CHILI DOGS
Boy, is this new Chili dog place popular!
We've been waiting forever!
What would you like?
Finally! I'm starv—
HELP!
a hero's work is never done.
Save some for us!!
'Strange, Isn't It?'
Previously...
So it's come to this, Metal Sonic!
You might know everything I'm going to do...
...but I know everything you're going to do!
By A. Rose

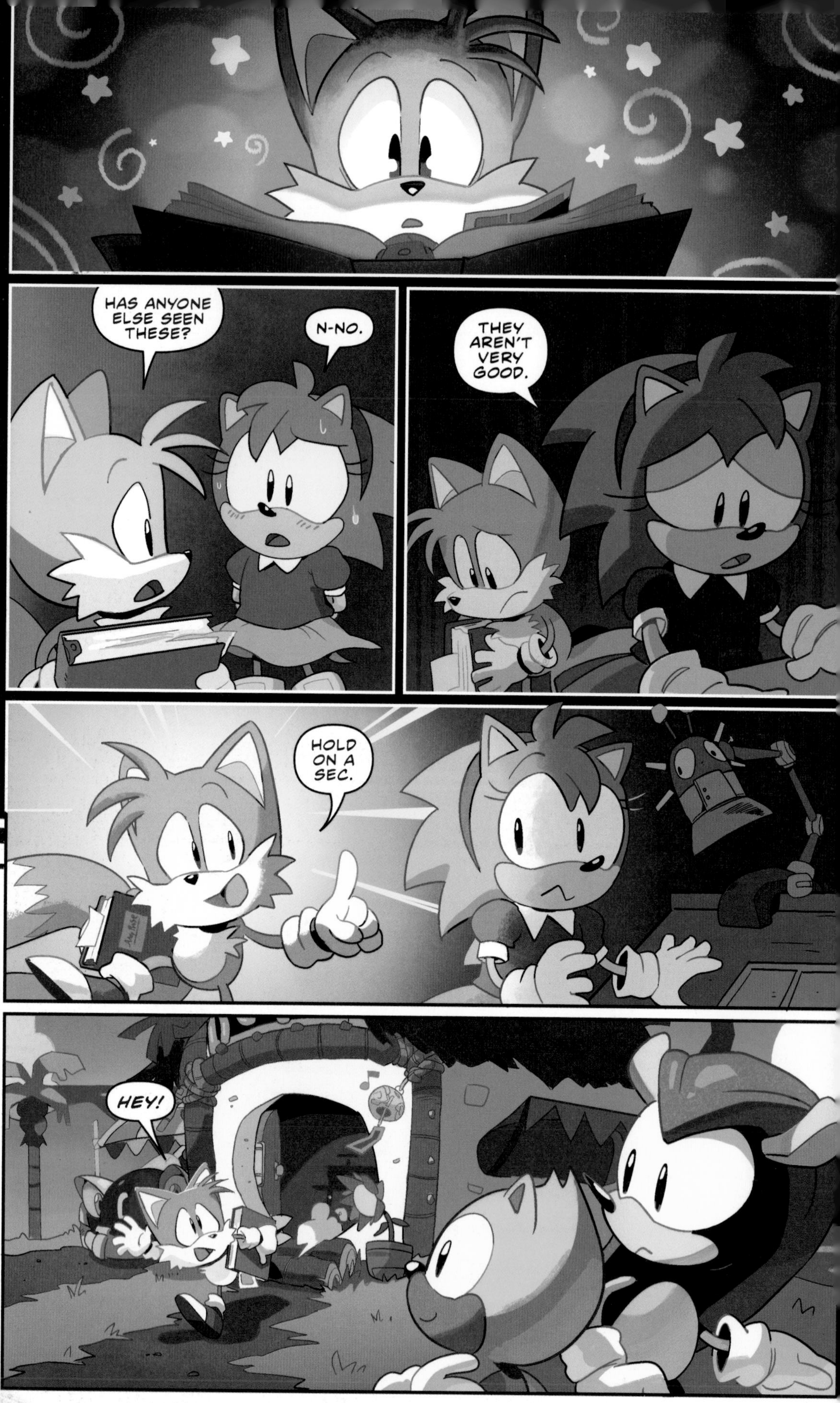
HAS ANYONE ELSE SEEN THESE?
N-NO.
THEY AREN'T VERY GOOD.
HOLD ON A SEC.
HEY!

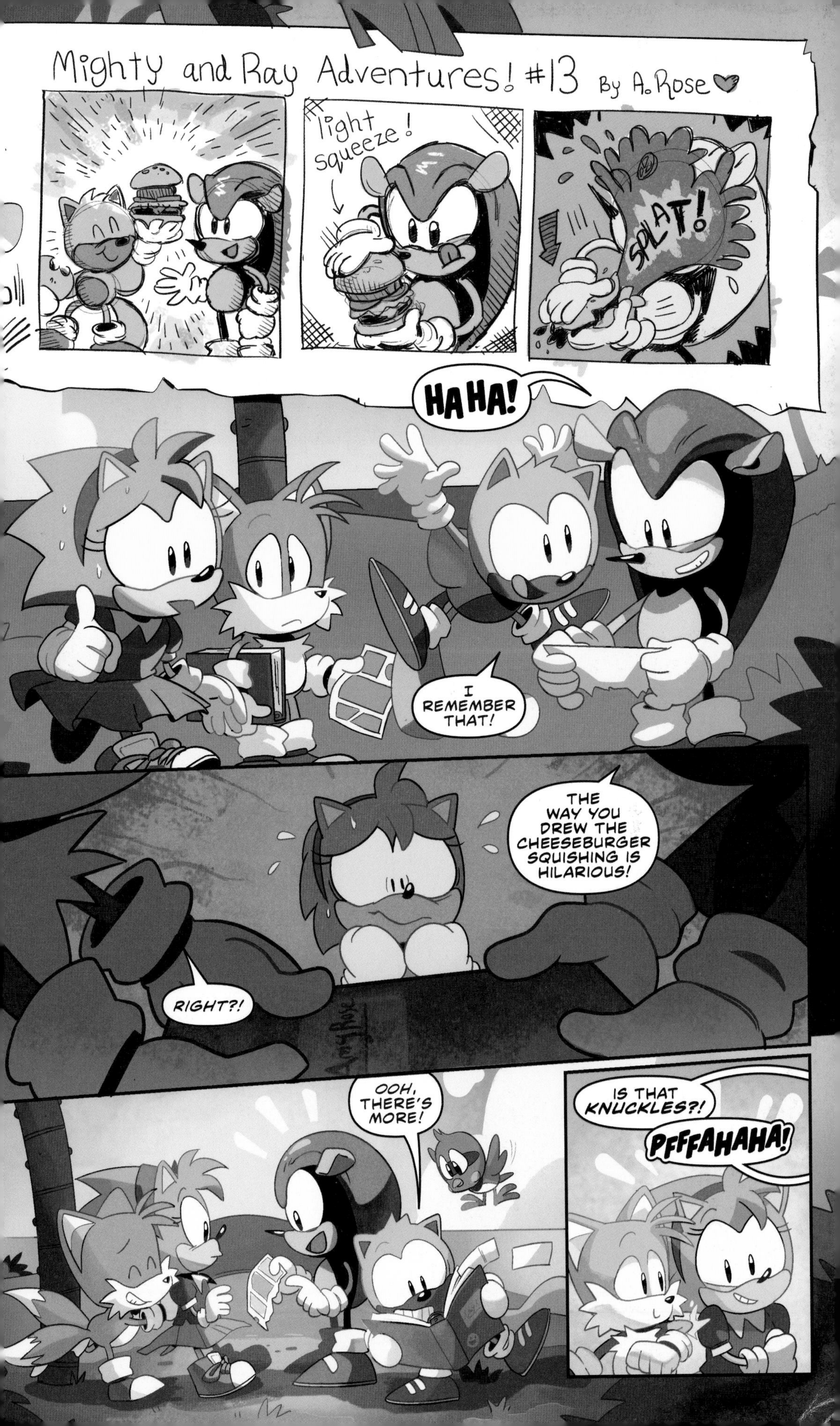

Mighty and Ray Adventures! #13
By A. Rose
light squeeze!
SPLAT!
HAHA!
I REMEMBER THAT!
THE WAY YOU DREW THE CHEESEBURGER SQUISHING IS HILARIOUS!
RIGHT?!
OOH, THERE'S MORE!
IS THAT KNUCKLES?!
PFFFAHAHA!

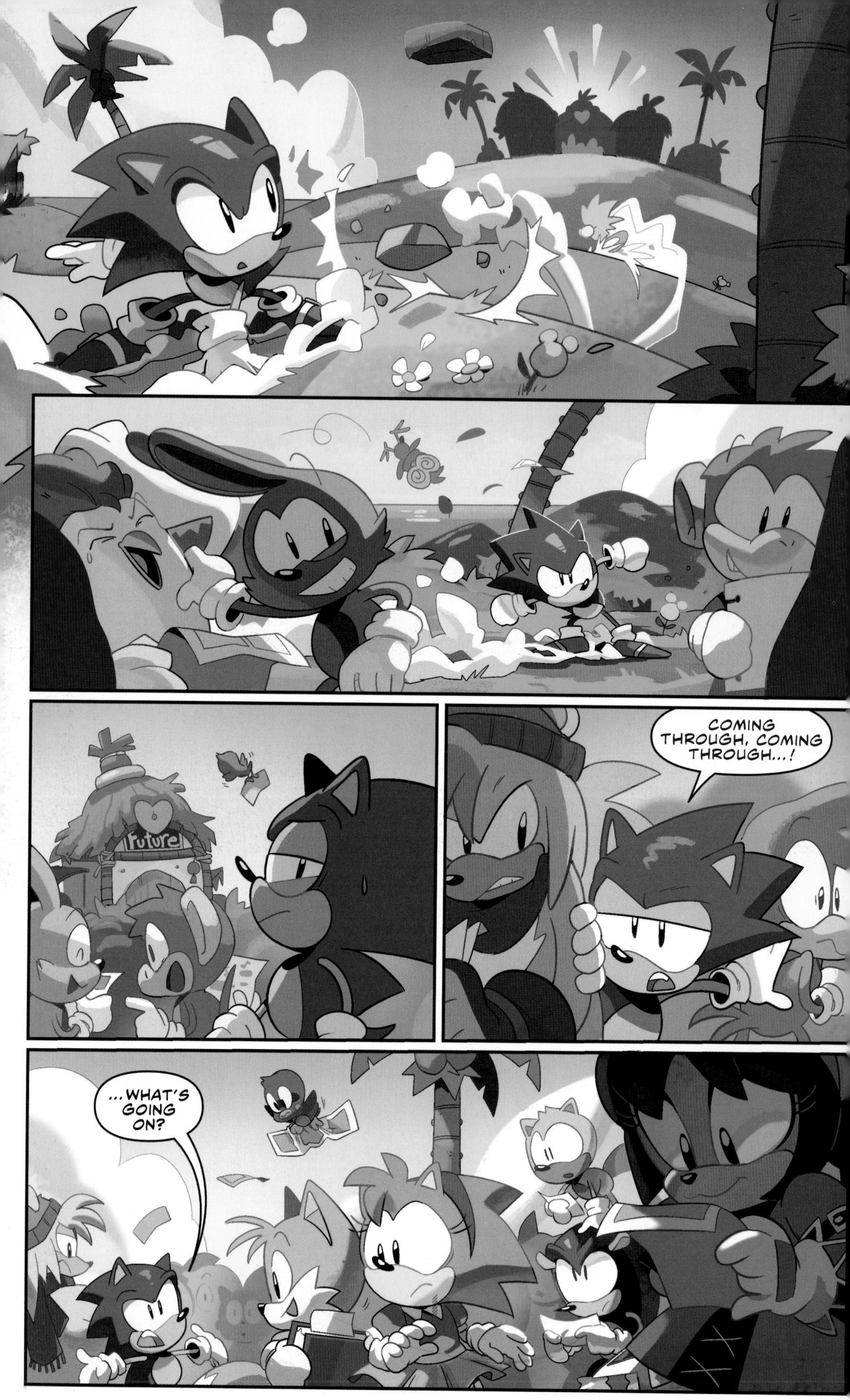
Future
COMING THROUGH, COMING THROUGH...!
...WHAT'S GOING ON?

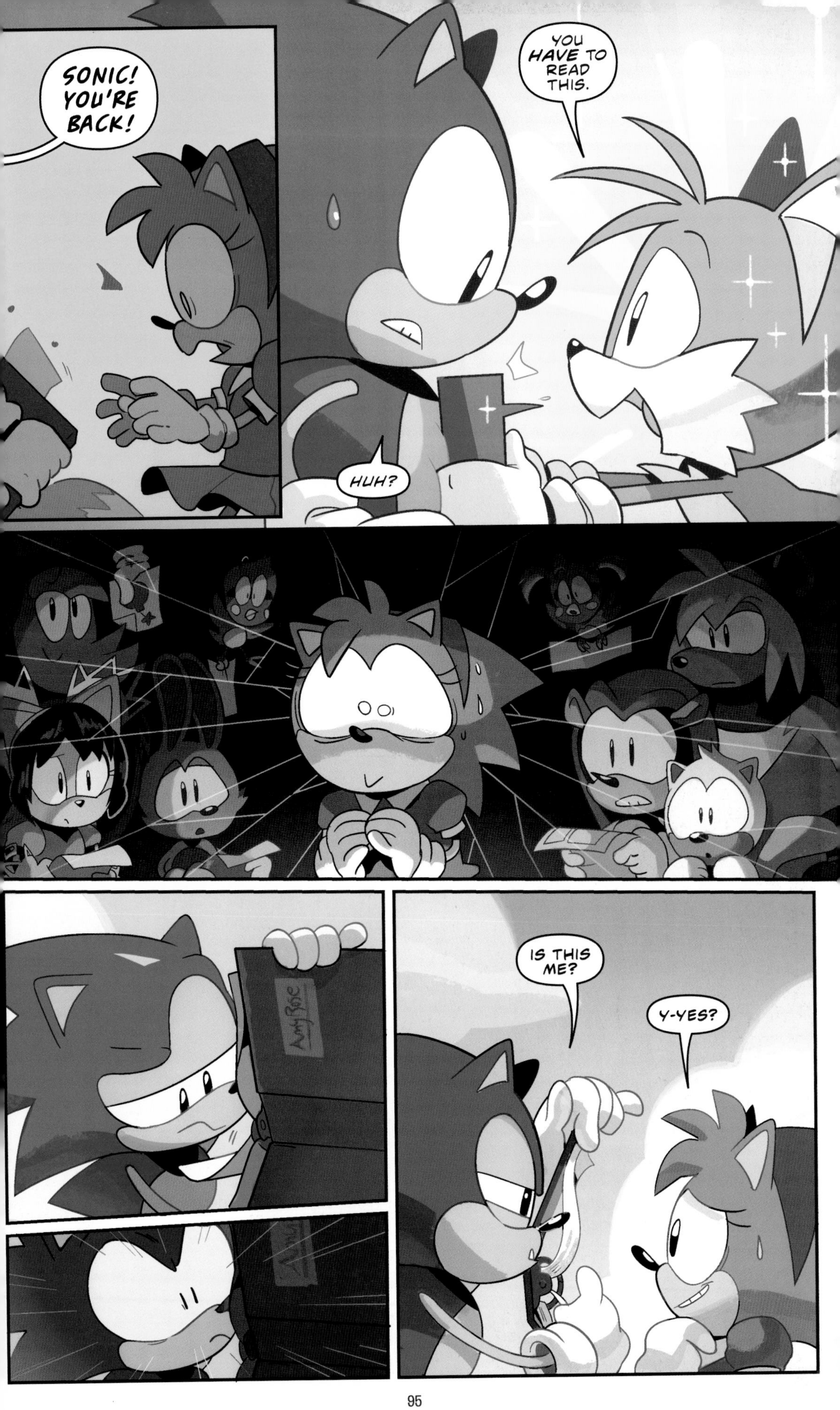
SONIC! YOU'RE BACK!
YOU HAVE TO READ THIS.
HUH?
Amy Rose
IS THIS ME?
Y-YES?

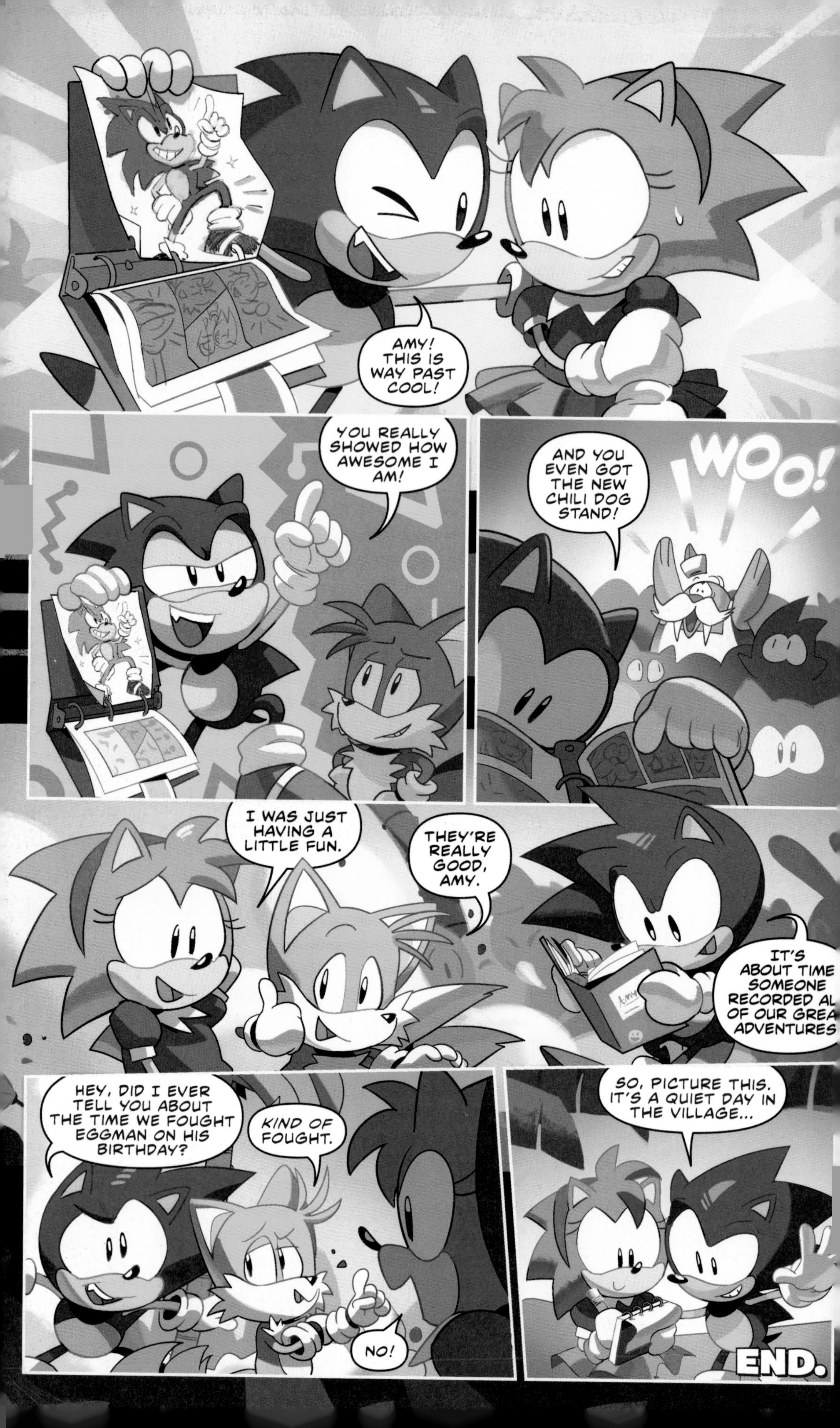

AMY! THIS IS WAY PAST COOL!
YOU REALLY SHOWED HOW AWESOME I AM!
AND YOU EVEN GOT THE NEW CHILI DOG STAND!
WOO!
I WAS JUST HAVING A LITTLE FUN.
THEY'RE REALLY GOOD, AMY.
IT'S ABOUT TIME SOMEONE RECORDED AL OF OUR GREA ADVENTURES
HEY, DID I EVER TELL YOU ABOUT THE TIME WE FOUGHT EGGMAN ON HIS BIRTHDAY?
KIND OF FOUGHT.
NO!
SO, PICTURE THIS. IT'S A QUIET DAY IN THE VILLAGE...
END.

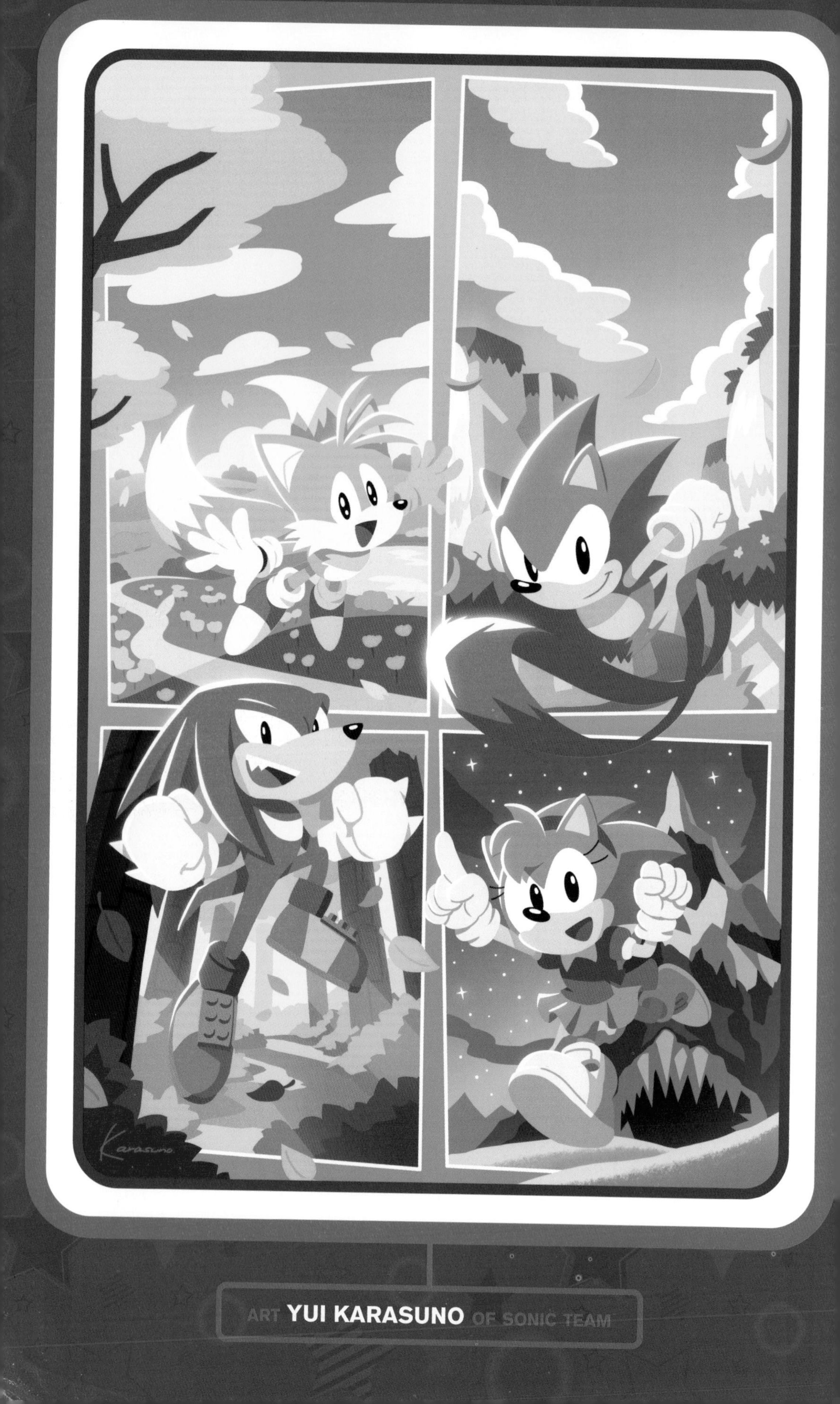
Karasuno

ART YUI KARASUNO OF SONIC TEAM

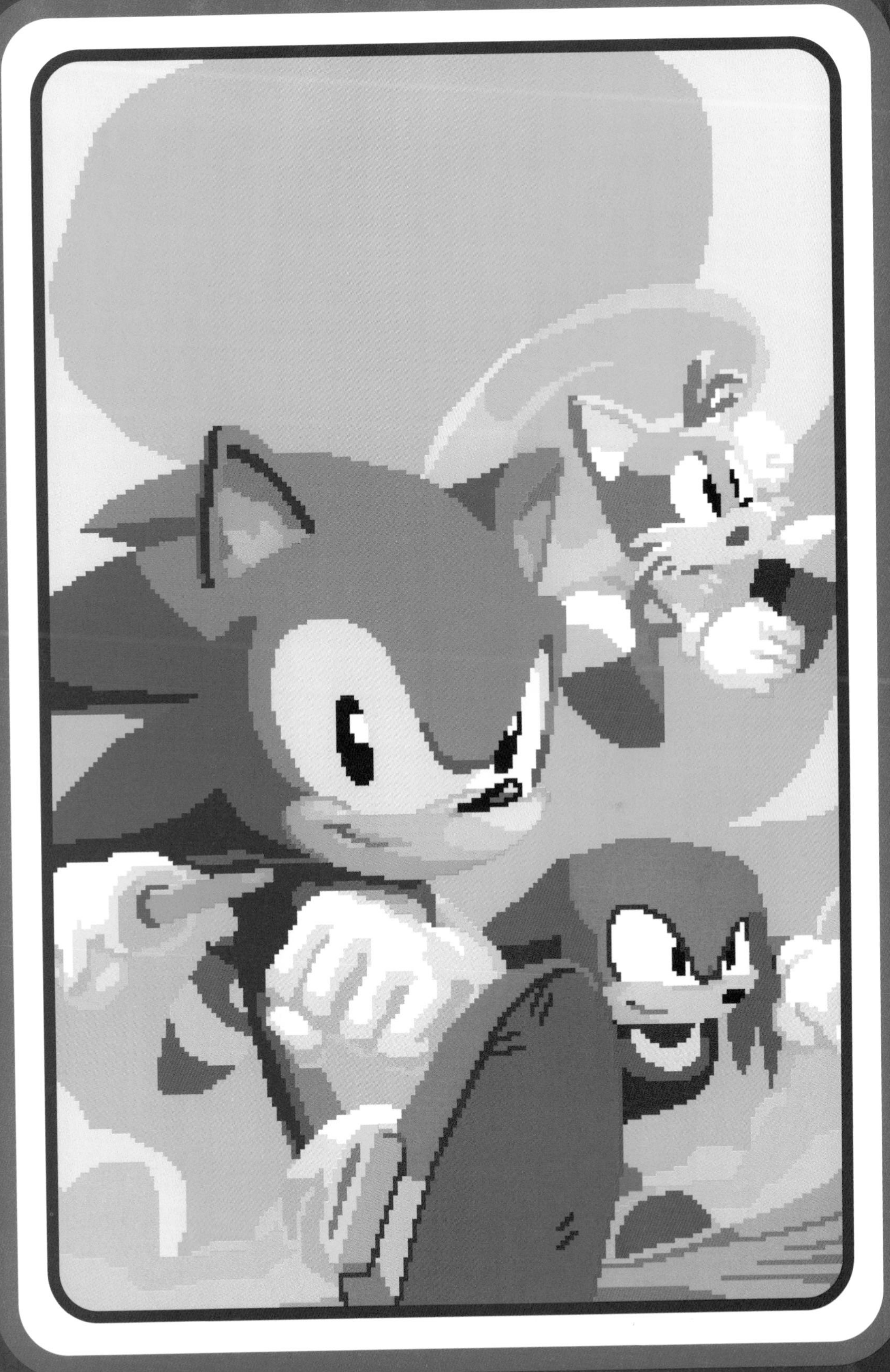

ART CHRISTINA-ANTOINETTE NEOFOTISTOU

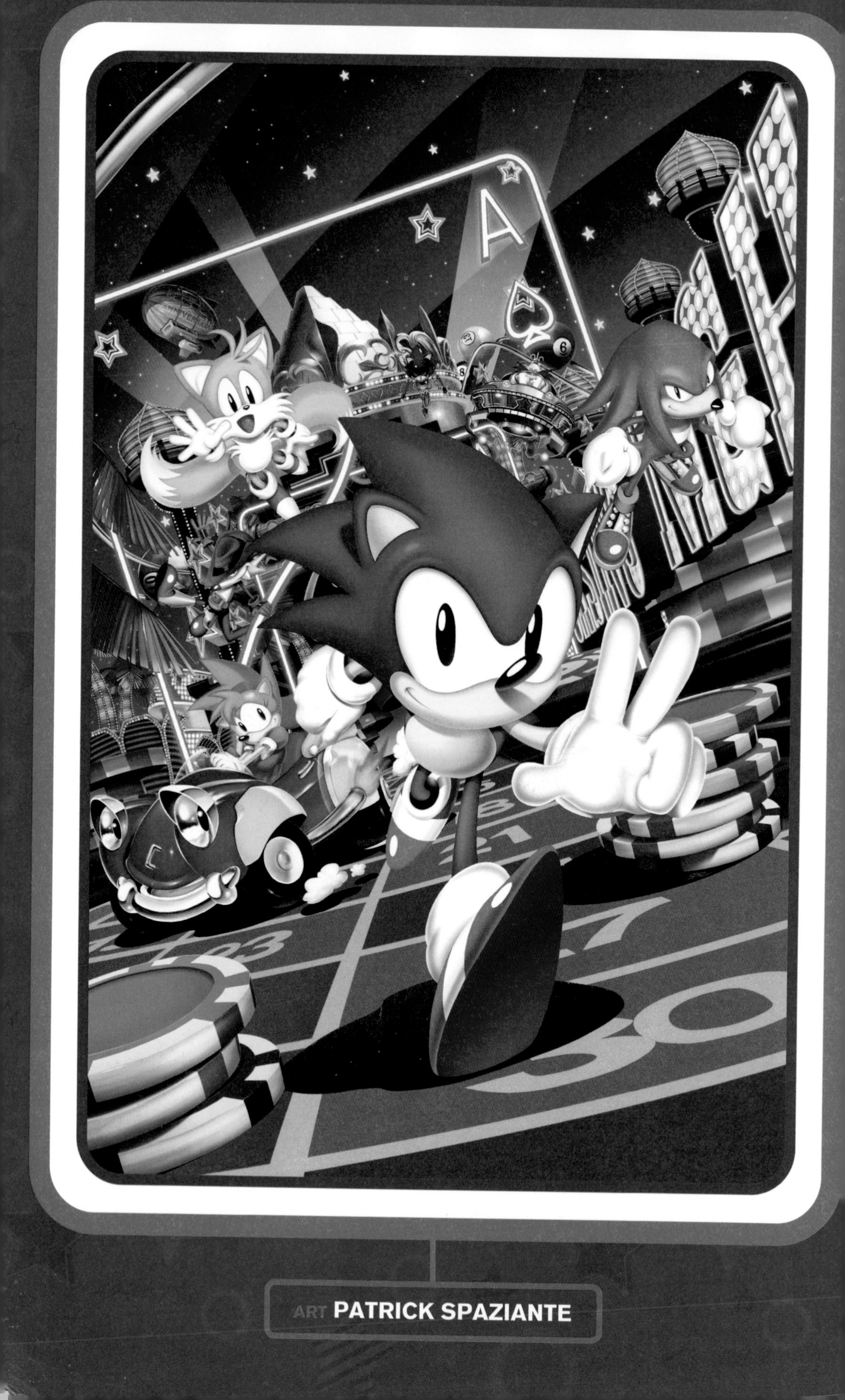

ART **PATRICK SPAZIANTE**

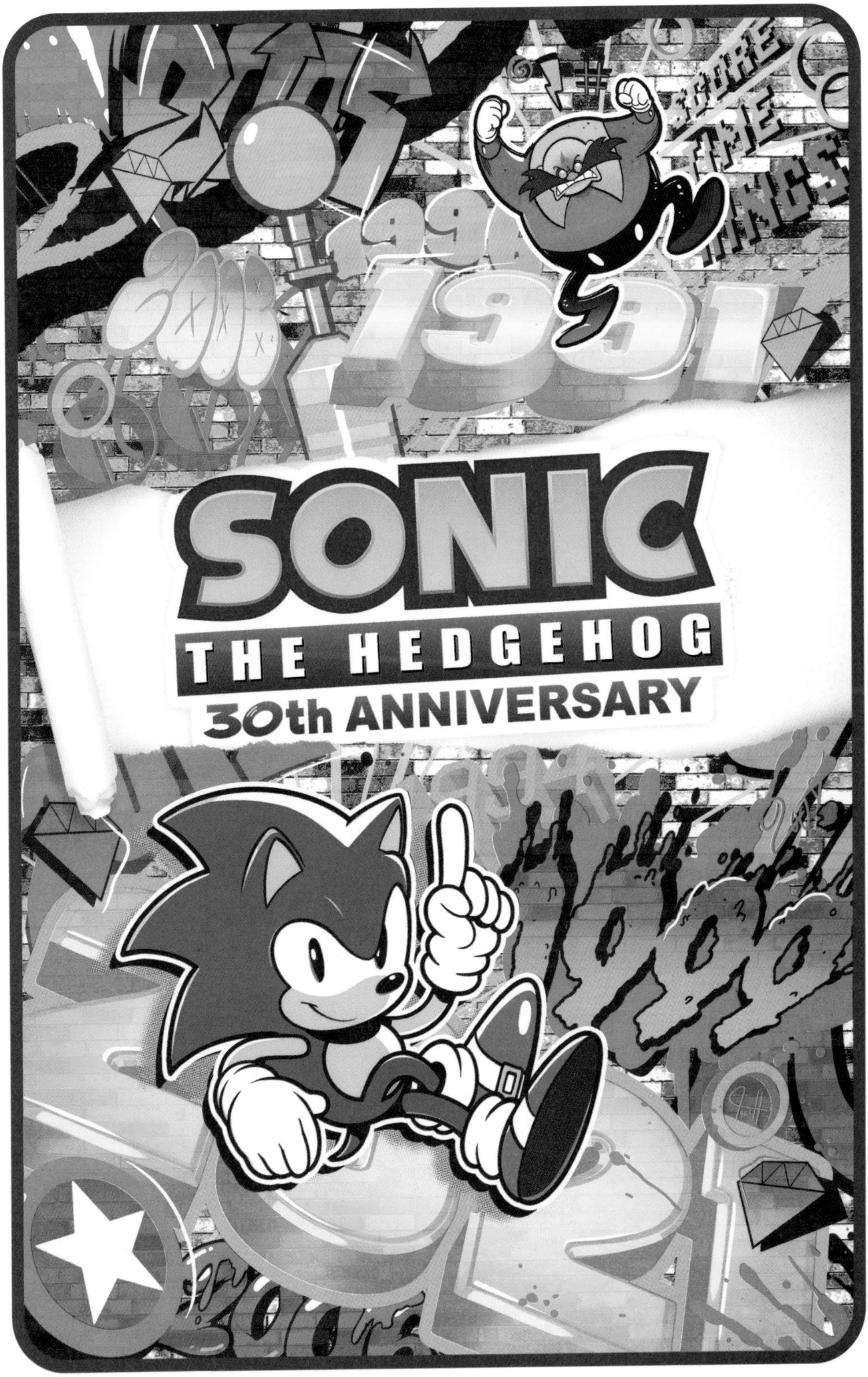
1991
SONIC
THE HEDGEHOG
30th ANNIVERSARY

ART TYSON HESSE

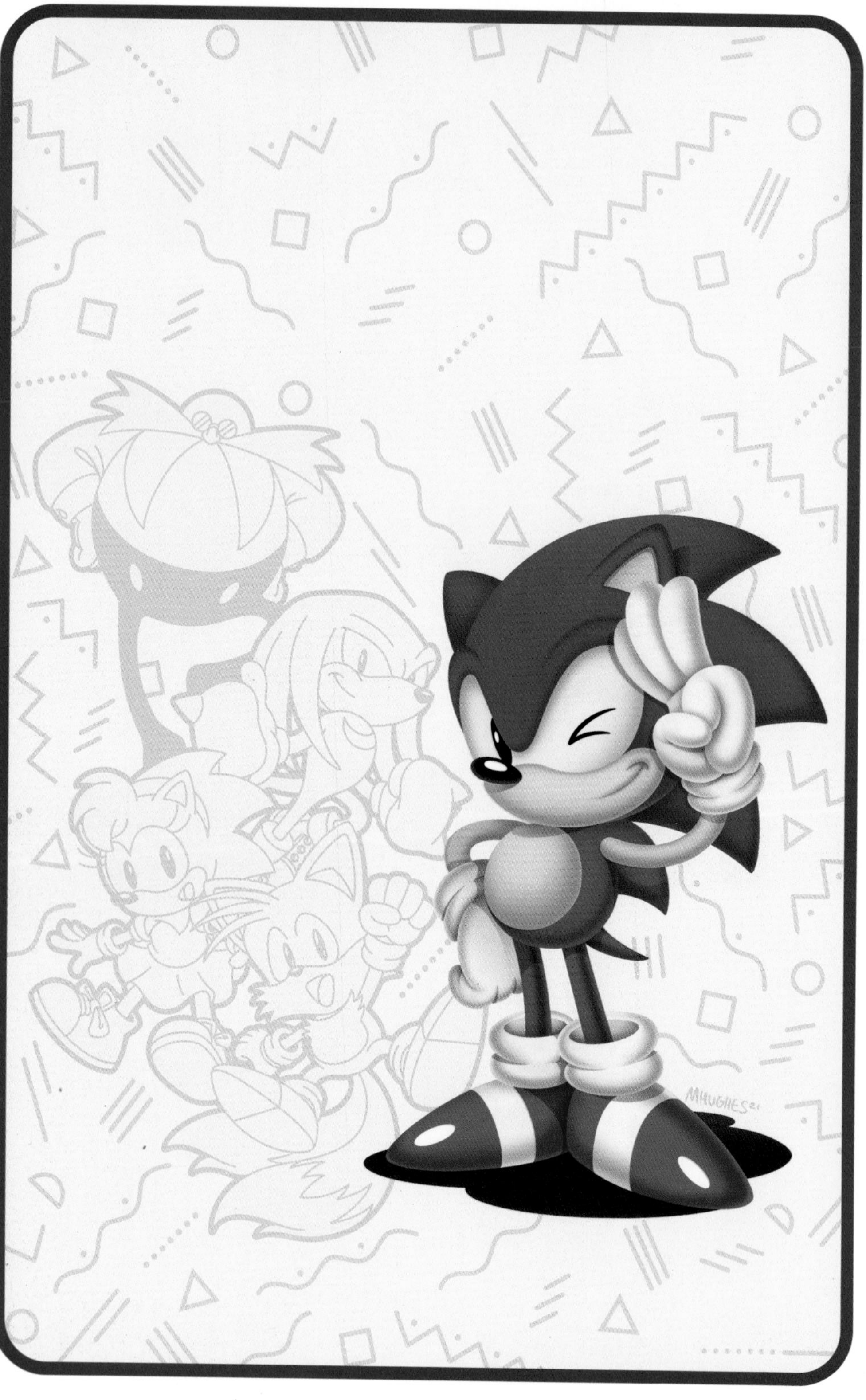
MHUGHES 21

ART MARK HUGHES

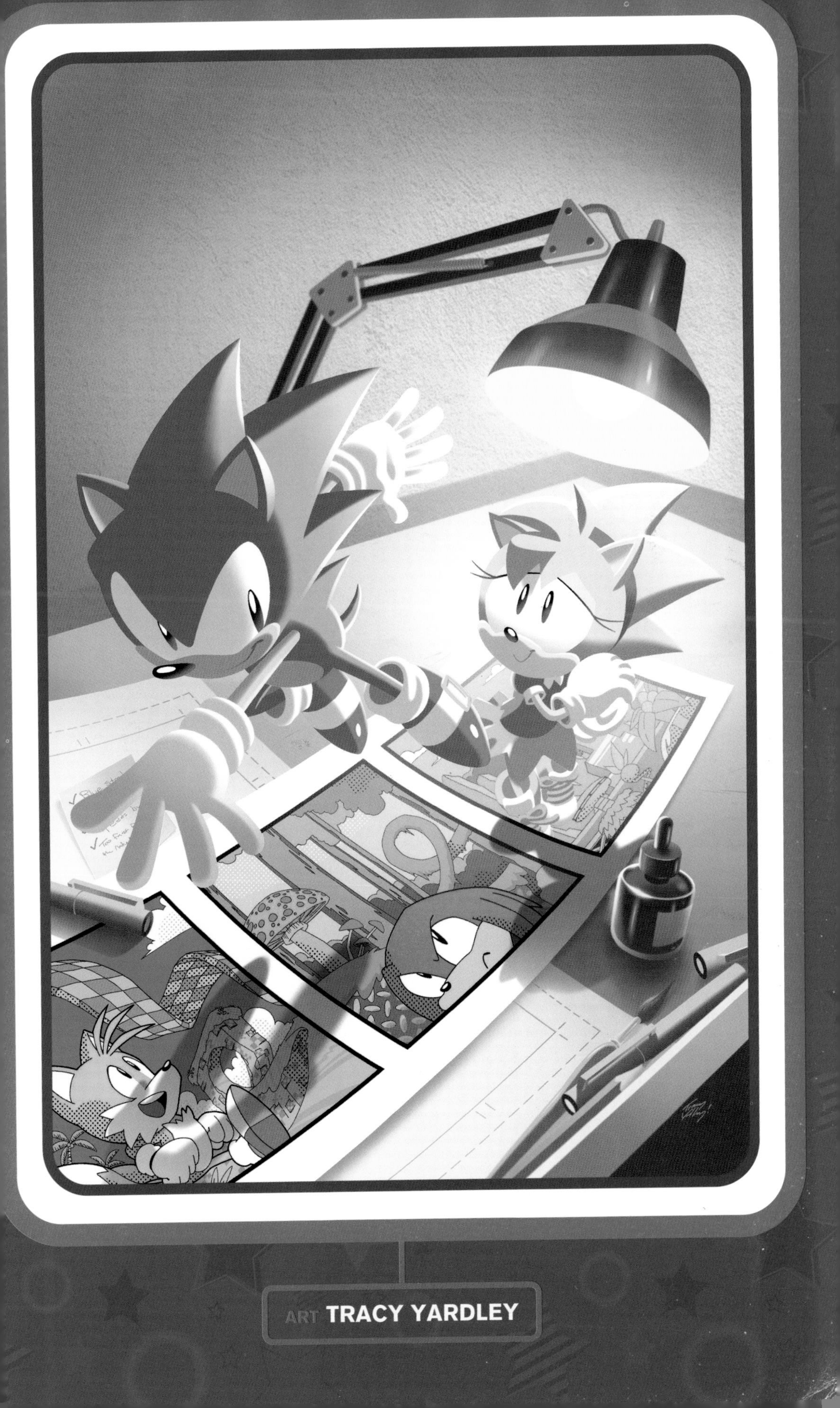

ART TRACY YARDLEY

FROM SCRIPT TO PAGE

Have you ever wondered how comics are made? Like in the story "Amy's New Hobby," they take a lot of hard work, thought, and often a little bit of help from your friends! Join us on a tour of the comic making process that brought you this collection as we go behind the scenes of how comics are made!

Just like Sonic assembled his friends (and foes) in "Seasons of Chaos," the first step to making a comic is putting together a creative team. Many comics have a writer, a penciller, an inker, a colorist, a letterer, a designer, editors, licensors, and all sorts of folks involved in the creation of the final comic.

"Seasons of Chaos" had a writer, Ian Flynn, who came up with the rough idea of the story that was presented to SEGA for initial approval. This process is called "pitching." The pitching process allows for creative conversations to happen early on, rather than writing the script and then having to make big changes. For example, at one point, "Seasons of Chaos" was going to be a silent story! Can you imagine reading it with no words and just the art?

When the pitch is approved, Ian begins writing the script. Like a movie script, a comic script describes the visual action of each page and the dialogue the characters say and think. Ian's scripts break the pages down into their individual panels and highlight important information like location, emotions, and other key details. Here are some script pages for "Seasons of Chaos."

NEL 1 – Spring Valley Zone – Exterior – Day

one in the style of a screen shot taken from a classic game.

ONIC, TAILS and AMY run through the "stage" from left to right. BADNIKS drift
azily in the background.

MY is at left and springing off a very large flower reminiscent of a game spring.

ONIC comes out of a SPIN JUMP off of a BADNIK to give TAILS a surprised look.
ONIC is at CENTER.

TAILS flies to the RIGHT and calls down to SONIC while pointing to something
glinting in the distance.

1   TEXT BOX
           Spring Valley Zone.

PANEL 2 - The GREEN CHAOS EMERALD rests in the center of an especially large
wildflower bloom.

SONIC takes center as he looks down at it in wonder. AMY and TAILS flank him and
peer around him at the CHAOS EMERALD, gawking.

2   AMY
           Oh wow!
           A Chaos Emerald!

3   TAILS
           You don't normally see them lying around in the open!

PANEL 3 – SONIC smiles, self-satisfied, and reaches for the EMERALD.

4   SONIC
           I guess I'll just help myself.

PANEL 4 – Same staging as the previous panel. SONIC goes wide-eyed in a "Wait –
what?" expression, hand still outstretched in mid-reach. A rush of BLUE whips past
him as METAL SONIC takes the EMERALD at high speed.

Scripts often have to go through
a few drafts before becoming
final. The "Seasons of Chaos"
script went through three rounds
of revisions before final approval
as the editorial team, a translator,
and the team at SEGA reviewed
the script and made notes to
correct punctuation, spelling
errors, and ideas to help make
the story the best it can be! And
while three rounds of revisions
may sound like a lot, the notes
on each round were pretty minor
as Ian's a talented writer!

PAGE FOUR

PANEL 1 – TAILS pivots in mid-air, straining to hurl SONIC higher. SONIC is flung
from TAILS'S hands in a SPIN JUMP.

PANEL 2 – SONIC strains as he reaches for METAL SONIC'S foot. METAL SONIC
looks back to see SONIC nearly grabbing him. Spring Valley Zone sprawls out beneath
them.

PANEL 3 – METAL SONIC accelerates away, a compression wave marking the jolt of
his thrust. SONIC is blown back by the thrust. (If you can render this after one of his
falling sprite animations, that'd be a great visual gag)

1   SFX
           BWOOSH

2   SONIC
           YOW!

PANEL 4 – SONIC closes his eyes and reclines in the air as he free-falls. SONIC holds
his hands above his head expectantly.

3   SONIC
           No worries. I'll just reach out and grab a perfectly timed
           air-support rescue from my bestest buddy in the whole world…

PANEL 5 – KNUCKLES glides towards us, hands held in front of him, catching
SONIC. SONIC hangs from KNUCKLES'S fists and looks up at him, baffled.
KNUCKLES frowns, serious.

4   SONIC
           --KNUCKLES?!

5   KNUCKLES
           Sonic.

6   SONIC
           What are you doing so far from home?

7   KNUCKLES
           There's trouble. You see…

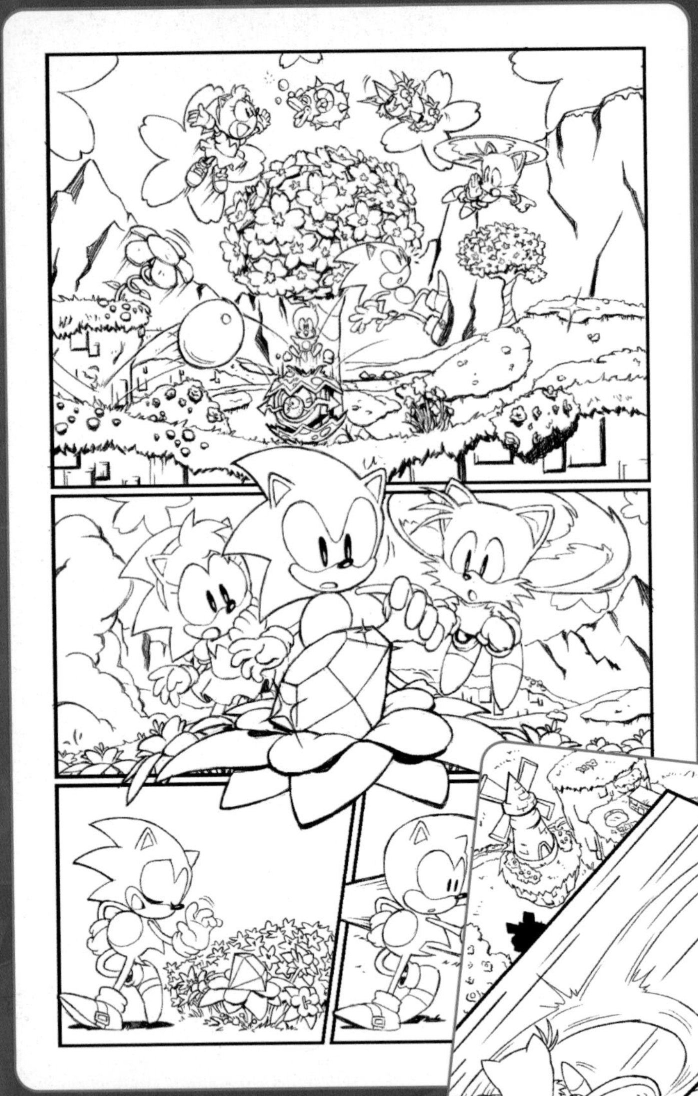

Once the script's approved, it moves to the art team! "Seasons of Chaos" was a group effort. While the majority of the pages were pencilled by Aaron Hammerstrom, both Thomas Rothlisberger and Tracy Yardley helped out too!

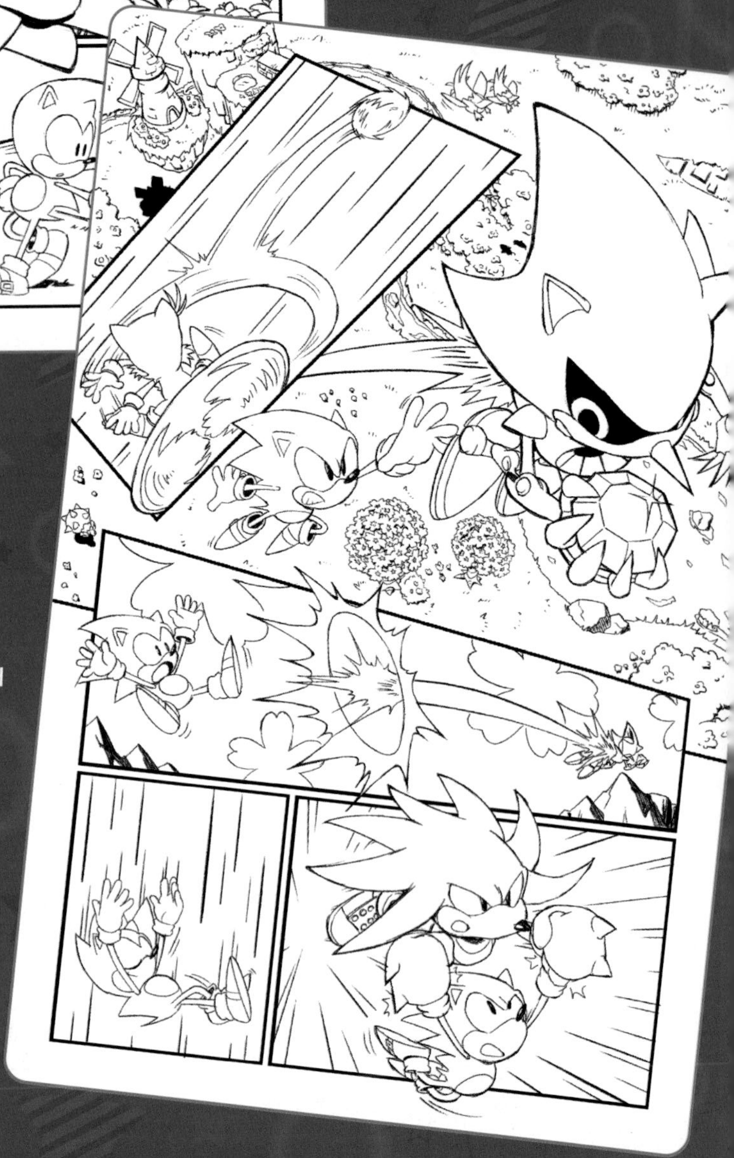

With the script in hand and plenty of reference material, Aaron roughed out all of the pages–loosely laying out the characters and action. From there, Aaron moved to pencilling the pages, taking those roughs and fleshing them out to be more clear and detailed. Check out some of Aaron's pencils and see how they match up with the script!

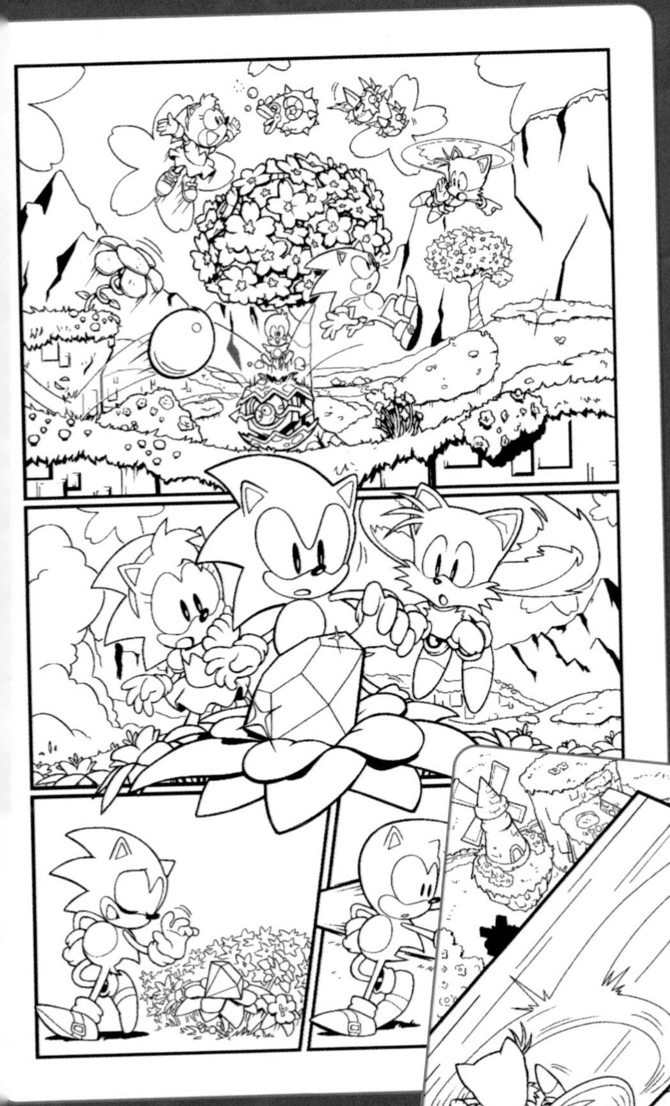

After Aaron finishes a page of pencils, they are handed over to one of the talented inkers on the story, Reggie Graham or Matt Froese. Reggie handled most of the front half of the story, while Matt tackled the back half. As inkers, their job is to refine Aaron's pencils further and prepare them for coloring.

nkers help define the weight of the lines on the page, giving additional depth, as well as lling in shadows and areas neant to be black. They also elp round out some of the ougher edges of the penciled rt. And they do it all while naintaining the original art as nuch as possible to keep the enciller's style! Look at how osely Reggie's inked pages esemble Aaron's pencils!

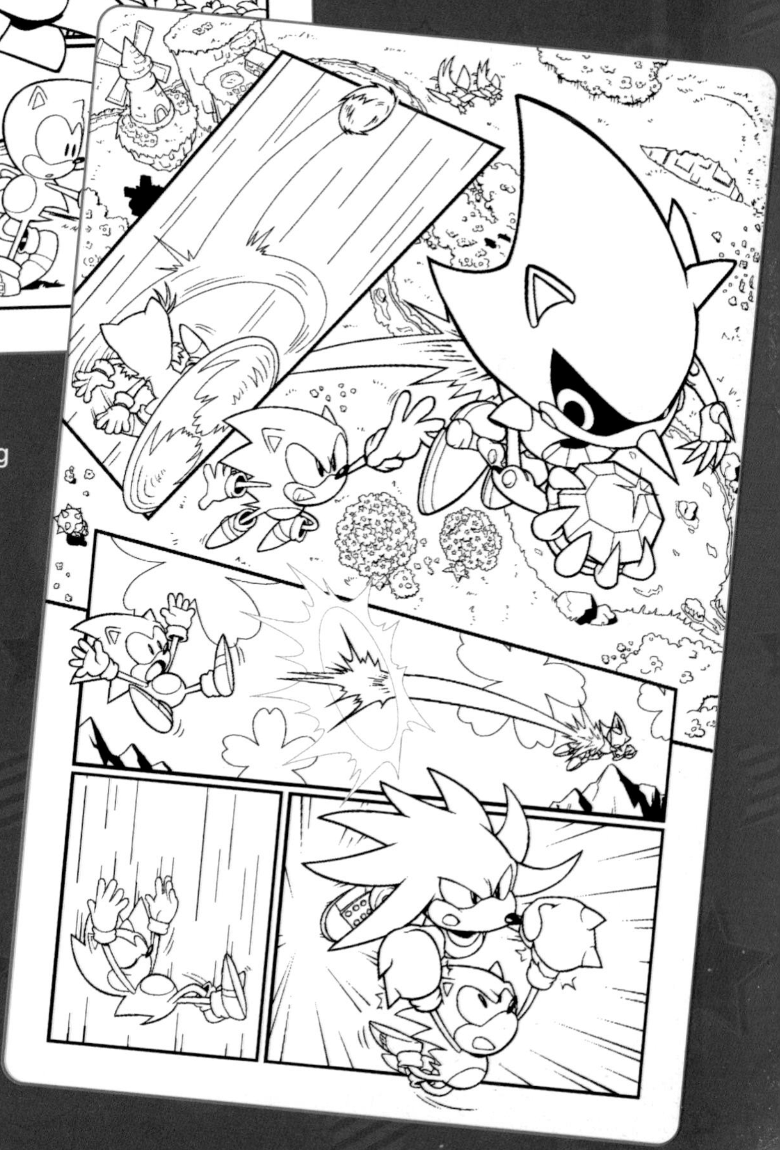

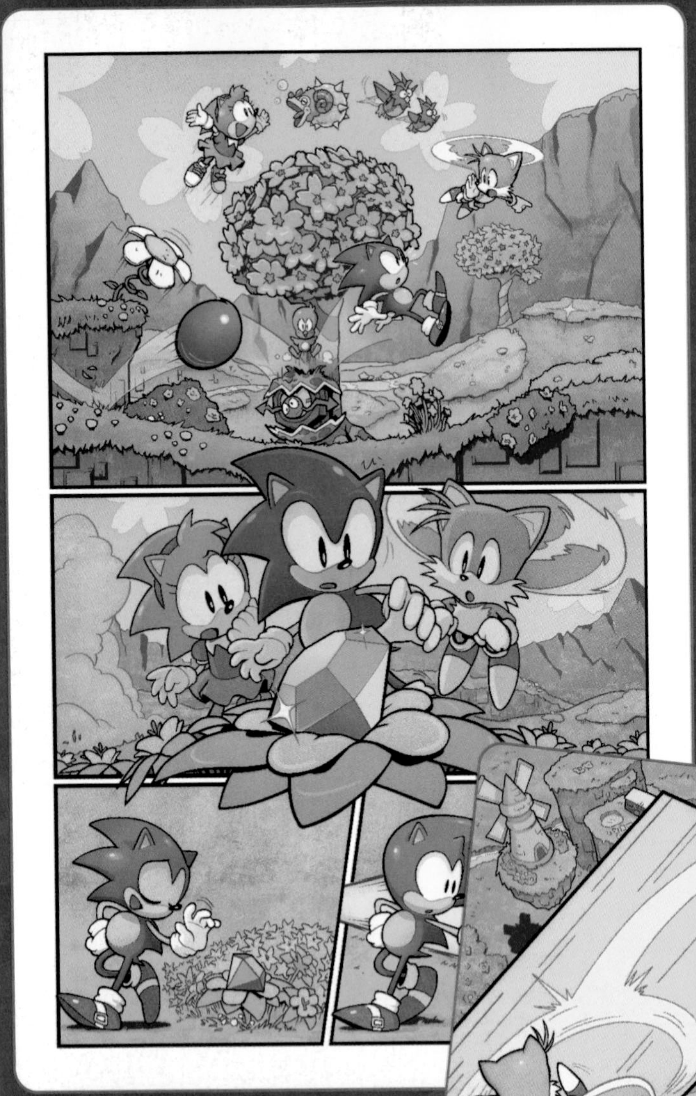

The next step of the process after inking is that the lineart (the combined pencil and inked pages) is sent to the colorist! Which in this case was a short journey since Reggie Graham was going on to colors directly from the lineart he finished (or received from the other inkers and line artists). Having pulled double duty on inks and colors, Reggie had a really clear vision of what the page would look like as it was finalized.

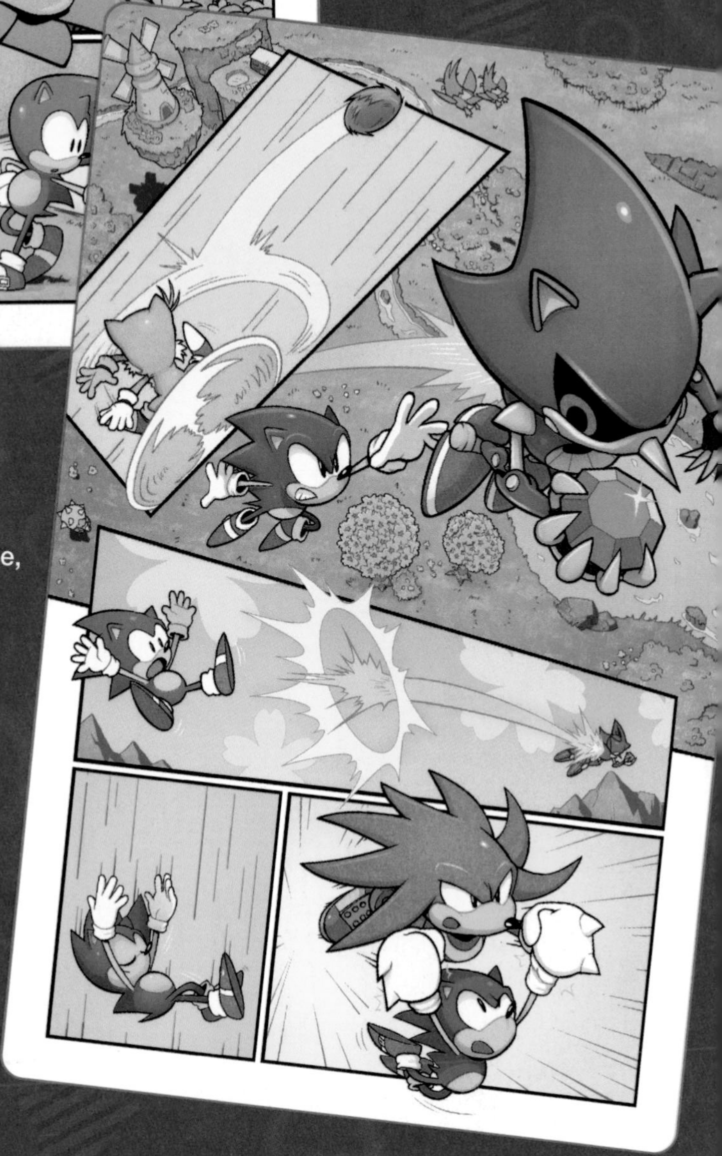

The coloring adds further depth to the world, using uniform colors on the characters to keep them consistent from page to page, while also creating special palettes for each seasonal zone in the story to make them visually distinct!

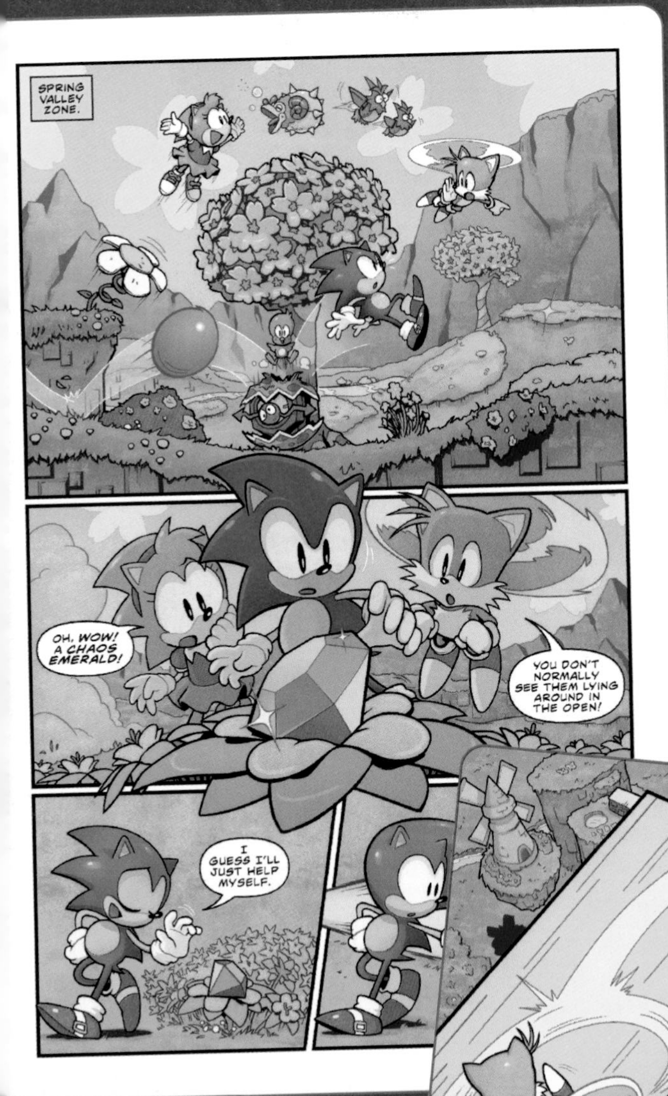
SPRING VALLEY ZONE.
OH, WOW! A CHAOS EMERALD!
YOU DON'T NORMALLY SEE THEM LYING AROUND IN THE OPEN!
I GUESS I'LL JUST HELP MYSELF.

Once the art has been finalized and approved by SEGA and the editors, the book enters the production process. Shawn Lee, Art Director, Design & Production at IDW puts all his skills to work. As a letterer, he puts all the dialogue and sound effects on the page (boy does he wish "Seasons of Chaos" had been a silent story)! Then as a designer, he assembles the lettered pages, all other material including covers, credits, design pages, and everything else, and makes it into the final product! His assembly even includes this "From Script to Page" behind-the-scenes feature!

With everything finally put together, the comic is reviewed once again by all the creators, editors David Mariotte and Riley Farmer, and the team at SEGA! When everyone's happy with it, the book is sent to print, ent to stores, and ends up ere, in your hands!

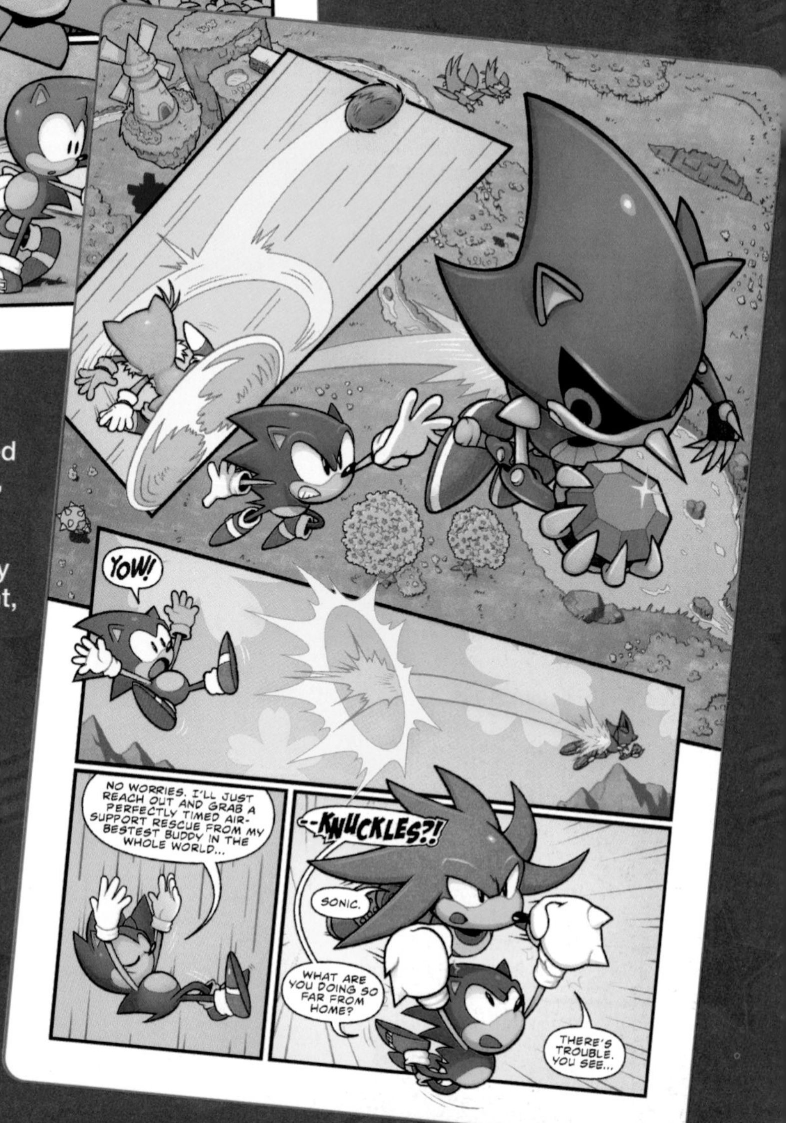
YOW!
NO WORRIES. I'LL JUST REACH OUT AND GRAB A PERFECTLY TIMED AIR-SUPPORT RESCUE FROM MY BESTEST BUDDY IN THE WHOLE WORLD...
--KNUCKLES?!
SONIC.
WHAT ARE YOU DOING SO FAR FROM HOME?
THERE'S TROUBLE, YOU SEE...

SONIC THE HEDGEHOG ™

SEASONS OF CHAOS

IAN FLYNN INTERVIEW

*Continuing the celebration, we spoke with **Ian Flynn**! Besides writing "Seasons of Chaos," Ian is the most prolific Sonic writer, having worked on around 300 issues of Sonic comics, Sonic resource books, and much more since 2006. To celebrate Ian's 15th anniversary working on Sonic, we chatted with him about his time on the franchise!*

IDW: Hey Ian, thanks for chatting with us.

IAN FLYNN: My pleasure!

IDW: Let's start at the beginning, how did you first encounter Sonic?

IF: Long, long ago, in the before-times and the fabled age of 1992, my dad came home one day with the Sega Genesis/ Sonic the Hedgehog 2 combo. It was the first major console for our household, and my brother and I logged an unfathomable number of hours playing it. Two cartoons and a comic book series were coming out around that time, too, so Sonic was inescapable.

IDW: From there, how did you first get involved with Sonic comics?

IF: My best friend (whaddup Jeff!) was a big fan of the comics. In the 8th Grade, he gifted me a copy because he "felt like I should have it." Little did we know

he'd just set me on the course that would define the rest of my life.

IDW: What have been some of the highlights of your Sonic comic career?

IF: My longevity with the franchise is a big one. To work on something you've loved your whole life is a gift. To be involved for as long as I have, to have my work rendered by so many talented artists, to meet so many awesome fans and watch them grow up over the years–it's amazing. It's humbling. It makes me feel old–haha.

IDW: Because you've been such a prolific Sonic writer and have introduced so many characters and elements to the franchise, you're often seen as a Sonic expert. How's that affected your life outside of the comics?

IF: It got me a lot of excited calls and emails from friends and family when the movie was announced, and that was the *one* thing I didn't have a hand in! Folks also assume I have some kind of greater authority over the little blue hedgehog than I really do.

IDW: Speaking of Sonic outside of the comics, we hear you've got quite a collection of Sonic goodies amassed over the years. What are some favorite pieces of your collection?

IF: The crown jewel of the set so far are my Fang, Bean, and Bark plushes from the limited *Sonic the Fighters* series that were exclusive to Japan (I think?). I also have some amazing custom-made toys and models gifted to me by some incredibly talented and generous fans. I'm still missing a Blaze the Cat figure from the old Jazwares line, though (shakes fist).

IDW: *Specifically to "Seasons of Chaos," much of your time writing Sonic has been his Modern interpretation. What are some of the differences you've experienced in writing Classic Sonic?*

IF: Classic Sonic is lighter in tone than Modern Sonic. The adventures are still grand, the perils still perilous, but it doesn't have quite the same dourness Modern Sonic stories sometimes have. Both are fun but in different ways.

IDW: *One of the things that makes Sonic so appealing is his friends and foes. Who's your favorite character to write, besides Sonic, and who do you think you've most improved at writing over the years?*

IF: I get this question a lot and I hate it because I love them all! But Knuckles has always been one of my top favs since the beginning. And I relish any chance I get to write Bean. I'm very happy I got to carry over his characterization, along with Fang and Bark, from my previous work. As for "most improved," that might be Sonic. I think I've come to understand him a lot better over the years.

IDW: *How has Sonic evolved as a character in the past 15 years that you've been chronicling his adventures?*

IF: He was created with the old '90s attitude, and that vision of "cool, irreverent rebel" died out with the decade. Who Sonic is has evolved with the trends, and I think he's begun to settle into a universal type of character that isn't so tied to the era he's currently living in.

IDW: *How've you changed in the past 15 years of working on Sonic?*

IF: I've gotten heavier and hairier, but that's about it.

IDW: *Are there any future Sonic projects that you can tease?*

IF: I do enjoy teasing everyone with my #KnowingSmile, but I have to play these close to the vest still. Rest assured I'm deeply involved with the Sonic series, and that's not changing any time soon.

IDW: *Anything else you'd like to add?*

IF: A big shout-out to all my fellow fans-turned-pro who got to share in the dream. A big thank you to all the editors and collaborators I've worked with over the years–y'all make me look good. Even bigger thanks to my wife and fellow *Sonic* creator alumnus Aleah Baker who has vastly influenced my critical eye. And a heapin' helpin' of "thank you" to all the fans who have shared their love and support over the years. Y'all are a boundless well of creativity and energy, and I hope I can continue to entertain you all.

Thanks so much for talking with us, Ian, and giving us insight to your many years working on Sonic, and the many more years that you'll be sticking around!

Art by Tracy Yardley

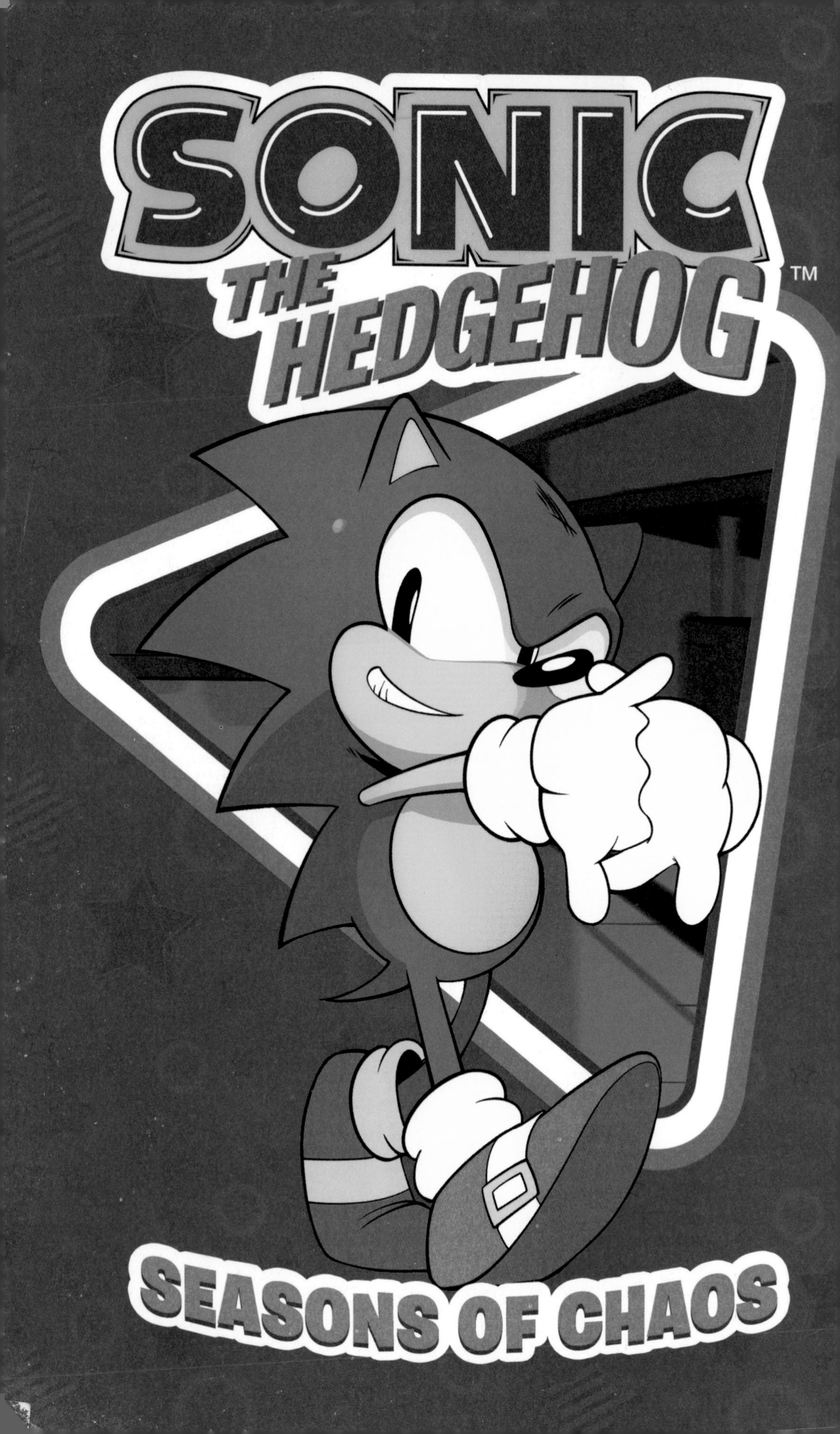
SONIC THE HEDGEHOG™
SEASONS OF CHAOS